VIOLET

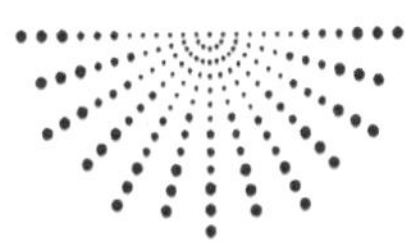

VIOLET

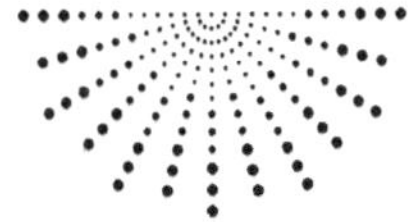

LILY HAMMOND

sapphicabooks

sapphicabooks

Dunedin, NZ

business@sapphicabooks.com

www.sapphicabooks.com

Violet/ Lily Hammond. -- 1st ed.

ISBN 978-0-473-38738-9 (print) 978-0-473-38739-6 (ePub) 978-0-473-38740-2 (Kindle)

For Valerie, with ever-deepening love.

There is no remedy for love but to love more.
- Henry David Thoreau

PROLOGUE

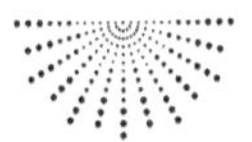

I was twenty-nine when the meat of this story begins. I've since realised it had its fingers in a much earlier pie, but for our purposes I suppose that is neither here nor there, yet.

A story must have several things, of which you are one, dear reader, and I another – your narrator, an easy task, since this is my own story I want to tell you. A story of mystery, and storms, and love – always and forever, love.

So then, we have everything, except for the beginning, and here is that. This tale of mine opens in a bookshop – my bookshop, on the eve of a wedding.

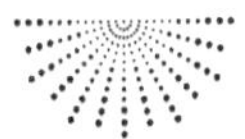

I remember that the room swam in a prism of light. Even the shadows glowed, floating on the periphery, a harmony of gentle illumination.

A sudden, squeezing embrace. 'You're standing there with your mouth agape.'

I tugged on the arms to loosen them and grinned. 'Since when do you know words like agape?'

Bronny let go and went spinning out under the light, her hair swinging out from her shoulders like spun-gold floss. She spread her hands wide, gesturing at the room. 'I'm getting married in a bookshop,' she said. 'I thought I'd better work on literizing my vocabulary.'

'There's no such word as literizing,' I pointed out, but my grin was even wider. Sticking my own hands in my pockets, I gazed once more around the room and sighed. 'It looks good though, doesn't it?'

She twinkled a wave at the fairy lights suspended in a glistening web from the ceiling, at more lights entwined with ivy that draped the ends of the heavy bookshelves, then twirled again to take in the sight of the long table set for the morrow's dinner, with an intake of breath that was half way between a sigh and a gasp.

'It's perfect,' she said. 'More than perfect, actually, though I don't know what word that would be.' She flashed me a radiant smile. 'Is there a word that means more perfect than perfect?'

I stepped over to her and laid a gentle kiss on her flushed cheek. 'You,' I said. 'You are, at this moment, the epitome of more perfect than perfect.'

She giggled at that and danced away again under the lights, reached out to touch a reverent finger to the bowls on the table, ready and waiting for the flowers they would cup in their crystal depths for the wedding dinner. Reflecting the lights above them, they were already exquisite, even without the perfection of roses.

Looking up, Bronny caught me gazing at her, and narrowed her eyes at me. 'You,' she said, pointing a pink nail in my direction.

'Me?' I pretended innocence, thinking I had an idea what was coming next.

'This should be for you, you know that, don't you?'

It was a conversation we'd had before. Bronny was convinced I should be the one getting married in the book-shop. Which, I supposed, did hold a certain logic, considering it was my own bookshop, and I was, and always had been, completely mad about books. I sniffed, gave her my most disarming shrug.

'I am yet to receive the appropriate proposal.'

She rolled her eyes and came back over, flung a casual arm about my shoulder again, and tucked me closer to her side, content for a moment to be silent. I risked a glance up at her. Bronny was tall, one of those willowy creatures who belonged in a Pre-Raphaelite painting. Whereas I was best, I thought, described as a Picasso, during his cubism phase.

'Thank you,' she breathed at last, and I relaxed against her, glad not to hear another rendition of grief over my lack of a partner. I was content enough to be single, and besides – I did have the bookshop. 'It truly is beautiful.'

It was. The lights on the ceiling would turn the dinner into something magical the next evening. It was winter, the wedding service was set for three-thirty, and the reception was simply to be a dinner here in the bookshop as the natural light faded from the day, the group seated at one long table that reminded me of the dining hall in Hogwarts. I glanced up at the ceiling again and smiled. Definitely Hogwarts on a starry starry night.

'I could never have afforded something this marvellous without your help,' Bronny whispered, bending to speak confidentially in my ear.

'We've been best friends since kindergarten,' I reminded her. 'You know I'd do anything for you.'

She sighed, and I could hear the happiness in the sound. It came from deep within her chest, most likely from that red, beating organ in charge of making us fall in love. 'And Louise,' she said. 'Promise me you like Louise.'

'I love Louise,' I said, and it was only a slight exaggeration. I'd always thought it would be impossible for anyone to be good enough for Bronny, but Louise, she made the grade, I had to admit it.

'And we're still going to hang out together all the time,' Bronny said, making me find her hand and pat it.

'Sweetheart,' I said. 'You really don't have to worry about me.'

But looking up at her I saw her forehead crease anyway. 'I do worry about you, Fran. I can't help it. You're the most wonderful friend in the world, and I want you to have the sort of happiness I've found with Louise.'

This time I didn't just pat the hand, I gave it a good squeeze, pinching my eyes closed for a moment too, so they wouldn't leak the way they were suddenly threatening to.

'You're the best, Bronny,' I said. 'Why, if it wouldn't be like marrying my sister, I'd be the one saying my vows to you tomorrow.'

That made her giggle again, a sound that always made me think of pulled taffy or some other sort of confectionary. It was sugary and sweet, and I adored hearing it.

'Listen,' I said, and I was patting her hand again. 'There's someone out there for me, I just have to be patient.'

'You really believe that?' She blinked at me. 'I mean, I do – but you have to too. You haven't given up, have you?'

My turn to laugh. 'I'm only twenty-nine, Bronny – not quite over the hill yet.' Letting go of her, I spread out my arms at the bookshop. 'Besides, I have this.' The shop was where my heart had been happy to belong since the day the real estate agent had pressed the key to the old Georgian house into my sweating palm. I'd curled my fingers around it, feeling its slight weight like it had been forged from gold. To me, it was, even still. The bookshop was a dream I'd had since I was knee-high to a grasshopper, as my gran had put it when she co-signed the mortgage papers that allowed me to buy the place.

Haven, I'd called it, and a haven it still was, for books, for the best tea, coffee, and muffins in Bath – if I did say so myself – and for all the gays, lesbians, queers, and other letters of the alphabet who came from all over the southwest to browse, mingle, argue, and find love over the printed page.

I nudged Bronny. 'You and Louise met here,' I reminded her. 'It's only right that you get married here.'

'You still can too,' my best friend said. 'When it's time.'

I nodded. 'Yep. Especially now I know how wonderful it looks all gussied up like something out of the fairy tale section.'

Bronny tugged her phone out of her pocket and took a quick look at the time. 'Gotta get going,' she said, giving me a big smacking kiss on the cheek.

'Gotta get your beauty sleep,' I agreed. 'Big day tomorrow.'

She was picking up her coat and shimmying into it. 'That's right. Which brings me to the topic you have been studiously avoiding all night.'

I looked at her with wide, innocent eyes. 'I don't know what you're talking about.'

She patted a woolly hat onto her head. It was December outside, a few days before Christmas and the chill of the season was determined to latch on to any unwisely exposed piece of flesh.

'You better know what I'm talking about, Fran,' she said, waggling her finger at me. 'Louise and I are counting on you.'

There was no helping it – I grinned at her and laughed. 'Don't you worry your pretty little head,' I told her. 'Everything is under control.'

'Speech?'

'Written, practised with a great deal of embarrassment in

front of the bathroom mirror every morning for the last two weeks.' I wasn't exaggerating.

'Good,' she said, then winced. 'You really are okay with doing all this? I've asked such a lot of you.'

'I'm thrilled about it all, believe me.' It was true. She was my best friend. We'd seen everything through together, and I wanted nothing more than to give her the wedding day she deserved. Even if that meant giving my own speech and supervising those from her father and brothers, who were apt to be ever so slightly loose and fast with their mouths.

'It's all going to be fine,' I assured her. 'Now go on and get out of here.'

With a radiant smile, she blew me a kiss and was out the door a moment later. I watched her disappear like a ghost into the night, then turned to look at our handiwork one last time before I switched off all the lights and headed upstairs to my flat, already looking forward to pouring a glass of Sapporo beer, which was a Japanese brew, but I figured it would go just fine with yesterday's red Thai curry.

'Damn.' One of the intricate festoons of lights had come off its hook. 'How did you manage that?' I asked, interrogating the inanimate object. For a moment, I considered leaving it until the morning, but standing there wrinkling my nose, I knew that possibly wasn't the best idea. A vision swam into my head of coming downstairs in the morning to find that overnight the whole get-up of fairy lights and artificial ivy had come crashing down onto the table.

It would only take a minute to fasten the lights back into place, and make sure they would hold. I'd been about to take the ladder back downstairs to the basement anyway.

Bronny had done most of the trips up and down the

ladder. A lithesome form had its advantages. She'd been like a gazelle, up and down the rungs and I smiled as I got the ladder into place. I wasn't nearly so nimble, and she wasn't there to hold things steady, but it would only take a moment, and boy I did not want to come down in the morning, rubbing sleep from my eyes, to find the whole mess of lights on the table amid splinters of crystal bowls and fine champagne flutes.

The last secure step mocked me, short by a good few inches. I'd gotten used to being short and rather square, but right then I would almost have sold my soul to be six inches taller and slim and flexible with it.

I might not have been well-endowed with classically beautiful features, but I was up there on smarts, and all the brain cells in my head screamed at me to stay off the very top step. They even graced me with a full-colour image of me standing there, nothing to hold on to, wavering first to the left, then to the right, before pinwheeling in an ungainly freefall that would undeniably hurt when I came in for landing. Likely on the table right in the midst of those crystal bowls and fine champagne flutes.

So why then I heaved myself up into mid-air, I have no explanation. I simply did it.

For a long, drawn-out moment, I thought it was going to be all right. I even got so far as to reach up to the ceiling, snaffling the offending loop of lights and slipping it back in its hook. I had time to smile – triumphantly – and begin the first mental words of congratulations, and then everything wavered in front of me. The long room, with its heavy bookshelves making corridors pointing towards the wedding table, wobbled in alarm, and the table itself, almost directly under me, seemed to rise up to meet me in a wonder of slow-motion animation.

But it was the ladder wobbling under me, it was me swaying first one way then the other, arms flinging outwards, fingers grappling at slippery handfuls of thin air, and it wasn't the table coming to meet me, but the other way around. In a feat of gymnastic witchery, I twisted, aiming for an ungainly, sprawling landing on the floor, and I made it too. I know I did.

The thing was however, that I also hit my head on the way there. You'd think you wouldn't hear the resounding crack of your own skull upon the blade edge of a two-hundred-year-old oak refectory table, but you'd be wrong.

You hear it all right. Just before the world goes black.

CHAPTER TWO

There wasn't enough air in my lungs. They lay inside my ribcage like two deflated footballs – I could feel them there, empty leather sacks into which I was desperately trying to suck some oxygen.

'Franny! You fell right out of the tree!'

There had definitely been falling. Aerial acrobatics not being my usual thing, I wasn't likely to forget. There had also been landing, although that was slightly hazier.

'Bronny,' I wheezed. 'You came back.'

There was light against my eyelids, and I prised them open to squint against it. Bronny moved to peer down over me, a dark shadow with a halo of light behind her. I licked my lips, slurping more air into those tight bellows in my chest.

'Who's Bronny, Fran?' Bronny asked. Her head turned. 'Mother! Franny's had all the sense knocked out of her!'

I squinted harder at the shadow under the light.

'Francesca?' Another head joined the first, peering over me as I lay on my back. This one also wore a halo, threaded through with filaments of golden hair. 'Francesca? I did tell you not to climb that tree.'

Tree? I worked my jaw, and with relief air made it into my lungs and they expanded gratefully. 'Ladder,' I gasped.

The two heads bent closer and I felt someone land on their knees beside me. I winced for them. It was a hard floor – goodness knows I'd be acquainted with that one, having just landed flat on it from the top of a ladder.

The golden halo shook from side to side. 'You are far too old for climbing trees, I did tell you so.'

'Mother, she was getting my kite!'

I looked at the darker head, now by my side, then back to the golden one.

'Come along Francesca,' it said. 'Enough of this.'

'What if she needs a doctor, Mother? What if she broke her legs and arms?'

'She appears intact, if a little winded.' The head retreated, and the light was back in my eyes. I squinted and lifted a hand to cover it.

'Urgh,' I managed. 'Bronny?'

The little head beside me bobbed up and down, hard to ignore. 'What's bronny? Come on, Fran. Get up.' Hands poked at me. 'You don't have any broken legs or arms.'

I could almost hear my neck creak when I turned it to look at this chatty thing next to me with the prodding fingers. Fortunately, my neck seemed correctly to attach head to shoulders, and a sluggish assessment indicated I was indeed all still intact.

Except I did not recognise the person crouched on their knees next to me. My mouth flopped open – I felt it – but nothing came out. It was not Bronny.

I was also not in my bookshop.

There was a child, and behind the child was a garden. The light in my eyes was not the ceiling of fairy lights strung for Bronny's wedding, but a yellow sun, a high, bright bullseye in a powder-blue sky.

'What's the matter, Franny?' the small person next to me said. 'You didn't really hurt yourself, did you?'

I shook my head, though it was hardly in response to the child. There were words in my head, but none were in the right order for speech. The girl tugged at my hand and pulled me up. I went with her and a moment later the world looked just as odd from a vertical position as it had from the horizontal.

'Francesca, I've poured you a cup of tea. Come sit down before you get yourself into more trouble. My cousin Isaac will be here any minute with Violet.'

The child stared up at me, little frown lines embedding themselves between her beetled brows. 'Franny,' she whispered. 'Are you hurt? You're looking awfully queer.'

I blinked at her and did another of those inventories. Funnily enough, I felt fine. There were no broken bones, not even any lingering stiffness. Surreptitiously, I flexed one leg then the other. Both their usual, sturdy selves. There was also no ache in my skull. Not a hint of one.

It was then that I decided I must be dreaming. I was actually lying somewhere – on the floor of the bookshop, or more hopefully, in a hospital bed hooked up to some beeping machines that were very generously monitoring everything and pumping in this and flushing out that. They were keeping me high on a cocktail of marvellously sophisticated drugs, and this here, this world of sunshine and children, long-skirted women and tea in the garden, it was nothing more than a lucid dream.

The realisation brought with it a great deal of relief and a twitch to my lips.

'What are you smiling about, Franny?'

I leaned down and whispered my question. 'How far up the tree did I get?'

The girl's eyes widened. 'Almost to the very top!'

'Excellent!' I said, then sobered, looking around the garden searching for the tree. I guessed it was the one with a torn kite tail still tangled in its branches. 'Sorry about your kite,' I said.

She shrugged and tucked her hand in mine. 'That's all right.'

'Next time we'll take it to the park and fly it properly.'

Now she did look crestfallen. 'You won't be back for ages though.'

That was news to me. Back from where? I'd only just got here. Not that my dream companions necessarily knew that, I supposed. I gave her hand a squeeze. 'Well, we'll see what we can do, anyway. Perhaps you can visit me.'

She perked up. 'At the seaside? Oh, can I?' Hot little hand abandoning mine, she skipped ahead to the table, covered in a white cloth and laid out with teapot, cups, and scones. I followed and slid onto a chair to stare at the golden-haired woman. She was older than I'd had time to tell, with fine lines creasing eyes and brow. Her hair was arranged in kind of the puff around her head I recognised from books as belonging to the early twentieth century.

'Your tea's going cold, Francesca,' she said, and promptly sipped at her own rose-patterned tea cup. I stared in fascination, astounded at the level of detail I'd managed in this dream of mine. I looked down at my own tea cup, then further to my lap and the long skirt that covered thighs, knees, and yes, ankles too. Twisting slightly, I felt the pull of foreign undergarments and had to bite back a giggle. All of a sudden, I was certain I was wearing a corset. Me – who in real life never wore anything but trousers – here I was in long skirt, blouse, petticoats and corset!

I always been accused of having an over-active imagination, but I was surprising even myself.

'It's Frances,' I said.

Pale eyes nailed me in their sight. 'I think I'm aware of my own daughter's name – and you do not decide on one of your whims to change it.'

That was me told. And apparently, I was whimsical. It made my mouth quirk in a smile. I liked that. And the name Francesca wasn't too bad. Certainly not worth getting caught in the crosshairs of that gaze again.

'Mother,' the child interrupted, perhaps used to conversations such as these, if this dream version of me did indeed suffer from an abundance of whims. 'Franny says I might visit her at the seaside.' The child leaned against the halo-haired woman and plucked at the lace on her mother's sleeve.

I got a raised eyebrow over that cool grey eye. 'Did she indeed?'

'Yes, she did. Please say I can go, Mother!'

The seaside, I mused, absently lifting the cup to my lips and sipping. What had I done to get myself sent to the seaside? A smile bent my mouth over the vagaries of the human mind. Hadn't the seaside always been where you went for the sake of your health, to recuperate? The grey hospital machines beeped in my mind. I could think of worse things than to dream of spending a few days watching the tide wash in and out. Especially if, as it seemed, it was summer here.

'Remind me where I'm going again?' I asked, venturing my first unwhimsical contribution to the conversation and knowing I'd probably get an odd look. But hey, it was my dream, and I didn't think it was too much to ask to be filled in on its details. I'd wake up in a few hours, after all.

The odd look was more of chagrin than consternation. 'Francesca, really. I'm not at all certain this is a good idea.'

'Why's that?' I asked, not knowing what we were talking about, but sipping tea with the sun on my head and birds chirping at my back was very pleasant, and I thought I might as well enjoy myself. It would make an excellent story to tell Bronny when I woke up.

A thought intruded – I wasn't going to miss her wedding, was I? I shoved it away. There was nothing I could do right now, and this sleep, this dream, was probably the most healing thing for me.

The woman stared at me and I thought about her being my mother. Brought up by my grandmother, I'd never had a mother before. I gave her a radiant smile. She seemed a bit stern right at the moment, but I was sure underneath that there was honey and cream and other sweetness. She drew a deep breath, the cream-coloured lace at her throat moving.

'I don't know if you're quite responsible enough yet,' she said. 'It concerns me greatly.'

'Mother,' the girl said, standing up and spreading out her hands. 'Franny is twenty-two years old! She's practically an old maid!'

What? I was most certainly not twenty-two. I remembered being that age, and it hadn't been all that fun the first time around. I had been awfully healthy though, so maybe that was why I'd picked it now.

'Yes,' my mother said. 'And that's the problem, isn't it?' She leaned a little closer over the table. 'We should be taking care of business more important to you, Francesca, not running about after Violet for the summer.'

'I don't understand,' I said. I didn't.

She sat back in her chair, composed again, cup back in hand. 'We should be thinking of your future, making arrangements, looking out for your own prospects.'

The little girl, whom I judged to be about nine or ten, rolled her eyes. 'She means marry you off.'

That got me sitting up. 'What?'

'Don't be vulgar, Marigold,' my mother said.

'But I don't want to marry,' I said. That would turn this very quickly into a nightmare. I'd take the seaside with Violet, whoever she might be.

'Please! I do not wish to have this conversation again, today of all days.' My new relative took a deep breath and spoke more evenly. 'We've agreed, you'll spend this summer with Violet and then upon your return it will be time to give serious thought to your future.'

'To getting married,' Marigold clarified helpfully.

'Yes, thank you Marigold,' The woman said, looking straight at me. 'To the issue of you settling down, marrying, and having a family.'

I looked at her and swallowed. 'When do I leave for the seaside?' I asked.

Her shoulders relaxed a fraction. 'Tomorrow, as you well

know,' she said on a sigh and I wanted to ask more about this trip to the coast. And who Violet was.

My lips remained sealed, however. Everything would reveal itself in good time. Unless I woke first, of course, and then it would simply be a dream of mind-boggling clarity.

Leaning back, I tilted my face to the sun. After weeks of biting wind and rain, the chill slush of winter, it was nothing short of a miracle to feel the sun's warmth. Marigold moved around the table and sat down, helping herself to a scone, splitting it open and spreading it with a jam made of plums I could still smell as though they were fresh from the tree. Our little group around the table settled down to the quiet contemplation of our own thoughts and my eyes slid closed, drowsy with the scent of fruit and sugar, the warm breeze, the gossipy chatter of birds.

I yanked myself upwards, shaking off the doze.

'Are you all right?' my mother asked.

I nodded. 'I almost fell asleep,' I said. She nodded, and her gaze drifted off again to the pages of a letter in her hand.

I didn't want to fall asleep. The hospital loomed in my mind with its sterile rooms, its antiseptic smells, lukewarm tea, gallstones in the next bed, and the beep beep beep of machines that could well be keeping me alive.

Better to stay here and dream awake for a while.

CHAPTER THREE

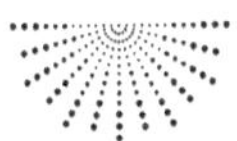

The sleeping mind is, don't you agree, a thing of wonder? Oh, the visions it can conjure.

I was winded and pressed a hand to the boning at my chest, feeling the corset squeezing me tight as I tried another deep breath.

'Francesca, you remember Violet?'

No. I did not. I certainly would though, if I'd ever met her before. Stumbling forward, I stuck out my hand, my tongue dry and tied inside my mouth. She flicked a disinterested gaze over my face, then drifted down to look at my hand. Her fingers were cool, the grasp brief before she dropped her hand and shuttered herself behind eyes that were open but unseeing.

'Isaac,' my mother said, kissing a saturnine man on the cheek, who glanced at me with a deep frown over cold eyes. 'Did you have a good trip?' I shivered at the sight of him – a dark intruder from a gothic nightmare, if ever there was one, and tuned out the rest of the greetings to go back to the more necessary examination of the heavenly creature called Violet. She did not appear to notice.

'Francesca!' the voice was curt, and I blinked, wondering how many times my name had just been said. The tone suggested at least twice. 'Be so kind as to show Violet to her room, please, so that she might refresh herself.'

Ah. That was a bit awkward. I leaned down slightly to the slim figure at my side.

'Show us the way, Marigold,' I said. 'I wasn't paying attention to which room.'

Even in the dimness of the entrance hall, I could see the roll of my new kid sister's eyes.

'This way,' she drawled. 'Honestly Franny. I have to do everything.'

A quick glance showed the elder cousins deep in congregation with each other and moving towards a room off the hall, heads bent together.

'Violet?' I asked, and my voice stuck for a moment in my throat.

She looked at me then wafted away again but fell into step as I followed Marigold deeper into the house, up a flight of stairs and down a hallway filled with small tables, flower vases, and urns sporting dusty peacock feathers. I tried not to sneeze, looking forward already to the fresh salt tang of the coast. Maybe Violet would mention which part of it we were actually going to, because I still didn't know.

Marigold stopped our procession in front of a door I would never have known to pick from the others and pushed it open.

'Here you go,' she said, and made a mock bow and flourish with her arms. 'This is your room for the night, Violet.'

I saw Violet look at her for a moment, then drift back off into whatever world she found more interesting than this one. But she stepped into the room, and I followed her.

'Does she ever say anything?' Marigold whispered as I passed her in the doorway.

'No idea,' I said.

'She's very peculiar.'

Perhaps. I thought there was a story to Violet, and I desperately wanted to find out what it was. I'd just met her, but the woman stirred me in places hidden deep under my layers of clothes. I waved Marigold away. She gave an elaborate shrug and disappeared back down the way we'd come.

'Can you close the door, please?'

Her voice startled me. Not because it was unpleasant, but because it was exactly the opposite. Rich and surprisingly deep, mellow. I hoped mine wouldn't be a squeak when I opened my own mouth. Reaching out, I pushed the door gently closed, me still on the inside. I wanted a conversation with this woman. Failing that, I'd settle for simply looking at her a while longer.

Her shoulders relaxed as soon as the door snicked shut.

'Oh, thank god for that,' she said, and went rummaging in the pockets of the coat she wore. When she dragged out a silver case, plucked out a thin cigarette and popped it nonchalantly in her mouth, I gaped at her.

'What are you doing?'

'Smoking,' she said shortly. 'What on earth do you think it looks like?' She flung herself into a padded armchair by the window. 'Don't tell me you're a good little girl who's going to go running to mummy about naughty Violet?' She lit the cigarette with a click of a lighter and blew out a cloud of blue smoke.

'Those things will kill you,' I said. Everyone I knew had quit the nasty habit years ago, when we couldn't avoid the knowledge we were no longer teenagers and smoking was no longer cool.

She laughed, a sound that made me think of chocolate mint waterfalls. 'Well, that's a new one, I must admit.' She folded her legs. 'Usually I get told it's unladylike.'

Not where I came from. Just stupid. I licked my lips.

'But,' she continued, blowing a cloud of smoke at the ceiling this time. 'It's 1916, millions of boys are getting murdered at the Front, and it's long past time to worry about ladylike.'

1916. I needed suddenly to sit down and did so.

'What is the matter? You've gone white as a sheet.' Her gaze narrowed. 'Don't tell me you're another of these who refuses to face the facts of this new world? You can't go hiding amongst the dahlias and the silverware forever, you know. The world is a different place now, and we simply must all get used to it.' Cat eyes blinked at me. 'We are not going to solve anything by hiding our faces from it, and if you're one that does that, then I don't think we're going to get along.' She seemed to give up on me with that, and flung her arm out, the cigarette sending a little rill of smoke towards the window.

'Like Elizabeth,' she said. 'Take my dearest stepmother. Two thirds of the boys in our village are dead, and she worries about who will help her prune the roses and whether she ought to matchmake between the vicar and Mary

Rottham who is very virtuous but has a terrible lisp, as though that means anything at all.' She sniffed and shook her head. 'The vicar would have preferred Mary's brother Robert, but of course you can't point that out!'

My fingers dug into the bedclothes beneath me and she shifted her gaze back to me, eyebrows raised.

'Don't you talk?' she asked. 'Not even to tell me what sort of person you are? We shall have a very dull time of it, if you don't talk.' The cigarette pointed at me. 'Of course, that is the plan, and you've probably been chosen exactly for your sensible dullness. You will make sure I eat my meals and embroider a border of roses, or if slightly more daring – sunflowers, on a snowy white tablecloth, and you will suggest you read out loud to me the latest religious tracts after dinner, and we shall have a very jolly time indeed.'

'I doubt that very much,' I said.

Only the one eyebrow raised this time, and it was very charming. She had a pale face, a rather large nose, and was too thin – if indeed we did make it to the seaside, I certainly would want to make sure she ate every meal – but the constantly mobile features seduced me. Her lips clamped around the cigarette again and I realised she was watching me watching her.

'You doubt which part, very specifically?' she asked, then jumped forward in chair to narrow her cat's eyes at me. They were wide, green chips of emerald. 'You want a cigarette?'

I shook my head automatically. 'I quit,' I said without thinking. I was thinking about the dark rim outlining the green of her eyes, the dark brows making perfect arches over them.

'You quit?' she asked, surprise in her voice, then threw back her head and laughed. 'You know, that makes me think we might get along after all.'

Which made me smile. 'There won't be any reading of religious tracts, for certain.'

She relaxed back against the chair, sprawling there as though loose-jointed under her coat. 'Good, because while you say you have quit cigarettes, I have quit the church.'

A sidelong glance accompanied the bald statement, likely expecting to see a reaction of horror and despair. But this was a dream, I was only visiting 1916 from a hundred years in the future, from a hospital bed and the marvellous and sophisticated cocktail of drugs.

'The church and I are not really acquainted,' I said and watched her mouth fall open. She had small, neat teeth the nicotine hadn't yet stained. 'How old are you, Violet?' I asked suddenly.

Her mouth snapped shut. 'Twenty-four,' she said. 'And according to my stepmother, I should be married by now and living in husband's house with a multitude of servants and a nanny for my three or four children.' She gave a theatrical shudder. 'I will not bring children into this world.'

That was all right. I wasn't keen on the idea of bringing them into my world either. The planet was pretty much going to shit in the year of my headlong plunge from the ladder. But good luck avoiding children in a world where marriage meant to death do us part with a man, and there was no reliable birth control. She saw my wince.

'Why are you not married?' she demanded, looking around for something to put out her cigarette out on. She settled on the dirt of a pot plant and stubbed it out vigorously. 'You're not ugly. Or if you are, there's a certain charm to it.'

'Thank you, I think,' I said, narrowing my eyes, then loosening into a shrug. 'Because you have saved me from it,' I answered, remembering the conversation over tea and scones.

'I?'

'Yes. Thanks to you, I have a summer-long reprieve from the job of marrying and procreating.'

She tilted her head to the side and gave me a crooked smile. 'We shall have to make it a summer to remember, then.'

I smiled back at her.

'An excellent plan,' I said. 'Do you know exactly where we are going?' I rocked back where I sat, digging my fingers deeper into the blankets, supposing that the French Riviera would be too much to hope for.

'Well, I did argue for somewhere on the Continent,' Violet said, and she sighed, a genuine sound, perhaps the first she'd made that wasn't calculated for show. Her eyes sought mine. 'I argued very strongly for France.'

1916. 'But...'

'Yes indeed. There were a great many buts when I said I should like to go to France.' She leaned forward. 'I'd make a lousy nurse, I know. I'd be terrible at anything that required me to wear a uniform and follow orders – I'm just not made that way – but nor am I made to sit at home and knit endless pairs of socks. Even if I was just in Paris, I could get a proper feeling for things.'

'And do what?' I asked.

She paused before answering, and I saw her chest rise and fall with her breath. 'Paint,' she said. 'Paint it. Tell the truth.'

'You are an artist?' I asked.

Her face fell into an expression of stormy clouds. 'You've no need to say it like that.'

'No!' I said. 'You've taken me by surprise, that's all.'

But her bravado had fallen, and she looked away from me, green eyes veiled. I wanted to go to her, kneel on the floor in front of her and absurdly take her hand, beg her to look back at me. See those deep sea-green eyes light back up and feel the cool caress of her fingers against my palm.

I ducked my head down and closed my eyes. This was awkward, I thought, deciding the dream was feeling all too real.

'Sorry,' she whispered. 'It's just that everyone reacts like that. Everyone who surrounds me anyway.'

Damn it. It *was* a dream. Levering myself off the bed I walked over to her and sank to my knees in front of her. She gazed at me in wide-eyed surprise and I took her hand in mine. It was just as cool and arousing as I'd imagined.

'We are going to have the summer,' I said. 'Just the two of us in a house somewhere by the beach. I think it's wonderful that you want to paint.'

She interrupted me. 'I don't want to,' she said. 'I need to.'

A nod. 'I have dreams too.' Although I wasn't going to tell her what they were. Not when they currently involved lying my head against her breast and listening to the sharp beat of her heart. I continued instead, hoping my voice would stay steady. 'We can use the summer to turn them from dreams into plans.' My smile was hopeful.

She looked down at me, brow in faint knots. 'You think so?'

'Sure,' I said, getting to my feet before I kissed her white knuckles. 'But you gotta quit the cigarettes. They really will kill you.'

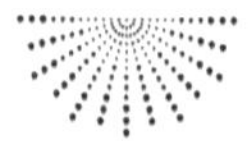

It had been odd to not only go to sleep inside a dream, but to wake to the same dream, as though it had continued on, a parallel world. Musing on which made me think of something, standing in the hallway by the front door, trussed back up into clothes that felt oddly familiar to my body, if not to my mind, and with a trunk at my feet for the upcoming mystery journey.

My hands were gloved. Gloves were worn on every occasion when one left the house, it seemed. I had on a hat too, jammed onto clumsily-dressed hair and lodged there with long, spiked pins, but it was the gloves I wrestled with.

'What are you doing, Fran?' Violet wafted up and anchored herself to my side, tucking an arm around mine, and gazing at my bared palm with bored curiosity.

'Nothing,' I said, and pressed my hand against my thigh, hiding the twin lifelines that had always fascinated and baffled my grandmother, proprietor of a New Age bookstore in Glastonbury carrying almost an acre of tomes on palmistry.

'You are lying to me,' Violet said, and if I wasn't prepared to mention the map of lines on my hand, then for the moment, it was more than I could articulate, with the heat of her body up against my own and the warmth of her breath on my cheek. We were the same height, but if Bronny had been willowy, then Violet was a twig. Too thin, she was all unpadded angles. It made me strangely protective, as though her bones were those of a bird's.

'What?' I asked, finally realising I had to reply.

She whispered, and her breath was sweet as well as warm. 'I said, you are lying to me. You are not doing nothing. There is definitely something on your mind.' Reaching out, she touched my hand, wrapped her fingers around it and turned it palm up. Her fingers moved to trace the lines upon my palm. 'Is this what you were looking so intently at?'

I couldn't move, couldn't remember how to breathe, let alone string words together. The sensation of her fingertips on my palm lingered even after she dropped it. I sought out her eyes, trying to discern if she knew the effect she was having on me, if she was knowingly initiating it. But they stared back at me and I could read nothing there but moss and jade.

'The car is ready.' Violet's father stepped past us and out onto the driveway, breaking the spell I was under.

Violet widened her eyes and squeezed my arm. 'We're almost free,' she whispered. 'Or at least, it's freedom of a sort.'

Her father looked back through the doorway. 'Come along, Violet. Don't drag your heels, lest I change my mind.'

Fingers of bone and flesh pinched my arm, and Violet gave me the quickest of leering smiles, then was out the door after her father. My mother, at least she was my mother for the purposes of this extraordinary dream, touched the arm still warm from Violet's body, and I startled, turning to see her looking seriously at me.

'Is everything okay?' I asked, and the frown she wore deepened. 'I mean, is there anything amiss?' I'd been making an effort all morning to tone down my twenty first century colloquialisms, but it was hard. Marigold had already told me twice I was talking very oddly.

The skin on my mother's brow smoothed a fraction. 'A word, Fran, just for a moment.'

I half turned to the door, lifting a hand. 'But the car is here.'

'A moment, Fran. That is all. It is Isaac's government car, it will not go without you.'

At least she wasn't calling me Francesca. It had to be a good sign. Following her gesture, I ended up in the drawing room and stood awkwardly there rubbing my palm with its twin lifelines against the linen of my plain blue skirt.

My new mother stared at me, hands clasped together as if to stop them from spontaneous wringing. I bit my lip, not knowing what was coming. Or expected of me.

For the first time, I questioned myself. If this was a dream, even perhaps some sort of coma-induced hallucination, it was damned strange.

But there was no time to contemplate anything. I breathed in, then out, watched the woman who said she was my mother do the same, a hand moving to toy with the lace at her throat. Today it was a lavender colour.

'It's going to be all right,' I blurted, unable to stand the tension any longer. 'I promise, it's going to be all right.' And it would – I would wake up in a few hours, or a day or two, perhaps, at the most, and this would all fade away as the sun did at the end of the day.

She stepped forward and took my hands in her own. Hers were cold, as if her nervousness blocked the circulation from reaching her fingers.

'What is it?' I asked.

She smiled at me, and something inside me responded to it. A mother's smile, it was. There was a lump in my throat.

'She's fragile, remember that, Fran.'

'Violet?' I said. 'She seems all right to me.' A little vulnerable, perhaps. But I was sure I'd sensed a strength wound like tendons around her bird bones.

'You know she's not. Not really. That's why we thought you'd be the best one to go this summer – someone her own age, but sensible.' Her face threatened to crumple. 'Oh Fran, you need to be your most solid, your most sensible.' She blinked watery eyes at me. 'Make sure she eats, moderate exercise, lots of fresh air, and for goodness sakes, keep all excitement far away from her.'

What on earth was wrong with her? I asked it out loud. 'What on earth is wrong with her?'

She squeezed my hands again. 'She is just over-excitable, that is all. And then she wears herself out and makes herself ill.' She swallowed. 'We wouldn't be letting you go, if it were anything a change of scenery won't help.' Her frown deepened.

'Then why are you squeezing my hands so tightly?'

With a self-conscious laugh, my mother let go and stepped back. 'I'm sorry Fran. I will miss you, that is all.' She brushed a stray hair from my cheek and smiled maternally at me. 'I just want you to be sensible. It is your first time away from home, after all. But I am worrying needlessly, I know. Already you are blossoming under the responsibility.' She smiled. 'You look brighter, more solid, somehow, than I've ever seen you.' A couple rapid blinks and she changed to looking vaguely around the room. 'Now, Mrs Kellow has written to Violet's father to say everything is ready for you, and she has organised for a cook, and a girl to come in and do for you.'

'Do for us?'

A quizzical look. 'Yes, the heavy work – but that's all you get.'

'I don't understand.'

'Oh Fran, now is really not the time to be obtuse. You girls wanted a measure of independence, and we have been convinced that it might be good for you.' She waggled a finger at me and I noticed the wedding ring, but I'd yet to find a male in the household other than an old fellow who helped with the gardening, and heavy lifting, and who was in fact right this minute heaving my trunk out the door.

My mother was still talking. 'You must seek out Mrs Kellow's council if you've any need. She knows her way around and is pleased to keep an eye on the two of you.' She barely paused for breath. 'But that does not mean you cannot pick up after yourselves, and while she lives close, you will be responsible for yourselves a great deal.'

It sounded pretty good. 'I understand, Mother,' I said, and did my best to look sensible, reliable, and responsible – which wasn't hard, because I've always had one of those faces people seem to find truthful and trustworthy without any effort on my part. Besides, I was actually the grand old age of twenty-nine and used to living on my own. I thought I could manage this house by the sea, and Violet too, although she might be a little more of a handful.

'Why have you gone red, Fran? Is something wrong?' She went back to a sudden wringing of hands. 'Oh I knew this was a bad idea. I will go and tell Isaac right now that we are not going through with it.'

'No!' I'd almost yelled and put a hand on her arm. 'I mean, please, Mother no, we will be fine, I promise.' I tried a smile. 'In fact, I guarantee we will come back better than new, the both of us.'

Her shoulders slumped, and she gave a weary nod. 'It is all arranged anyway.' The smile she gave me was equally weary but beautiful all the same. 'Kiss my cheek, then away with you – but mind I expect weekly letters.'

'You are not coming to the station?'

She shook her head. 'No, my dear, Isaac is going straight on to London – and you know how I dislike goodbyes.'

I knew no such thing of course, but nodded anyway, and gave her the kiss. Her cheek was soft, cool, and she smelt of lily of the valley and nervousness. I wished I could reassure her there was nothing to be worried about.

But I wasn't sure about that myself. Not quite.

CHAPTER FIVE

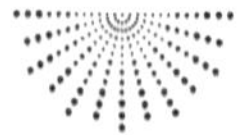

I don't know what I was expecting, but riding to the train station in a lurching, juddering two-horsepower-if-you're-lucky ancient jalopy was really helping the whole 1916 thing sink in. Because it seemed the clothes, manners, and house hadn't been enough. It took a classic car and a steam train to do that.

'What are you looking so flustered about?' Violet asked, settling into the seat opposite me on the train, her penetrating eyes looking me up and down. It was the first time she'd spoken since I'd climbed in the car for the tense and silent trip to the station with her father.

I shook my head. 'How long does it take to get there?' I asked, wishing I could just ask where the hell we were going. Yes, I was getting grumpy.

It was feeling less and less like a dream with every passing minute.

Violet shrugged and tugged her gloves off. 'No idea, I didn't recognise the name of the town when my stepmother prattled on about it. All I know is that Father is sending me away and there is a house somewhere and I am to live in it for three months.' She waved a hand vaguely in the air then leant forward and zeroed in on me. 'Now,' she said. 'Show me your hands.'

'What?'

She narrowed her beautiful eyes at me. 'You heard. Show me your hands.'

I looked down at them, knotted in my lap, gloves still on. I shook my head.

'Why not?' The voice didn't demand or tease, it was simply curious.

There was no answer. I sat mute, hands gripping each other in my lap, staring into her deep green eyes.

'Please?' she asked. 'Just for a moment.'

'Why?' I croaked.

She tilted her head at me. 'Because when we were at the house, you were looking at them.'

I licked my lips. They were dry. 'I didn't realise it meant anything odd to look at one's own hands.' A tiny voice at the back of my mind congratulated me on my appropriate word choice. I told it to sod the hell off.

Violet smiled at me, almost indulgently. 'You forget, Fran.'

I had to clear my throat. 'Forget what?'

'That I am a painter.' Her voice was almost a purr. 'Which means I notice details. Such as the expression you had on your face while frantically tearing your gloves from your hands.' She blinked. 'Now give them to me.'

I did. I offered up my hands and laid them on my knees between us, fingers curled upwards like dead spiders.

She laughed, took them in her own hands and peeled off the gloves. First the left, then the right. It was the right hand I'd really been trying to see.

My grandmother had shown my palm to anyone who would look, pressing it under their gaze, demanding that they see what was there. They'd all puzzled over it, heads bent over the lines on my palm like they were looking at map of a country they'd only just learnt existed. No one could say what it meant. Not for sure.

'You have two lifelines!' Violet lifted her face to mine, surprise written large across her features. 'I've never seen anything like it.'

'No one ever has,' I said, and she pounced on the left hand and spread its fingers flat, peered at that one too.

'Oh,' she said. 'It's only like that on your right hand.'

A nod was as much as I could manage.

'What do you think it means?'

'Why does it have to mean anything?' I considered tugging my hands from her grasp and tucking them out of sight under my arms, but I liked the touch of her fingers too much and left them where they were.

She smiled, and to me it was a wicked tilting of her lips. 'If I were a fortune teller, and you were to cross my palm with a gold coin, I would tell you it means that you are going to have the choice between two very different lives.' Her fingers stroked the lines on my palm.

'Two different lives?'

'Yes,' she said, eyes locked on mine. 'Perhaps, shall we say, between a life of convention and duty, and…'

'And what?'

But she folded my fingers closed and pushed my hands back to me. 'I would think that was obvious, wouldn't you?'

I shook my head. 'From where I'm sitting, believe me, nothing is obvious.'

Leaning back Violet opened her purse. My hands felt suddenly cold without her touch. 'Watch out now, I'm going to do something scandalous.'

That made me shake my head. 'Nobody's watching.'

Her mouth turned down. 'Oh Fran,' she said. 'That is where you're wrong. Somebody is always watching.' She lit a cigarette and gazed out the window at the scenery passing in a blur of green that matched her eyes. The smoke wreathed itself around her head.

'I don't think anyone much will be watching where we're going for the summer.'

That made her shake her head and turn to look at me. 'But is that not your job, Francesca? To watch your crazy cousin and make sure she doesn't do anything to get herself in trouble?'

It was my turn to look out the window, perfectly clear on the fact that she was right. Also perfectly clear on the fact that I wasn't quite the Fran everyone had been expecting.

Which might be okay, except I had no idea where we were even going, let alone what I was supposed to do about it.

'Wake up,' I whispered.

'What did you say?'

I shook my head. 'Nothing,' I said.

That made her glare at me, and probably justifiably.

'Good grief, Fran, if you say that one more time when it is patently a lie, I swear I will come across the compartment and throttle you with my bare hands.' She leant forward, eyes narrowed. 'Now I would like to have decent, interesting conversations with you. You are interesting. There is something different about you, and I would like to find out what it is.' Her feline eyes blinked. 'So don't you dare bore me with stupidity!'

I stared at her a moment longer, then looked away. I wanted to wake up. For the first time since this dream started, I wanted to wake up. It was no longer relevant if I was lying in a hospital bed somewhere with a catheter and an I.V. I'd even put up with finding a tube stuck down my throat if it meant I could wake up.

My gaze went back to Violet's and I took a breath. 'I think I'm dreaming,' I said.

The train whistle screamed, and I jumped, clutching at the seat, white-knuckled. Underneath the carriage, steel sparked against steel as the great metal beast we were aboard gathered speed, hurtling me towards god knew what.

Violet looked at me, cigarette forgotten for a moment in her hand, then she reached over and stubbed it out in an ashtray under the window. Her hand touched the knuckles of my own.

'You'd best start at the beginning,' she said.

'No.' I shook my head. 'You wouldn't believe me – even if you're part of my own imagination, you wouldn't believe me, so it would achieve nothing.' I turned my right hand over under her fingers and stared at the twin life lines.

If I thought that would put her off, I had never been so wrong in my life. It had the exact opposite effect because a moment later she had picked herself up and switched seats, landing next to me, her presence a warm and immediate thing I had to close my eyes against.

There was a touch on my cheek, and then my hand was lifted again in her own and cradled there. Her fingers had heated, and my own thawed beside hers.

'Tell me what you mean,' she whispered, and her breath was hot against my face and it tasted of cigarette smoke, and something else, tea, plum jam. I kept my eyes closed, wondering how it was possible for a dream to feel this real. Searching my mind, I tried to remember other dreams, compare them.

'I used to have a recurring dream,' I said, leaning back against the seat, the train a rhythmic vibration under me now. 'I still have it every now and then.' A short laugh, and her fingers tightened on mine. I liked the touch. 'It haunts me,' I told her and myself. 'Literally.'

'Don't ramble,' she said to me in a low voice. 'Tell it straight.'

That made me open my eyes, and I turned my head slightly and looked at her. Violet's eyes were large and so very green from this close. Her breath touched my lips and I parted them slightly, breathed in a sip of the air she breathed out.

'You have the most marvellous eyes,' I said, before I could stop myself.

They blinked slowly, looked at me from a fringe of dark lashes. 'You can swim in my sea-green gaze later,' she said, and her voice was amused, wry.

'Can I?' There was no censoring myself when she was this close. I threaded my fingers through hers and watched her look back at me. She blinked again, fast this time, three times, then looked steadily at me.

'That is a conversation for later,' she said eventually. 'Right now, you are telling me about your dream.'

'Right now I am dreaming you.'

She had beautiful lips too. A wide mouth, made for laughter, long speeches, mobile, always on the move. I looked at it but stayed still.

'I am not a dream,' she said.

Back to her eyes, holding me steady in their gaze.

'Are you not?'

She took my hand, untangled our fingers and pressed mine against her cheek, slid them down her jaw to the hot skin of her neck at the collar of her blouse. 'Does that not feel real? Do I not feel flesh and blood?'

It did. Oh, how it did. Her pulse leapt under my fingers and I felt the blush of heat spread across the base of her throat. I closed my eyes against it all, bathing in the sensation, splashing around in it, drowning in the tide of it washing over me.

'Fran?'

'What?'

'Come back to me.'

I shook my head. 'You are not real.'

She moved my hand down further, and I felt the swell of her breast through her clothing, then her heart.

'Is it not beating?' she asked.

It was. Fast. Her chest rose and fell under my hand, her breathing rapid, almost panting. She dropped my hand as though suddenly scalded and it fell back in my lap. I opened my eyes to find her fishing on the opposite seat for her cigarettes. She didn't speak until she had one lit, gulping in the smoke.

'Tell me about your recurring dream.' She didn't look at me, but past me, out the window where a world I hadn't been born to flitted past. 'Begin at the beginning and tell me the story.' She glanced at me, and her mouth was twisted into something briefly humorous. 'We've only room in this relationship for one crazy woman, and that spot is taken.'

'I'm not dreaming you?' I asked.

'No, you are not.' She looked at me again, for a beat longer. 'I should be offended that you would even consider me unreal.'

I shook my head. Took a deep breath. 'For years I've dreamed of being haunted by a woman.'

She raised an eyebrow and I was forced to elaborate.

'In the dream I am doing something, going somewhere, something inconsequential, perhaps. But this woman is there, and I know she is a ghost, a spirit, but she follows me, watching me.' I turn to stare sightlessly out the train window. 'It is always the same. I am somewhere, and it is dark, and she is there, watching me.'

'She follows you?'

'Always.'

'What does she look like?'

I shrug. 'I don't know. A woman. Just a woman. Young.'

'How do you know she is a ghost?'

I had to think about that. 'She is not completely solid.'

'Does she simply watch and follow you?'

'Yes. That's all. She won't interact with me, she is just there, watching.'

'Why are you telling me this?'

'You asked me to.'

She sighed, as though I was a recalcitrant child. 'You began this story of your own volition. I am asking why.'

It was a good question. I turned my hand over in my lap and looked at the twin lines that swept across my palm.

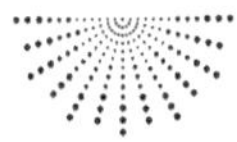

CHAPTER SIX

I looked around at the railway carriage. It was small, panelled in a dark wood, two upholstered bench seats facing each other, under a netting shelf for our bags. A sliding door cocooned us from the rest of the passengers.

'There is no one to overhear our conversation,' she said, watching me. She was still back in her original position, and leaned against the window, staring unblinking at me. Our knees brushed against each other when the train jerked.

'Where are we going?' I asked.

Her head, small and neat, tilted to the side. 'Why do you not know?'

'Do you always ask questions instead of answering them?'

She appeared to consider it. 'Quite often, I believe. My stepmother names it my *appalling habit*.' She smoothed her cream-coloured skirt over her knees. 'Now tell me, if you please, why you seem not to know our destination? This has been planned for a number of months, I do not understand why you are asking such a basic detail.' Her humour warred with her interested confusion and won briefly. 'Did you hit your head hard yesterday? Your sister informed me you fell out of a tree trying to fetch her kite.'

Here was my opportunity. Did I dare take it? Where was I, really? Was I lying in a hospital bed, in a coma? Or had I somehow slipped through time and a dream to land here? I rubbed at the lines on my palm again.

'I did hit my head,' I said. 'But I don't remember falling from a tree.'

Her green eyes were fixed on me.

'I fell from a ladder.' A pause, waiting for her to interrupt. She didn't. 'I was trying to hook some lights to the ceiling of my bookshop because my best friend Bronwyn is getting married and we are having the reception there.' I paused, watching Violet, watching her watching me.

'You are telling me another dream?' she asked.

I shook my head. 'Which is the dream?' I waved a hand around at the train compartment where we sat. 'Is it this? To me, it is this.' I clasped my hands back together and leaned forward, looking at her. 'You're going to think I'm crazy.'

It was her turn to shake her head. 'No, I don't think so.'

What the hell – it was a dream, right? And if it wasn't, then I obviously wasn't capable of coping with it all in silence. Something about the way Violet looked at me, listened, made me want to tell her everything.

'My name is Fran Madden,' I said.

She nodded. 'We are second cousins, I believe. My mother – my real mother, was your mother's cousin. So we're twice removed, or some such nonsense.'

'Have you met me before?' I was risking getting side-tracked but couldn't help it.

'Yes, but not for six or seven years. There was some

distance between our parents, after my mother died and my father remarried, I believe.' She waved a hand. 'It sounded boring, so I never asked for explanations.'

I laughed. 'Do you find many things boring?'

'Most things in my parents' world are dull.' She smiled. 'But you are not. You are the most interesting thing I've met in a long while.'

That made me narrow my eyes at her. 'In a long while?'

'Yes, at least since I ran away to art school for three months.'

'What? You ran away to art school?'

She settled back against her cushion with the comfort of a cat. 'Yes. But surely you must know this?'

Ah. We had come full circle. 'No,' I said, 'And that is the point I was making before. I know nothing, because I am not your second cousin once, twice, or anytime removed, although I do not know how this has come to be.'

'You are not making yourself very clear. Do you think you could try to?'

I wanted to kiss her. Right then, with a desire perhaps not sudden, but terribly strong. It was the way she looked at me, a slight smile playing around her lips, yet not mocking. She was prepared to believe whatever preposterous story I was about to tell her, and that was an astounding thing.

'What on earth are you thinking?' she asked, a loose frown replacing the smile.

I shook my head, fibbed. 'Trying to figure out where to start.'

'Where you left off would be fine. You fell off a ladder and hit your head while doing something with lights for your friend Bronwyn's wedding.' Her eyebrows raised in perfect arches. 'You own a bookshop.'

'Haven,' I said. 'That's what it's called. Haven for Books.'

She cocked her head to the side. 'I like it,' she decided. 'Tell me more, please.' I opened my mouth and she must have seen that I was about to question the way she seemed to be accepting what I had to say. 'No, just tell me the story,' she told me. 'We can discuss my feelings about it, and other such things, when I have heard the entirety of it.'

I stared at her for a long moment and she held my gaze. 'You know what?' I said. 'Okay. You have a deal. That's what we'll do.'

She lit another cigarette. 'I'm all agog,' she said, and made me laugh.

'Where was I?'

She held up a bony hand. 'Ladder, bookshop, wedding.' She ticked them off on her fingers. 'Although not necessarily in that order.'

'Right.' I looked around the compartment. 'I'm parched,' I said.

Violet shook her head. 'No, you must tell your story first. Then we will go to the dining car and have some luncheon.'

It was probably that moment that I really did decide to tell her my fantastic tale.

'This Fran Madden,' I said, pointing a finger at my own chest, 'is twenty-nine years old and lives in Bath, in a flat above her bookshop.'

'Haven for Books.'

'Yes.' I almost told her the type of books we specialised in at Haven but decided against it. TMI, I said inside my head.

'Are you married?' she asked, and there was an avid curiosity in her voice. She was enjoying this.

'No,' I said.

'Why not? I think my stepmother will throw me down the cellar steps if she has not married me off by the age of twenty-nine.'

I realised I hadn't told her the biggest part of my story. My throat closed on the words. I had no idea what would happen once I said the words.

So I said them quickly. Forced them out. 'It was 2016 when I fell off the ladder.'

She gazed at me.

'And 1916 when I woke up.'

She mouthed the words twenty sixteen to herself.

'The year two thousand and sixteen,' I said helpfully. 'One hundred years from now.' I blinked. 'One hundred years and some months, I suspect, because it was December there, almost Christmas.' I shivered at the remembered chill.

Her eyes were round cat's eyes. 'You are being truthful?'

'Yes.' She would believe me, or not. I waited.

'Two thousand and sixteen?'

'Yes. The twenty-first century.' I was almost apologetic by now.

She tilted her head at me. 'And where do you think the 1916 Fran is? The one I have, in the past, met.' She waved a hand. 'Vanished, just like that?'

My mouth went dry. For some reason, I flashed on my dream, but I shook my head. 'I don't know,' I said.

Violet shrugged. 'Perhaps she was always meant to step aside for you. She was one of the most colourless people I'd ever met, never expressed a single dream for her future when

I quizzed her about it.' Her eyes sparkled. 'Which you know I did.' She grinned. 'That would make the most sense, do you not think? And you know – this does explain the twin lifelines.'

I gaped at her, head spinning. 'You believe me?'

'I have no idea,' she said, then smiled widely at me. 'But I am willing to indulge in the extremely entertaining possibility.'

That was probably more than generous, and it filled me with a surprising satisfaction. 'I feel better for that,' I said.

'Good. Then let us go have something to eat. I find myself – rather surprisingly – with an appetite.'

I wasn't sure I could say the same, but I stood up feeling buoyant.

Violet paused in sliding the compartment door open. 'When you told me that,' she said. 'The last bit – you had the strangest expression on your face. What were you thinking?'

'Besides that you wouldn't believe me?'

'Yes.'

I looked down at my hands, pulling the gloves onto them. 'I half expected the dream to burst, and that I would wake, and it would be over.'

'And you would be back in your own time?' Her frown deepened.

I nodded.

'But it didn't.'

'No.' The train swayed under me and I swayed with it.

She turned back to the door and stepped out into the corridor, not looking at me as I followed. She said something.

'Sorry,' I said. 'I didn't hear you.'

She cleared her throat. 'I asked if you minded.' She met my eyes, then slid her gaze away. 'Still being here.'

I was silent for a moment, long enough for her to look at me again, then shake her head.

'Forget I asked,' she said. 'It was a foolish question. Of course you'd rather be back in your own home, your own time.'

Reaching out, I touched her sleeve. She'd put her jacket and hat back on, as had I, following her lead, but I still imagined I could feel the heat of her skin through it.

'No,' I said, realising things had changed in the last few minutes. 'I think right now I would have minded if I'd woken up.'

I watched her lips move, but whatever she was saying had no sound. She subsided into a smile instead and nodded.

'I'm glad,' she said finally. 'I was just getting to like you.'

With that, I followed her to the dining car, listening to my heart singing a strange, unknown song.

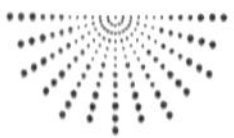

CHAPTER SEVEN

The sun slanted across the hills outside the train windows by the time we came whistling and clanking to a halt at a small station.

'We're here,' Violet announced, and I stared at her in surprise. We'd spent most of the trip – since my big revelation – in silence, or quiet, inconsequential talk of the weather, the food, the view. I'd been content to give Violet time for it all to sink in, to decide whether she should try believing it. As for me, I spent my time sneaking glances at her.

She was not, perhaps, conventionally pretty, but everything about her appealed to me – in fact, I found her intensely beautiful. With hair of a rich darkness, and her magnificent eyes underneath it, that incredibly mobile mouth and a chin endearingly pointed, I had to admit, an hour or two into the journey, that I was risking becoming completely smitten.

I looked at Violet, and before long it was the bookshop, the wedding, the hospital with its beeping machines keeping me alive that were the dreams, not this train carriage, not the woman sitting opposite me, quietly smoking a cigarette and gazing out the window with eyes the same colour as the hills and valleys she was looking at.

'But we're...' I began, sitting up and peering out the window.

'Precisely nowhere,' Violet said. 'Nevertheless, this is the end of the line for us.'

Her words made me shudder, an edge of my grandmother's New Age superstition creeping under the skin to bring me out in goose bumps. 'Don't say it like that.'

She looked at me in surprise. 'Like what?'

'The end of the line for us.' But I was being silly and so I shrugged, getting up and reaching for her carpet bag, tugging it down from the luggage rack and passing it to her. I smiled. 'Pay no mind,' I said. 'I was just having a moment.'

She looked at me with her sea-green eyes then shook her head. 'No,' she said. 'It's all right. I quite understand.'

That took me by surprise. 'You do?'

A slow smile crept over her face. God, but I loved her mouth. 'We've just properly met. It would be a tragedy were it to be *the end of the line* for us. I'm sorry. I was insensitive with my words.'

I didn't know what to say. 'Really, there's no need to apologise. I spoke without thinking.'

She burst into laughter. 'Come along. We'll be here all day if we continue to take turns apologising like this. At least there's a house somewhere here waiting for us.'

I turned my attention to my own bags. 'With a cook, and a girl from the village to do for us.'

A questioning look. 'I thought...'

'I was told just before we left,' I explained.

Her laughter was nervous for the first time. 'This is going to take some getting used to.'

I followed her from the train. 'You're telling me,' I said, little more than a mutter.

We landed like twin pieces of driftwood onto the station platform.

'I can smell the ocean,' I said, delighted. The briny scent lifted my spirits.

Violet sniffed the air. 'I've never been to the seaside before,' she said.

Gaping at her, I searched her features for an explanation. 'Really?'

'It's true.'

'Did you bring painting equipment?' I asked, excitement for her already threading through my veins. I couldn't see the ocean from the station, but I could smell it, and I couldn't imagine a painter seeing it for the first time and not wanting to paint it.

Her face had fallen, features suddenly angular and awkward. She shook her head.

'But...' I said.

'I suppose that is part of my story,' she told me, switching her bag to her other hand and shuffling a little where she stood. 'Which apparently you are unaware of.'

I touched her elbow, meaning it to be a comforting gesture. 'At least we won't run out of conversation too soon.'

Her face relaxed and she laughed. 'There is always that, indeed.'

I nodded and went back to looking around. A porter was busy heaving our trunks onto the platform. He straightened and looked in our direction. Nudging Violet, I whispered to her. 'What do we do now?'

She pursed her lips. 'I believe we are to be met here.'

As if Violet's words had conjured her, a woman red of face bustled up to us.

'You girls will be the Misses Farningham and Madden, then,' she said, beaming. 'I'm Mrs Kellow, and I've the pony and trap, to take you to your summer cottage.'

She spoke in a wheezing rush through a constant smile that left both Violet and I speechless. We needn't have worried, however, because a moment later Mrs Kellow turned and was ordering the porter about, waving her hands in frantic signals regarding our trunks.

Violet slipped a hand into mine. 'I feel suddenly tired,' she said, while I simply swallowed at her touch. I knew the gesture meant little – it was common for women to link arms in public and no one thought anything of it, but it was a custom gone by the time I was born, and to me, her touch made me desire a great deal more than friendship.

'We will be there shortly, it seems,' I said, dredging up my voice and she nodded against my side.

'Girls!' Mrs Kellow called. 'Let's move, shall we? I've Mr Kellow's supper to tend to at home.'

An exchanged glance, then Violet and I were following the barrelling figure toward a wooden wagon hitched to a disinterested horse. The porter had heaved our trunks aboard and stood there listing somewhat to the side. He had a club foot, which I guessed was why he was here being bossed around by Mrs Kellow rather than on the Continent taking orders in the mud of Flanders.

Violet nudged me. 'Tip him,' she whispered, and flustered

for a moment, I searched for my purse and fumbled with it, pulling out a coin and plastering it to his waiting palm without checking its denomination. It must have been acceptable though, because he suddenly grinned at us with tobacco-stained teeth and touched a hand to his cap, before turning and making his limping way back to the station.

'Climb aboard, girls. Your supper will be waiting for you too.'

We did as we were told, and I felt about four years old as I did so, moving past the trunks to sit on a wooden bench behind Mrs Kellow where she sat with the reins in her hands. A backwards glance at us to make sure we were situated, and she got the whole contraption moving. I hung onto the sides as we lurched around out onto the road.

'How far is the cottage, Mrs Kellow?' Violet asked, and I looked at her, seeing dark smudges under her eyes.

'Not far, my dear. We'll be there in ten minutes.'

Violet turned to me. 'Walking distance,' she mouthed, and I nodded. At least, then, we wouldn't be completely isolated.

'It's a lovely spot,' Mrs Kellow said. 'The view is stunning. Most popular with all our visitors.'

'You own the cottage?' I asked.

'Mr Kellow and myself, that'd be right,' she replied. 'Mrs Snell who is cooking for you is my sister, and she will come mid-morning and make the luncheon and supper, but she will not stay to serve.'

I took this to mean she would only be there a few hours a day. I was glad. A glance at Violet told me this suited her as well.

'I'm sure we will manage perfectly well,' I said. 'You're very kind to organise everything.'

Our companion laughed. 'Oh I'm paid well enough to be very kind for sure, love!' She twisted in her driver's seat to give me a wide grin. 'But it's my pleasure. I enjoy organising the hospitality, and you two look as though you will give me little trouble.' Her eyes wandered to Violet sitting opposite me and nodded her chin at her. 'Is she not well with the travelling?'

'It has been very tiring,' I said, but in truth I was a little concerned. Violet was drooping with fatigue.

Mrs Kellow and I carried the trunks into the cottage between us, humping them upstairs to two little bedrooms and depositing them each under twin leadlight windows.

'The view!' I exclaimed. Mrs Kellow paused a moment to give it an appreciative sniff.

'Did I not tell you?' she said.

The sea, glossed by the last tendrils of sunshine, spread out in a glorious display of aqua waves that deepened to turquoise as the bay spread out below us. I could have sat and looked at it until there was no light left by which to see it.

But I had left Violet wilting on a sofa downstairs.

'Your supper will be in the larder,' Mrs Kellow said, moving back to the stairs. 'I suggest you feed that young lady up, then tuck her into her bed. She is exhausted. Her father said her health was somewhat precarious.'

'I'm going to do exactly that, Mrs Kellow,' I said, following her down to the front door where she turned and nodded at me.

'My husband and I are next door, about half a mile on down the road. You come and fetch me if you've any need, I shan't mind. I promised your cousin's father I would keep a look-out for you.' She smiled, matronly and pleased, then set off down the path back to the horse and wagon with a wave of her hand.

I watched her go, solitude falling over the cottage and the garden like a curtain, until there was only the light, the scent of grass and flowers and ocean, and the sweeping hush and tussle of the tide below us. I breathed it in until it felt like the very air in my lungs was made of such things, and then I moved gladly to go to Violet.

She sat where I had left her, head turned with bright eyes towards the window. She didn't stir when I came into the room.

'Don't turn the light on yet, Fran,' she said, gaze still fixed on the view, spectacular even though the sea was tucked out of sight below the cliff. The sky was enough, blue and gold and infinite. 'I've never seen anything like this, you know.'

'It is beautiful,' I said, knowing now finally where we were, on the Cornish coast, which right now, was enough detail for me. I reached out and placed my hand on the back of the sofa, feeling the smooth and rough of the brocade upholstery, and thinking that surely that this was more than a dream. If I was in a hospital bed, hooked up to those machines, then perhaps it was only my body there.

My soul was here, slipped into another body that was just like mine, my twin, and I stood here in a golden, gathering twilight, the ocean on my breath, feeling real and unreal at the same time.

It was a different time, a different place, and yet, maybe it was the right time and place. Could that be possibly so? I was no longer in any hurry to wake up.

Violet moved, turning her head to look at me, and she was smiling. 'It is more lovely here than I expected, Fran.'

'I know,' I said, moving my hand to rest instead on her shoulder. 'Perhaps it won't be so bad after all.'

Her eyes were deep pools in the growing shadows. 'As good, perhaps, as a bookshop in the year two thousand and sixteen?' She said the date slowly, as if trying not to stumble over the unfamiliar numbers.

Her question, taking my own a step further, left me unable to answer straight away. A long moment passed, and her face fell, and then my heart fell with it. She turned away, back to the window.

'I'm hungry, Fran,' she said. 'Would you be able to see what there is for our dinner?'

I could have kicked myself. She sat in the shadows in the strange room, a small, slight figure, and I realised that possibly it wasn't just me worrying what would happen if this were all a dream I would wake up from at any moment.

If I woke up, where would that leave Violet?

I tightened my fingers on the bones of her shoulders. 'I don't want to be anywhere else right now,' I said, surprising myself with the truth of the words.

Her attention was back on me. 'You don't need to say that, Fran. Not just for my sake.' She looked back out the window again. 'I'm sure, if you were to wake up back to your own time, then I would simply have the real Fran here, and all would be perfectly well. I do not remember her being a particularly vibrant person, but I am sure we would get along well enough.'

My hand froze on her shoulder, and then I took it away. Her words had perhaps meant to hurt, and they did so.

'I'll go get us something to eat,' I said. 'We're both tired.'

She nodded but didn't turn back to me, and I found my

way out of the darkening room and through the small cottage to the kitchen, where I placed my hands on the table and leaned against it, hanging my head down and trying to think.

It didn't work. Nothing was clear. Straightening, I looked about for our dinner, found it, and busied myself setting it out on a tray. We'd eat looking at the view, the sun sinking in the west, the moon rising in the east.

And in the morning, I decided with a feeling of presentiment, I would either be here, or I wouldn't.

It was impossible to say which I wanted.

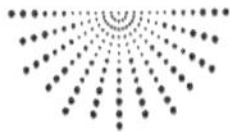

CHAPTER EIGHT

I dreamed of her again. Lying in the high bed, feather pillow under my head and the sea washing against shadowed sand below the cottage, I dreamed of the ghost woman who haunted me in the darkest recesses of my mind. She looked at me from shrouded doorways – it was always night in the dreams I had of her – and she followed me on feet that made no sound on the road and footpaths behind me. She was simply there, watching me, attached to me as though by some invisible umbilical cord.

I woke with her indistinct face in my mind and it hovered there for a moment, then slunk away into the tattered remnants of the dream and was gone.

What had roused me?

The curtains at the window were undrawn, the silvered sky visible, peppered with a hundred thousand stars, but it wasn't the inquisitive moon that had brought me awake.

A sound. I sat up, pushing the thick blankets down to my thighs and straining to listen. It had been the sound of a door opening that I had heard buried in the depths of the house.

And before that perhaps, the soft whisper of a bare foot on a stair.

I was out of the bed before I'd had time to consciously decide what to do. My feet, bare too and still warm from the bed, slapped against the wooden stairs that creaked a little under my weight. Perhaps it had been that noise that had woken me too.

Half way down I slowed and peered back the way I'd come. I should have checked Violet's room. I should have seen for sure that she wasn't there.

But I knew. It had been her step on the stairs I'd heard. We were the only two in the house and although perhaps in my own time I would have thought first of an intruder, here, I thought only of Violet, and that had me turning back, running down the stairs and to the front door.

It was ajar, and I pushed it the rest of the way open, stepping out onto the stone pathway that had cooled with the night air, and looking around the garden. She wasn't there.

I wanted to call her name, but it stayed stuck to my tongue and I made no noise except for my quiet steps as I traced the way down the path and out through the little gate into the grassy lane that spread parallel to the clifftop.

She was where I had known she would be the moment I heard the front door open.

I stopped several steps back from her and simply stayed there, looking. Silhouetted by the sky, haloed with stars, Violet stood with her head tipped back, then leaned forward and gazed out at the sea.

'I do not know what to think,' she said without turning.

'About what?' I asked, wrapping my arms around my

middle. It was cool outside, the air damp from the sea beneath us, and I wore only a long, white nightdress.

She spread fingers to the horizon, as if to touch it from where she stood. 'This,' she said. 'The ocean.' She paused, and I watched her considering it all. 'It looks eternal,' she said. 'It will outlive us; do you not think so?'

I made no reply, thinking of how in my own time we poisoned the oceans with our plastics and our waste.

'I thought the world had changed,' she said. 'The actual world, the structure of it, everything. It seemed impossible that it wasn't everything that had changed, but now I see that I was wrong.' The hand pushed at the air over the sea and I watched, wanting her to step back from the edge. 'This,' she said. 'This lasts. This goes on unchanged, no matter that our society worships a mechanical god now, no matter that there is no god at all anymore.'

She turned to me. 'And if this goes on unchanged, uncaring even, then there really is hope.'

'For what?'

'For art,' she said, then tipped her head to the side. 'For love?'

'Is that a question?'

'If it is, then do you know the answer?'

I thought for a moment. 'I think love means everything.'

Violet stared at me for a moment, then she stood there in the moonlight and laughed. 'I didn't take you for a romantic.'

'Looks can be deceiving.'

She tipped her head in acknowledgement. 'I should have known – a bookshop, after all.'

'What do you mean?'

An impish smile. 'All that time spent among stories. How could you not be a romantic?'

It was my turn to point to the ocean. 'There is also this,' I said. 'Art, love, oceans.'

She closed her eyes and spread both arms wide, a slight figure in white, the sea breeze playing with her loose hair.

'How I want to live,' she said, and her voice was full of a beautiful fury for the world.

'Then you must live,' I said. 'Live as your heart tells you to, and don't let anyone say you should do otherwise.'

That earned me a smile, tinged with sadness. Stepping away from the edge finally, she came to my side and linked an arm through mine.

'But I tried that, Fran,' she said. 'And I failed.' She shivered against me.

'Come inside,' I said. 'Back to bed. You are cold.'

We moved toward the house even as she shook her head. 'I do not want to go back to bed. I want to see the night, I want to watch the stars wheel overhead like they have since before we were here to start counting the years.' Her eyes glittered, themselves like stars. 'I want to watch the tide come in, bringing with it waves that have visited far shores, and then I want to see it wash it all out to sea again, waving farewell in the early dawn with fingers of white spume.'

'You should have been a writer,' I said.

She laughed and leaned against me as I led her through the gate to the cottage. 'My fingers do not know how to properly hold a pen. They were made for brushes, charcoals.'

There were so many things I wanted to ask her. 'Why did you not bring any supplies with you?'

Her face shuttered and we paused for a moment on the

doorstep, not quite within the house and neither without it. I held her arm in mine, feeling her body shivering against my side, and seeing her face a pale moon with cast down eyes.

'Remember I said that I had failed?' she said, lifting her gaze to mine again, but it was not the same, all shadows and pain.

'What did you fail at?' I said, barely above a whisper. 'Fail is such a harsh word.'

She turned her head and stared inside at the strange cottage. 'I failed at my attempt to live,' she said, and did not look back at me, but stepped into the house which swallowed her up into its darkness.

But I was Fran Madden from the twenty first century and from a child of a practical bent, even while confessing my belief in love above all else. There was a switch inside the doorway and I flicked it on, spreading a yellow light where before there was only dimness.

'Violet?' I called. She was gone from the entranceway.

'In here.' Her reply was muffled. I went into the front room, a long, low sitting room, and found her at the window. There was a rug on the sofa and I picked it up, spread it over her shoulders.

'Let me make you a cup of tea,' I said. 'If you want to stay up.'

'Just a little longer, Fran,' she said, turning to look at me with eyes wide again, but tired. 'And perhaps there is cocoa?'

It made me smile, her childlike request. 'I'm sure there is,' I told her. 'Let me go see.'

She nodded. 'I'm just going to sit awhile and look at the stars. I can almost see the ocean reflected in them.' She sank down into the armchair by the window and gathered the blanket tighter around herself.

I wanted to pat her, say something comforting, but she was already turned back to the sky outside, and besides, she wasn't a child, or a puppy, and I would be mistaken to treat her as one.

'Be back shortly,' I said instead, and tried not to linger for a reply I knew wouldn't be coming.

Upstairs, I found my dressing gown and tugged it on, deciding that tomorrow we would do some exploring, discover the nooks and crannies of the cottage, and the garden. There was probably a spot somewhere too, where we could sit and see the water; I would seek that out for us.

A smile spread wryly on my face. For us, I'd said. For Violet, that's who I wanted to do it for.

And another thing, I realised, as I found slippers and pushed my cold feet into them. I had just assumed I would be there in the morning – as though this were not, after all, a dream from which I would abruptly awake. As if this were real, and my life now.

Maybe it is, I told myself, skipping down the stairs and turning into the kitchen. I had spent a night in this world already, had been asleep in bed twice already, had dreamed – a dream within a dream – who had written that poem? I sifted through the inventory of my memory and pulled Poe's name from it.

> Take this kiss upon the brow!
> And, in parting from you now,
> Thus much let me avow —
> You are not wrong, who deem

That my days have been a dream;
Yet if hope has flown away
In a night, or in a day,
In a vision, or in none,
Is it therefore the less *gone*?
All that we see or seem
Is but a dream within a dream.

I stand amid the roar
Of a surf-tormented shore,
And I hold within my hand
Grains of the golden sand —
How few! yet how they creep
Through my fingers to the deep,
While I weep — while I weep!
O God! Can I not grasp
Them with a tighter clasp?
O God! can I not save
One from the pitiless wave?
Is *all* that we see or seem
But a dream within a dream?

A nod and I found myself letting the question go and searching through the cupboards instead on a quest for cocoa. It was there, a round tin of it, and I smiled at it, feeling quite absurd, quite unreal, and yet more flesh and blood than ever before. Violet was waiting for me, and she wanted a cup of cocoa.

A life had been hung on less.

The kettle upon the range was still warm, and the embers in the firebox still glowing from the tea I had made us before bed. Violet had wandered into the kitchen to watch me then, a cigarette in her hand, a gentle waft of smoke around her head.

'How do you know to do that?' she had asked.

I'd smiled at her. 'How do you not?'

She'd tilted that charming head of hers and raised an eyebrow. 'The cook and scullery maid do it,' she said, then grimaced. 'We have built our leisure upon their backs.'

'I can teach you to do it yourself, if you like. It's a skill you should have, if you feel like that.'

'I don't know how I feel, to tell the truth. What is it like in your time?'

'In my time we do for ourselves, unless, I suppose, we have a great deal of money.'

Both fine eyebrows were up in surprise now. 'What?'

I fed another piece of coal to the fire and blew gently on it, feeling the fledgling flames. 'It's true.' A brief glance at the ceiling, thinking about it. 'You are more right than you know about the world changing,' I told her. 'It is starting right now, during the war.'

She sat herself on the table and leaned forward, listening. I wanted to kiss her, but looked back at the fire instead, rethreading my thoughts.

'With so many men sent to war,' I told her, 'women were necessary to take their place in a great many jobs.' I smiled. 'Long story short, I guess – we got used to it, wanted more of it, demanded the right to work, to vote, to be independent.' Straightening, I looked with satisfaction at the fire in the range, then popped the kettle on the plate over it.

'Tell me more.'

'Well, by the…' I stopped.

'By the what?'

I reconsidered. News without warning of a second world war when the first was only part way done was perhaps a cruelty.

'By the 1940's,' I said instead, 'there were far fewer women – and men – in domestic service. Society changed. Women worked outside the home more and more often. We went to university, we got jobs, although it was still another twenty or thirty years before it became acceptable for women to continue working after marriage.' I looked at her. 'Now,' I said, 'now it is normal for a woman to work most of her adult life.' I grinned. 'And we definitely do not think it a requirement that we have a man to look after us.'

The look on her face had been priceless. A mixture of astonishment.

And envy.

CHAPTER NINE

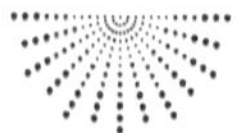

The kettle whistled, and back in the present – which was a relative term, if ever there was one – I roused myself and poured the hot water into blue and white Cornish mugs, adding milk from the larder and stirring the lumps from the drinks as best I could. It was a little bitter for my taste, and a far cry from a cup of coffee, but still it was hot and somehow comforting, reminding me of my childhood when my grandmother made me a hot cup of cocoa before bed every night.

That made me think of the dream, and the twin lines on my right palm, but I pushed the puzzle aside for the moment and loaded the mugs onto the tea tray instead.

Violet hadn't moved except to lift up her feet and tuck them under the blanket, wedged into the chair with an awkward abundance of angles. She heard me come in and turned to look at me.

'Do you tell the truth?' she asked, as if we'd been having a conversation while I was gone.

'Generally,' I answered, with a short laugh.

She shook her head, impatient. 'No; but there is a conversation for later, certainly, as to why only generally.' She blinked in the light from the lamp I turned on. The stars dimmed, but the swish and wash of the sea was still there.

'Then do I tell the truth about what?' I asked, passing her the mug of cocoa and sitting myself in the chair next to hers under the window, looking at her with a soft smile. Even with the dark bruises under her eyes, she was beautiful, her hair a wild tumble upon her shoulders, everything about her somehow contradictory, and yet harmonious. She fascinated me.

'The truth about where you are from.' I couldn't see the colour of her eyes well in the shadowed room, but the intensity of their expression was undeniable.

'Yes,' I said.

She waited a beat. 'Yes?' she asked. 'Just yes, that is all?'

I shrugged. 'The answer is only either yes or no. It happens to be yes, in this case.'

'It is a lot to believe,' she stated.

I did not ask if she was up to the task.

Violet sipped at her cocoa. 'And yet, I do,' she continued. 'It makes no sense that I should – absolutely none at all – and yet I do.'

'Why?' I asked her.

'That is a good question, and I do not know, exactly,' she replied. 'Perhaps because the alternative is that you are even crazier than I, and I simply cannot believe that is so.' She laughed, a silver tinkling.

'But that is flawed reasoning,' I said. 'Since I do not see you as being crazy, so we are both judging each other by...' I stopped talking.

'By what?'

'By what we think is in front of our eyes,' I finished. 'Tell me why you call yourself crazy.'

Her gaze drifted towards the window again and I saw her body tense under the rug, her bone fingers gripping the mug.

'Because it is true,' she said, and her lips tightened against each other.

'Crazy is a loaded word,' I told her. 'At least where I come from, it means many things, and mostly nothing much at all.'

Haunted eyes stared at me. 'I am banished here to this cottage far away from everything I want in my life, and I am so by my own father,' she said. 'To get me out of the way, to keep me out of trouble.' The eyes blinked slowly. 'And you are here to play nursemaid. Which is no kindness to you, although decidedly it is to me.' A cynical smile appeared. 'I am here while my father decides what should be done with me.'

'You will have to tell me the whole story,' I said, although already I was guessing at some of it.

She shook her head. 'Probably, but I am tired. I think I should return to my bed after all.'

I put down my cup. 'Do you need help?' She'd stood and was swaying on her feet.

'No, Fran. You have been kind enough already. I can find my own way.' She walked to the door then looked back. 'But I am glad you are here with me,' she said.

'You barely know me.'

Her head tilted to the side in its habit. 'And yet, you're already more interesting than I could have imagined.' Even though her face was drawn with tiredness, she offered me a grin that showed some of her earlier spirit. Then she was gone, and I heard her quiet footsteps on the stairs.

I sat on where I was, the house settling back down to sleep, curling around me like a cat, the breeze twitching like whiskers around the eaves. After a while, no answers having come to me about anything, I got up, stretched, turned the lamp off and carried the two mugs back to the kitchen. It was warmer there, and I rinsed the mugs and threw some more coal into the range, knowing I would want it still burning in the morning so that I could sit bleary-eyed over a cup of tea, wishing it was coffee.

For a moment the loss of my bookshop and my life bit into me like a sharp-toothed animal. I wanted the smell of dark roast brewing, mingling with the inimitable scent of books, that taste of ink on page. I wanted the familiarity of wedding preparations, of Bronny's loose-lipped smiles, of all my regular customers, popping in and out to browse, chatting over the stacks, their bright hustle and bustle filling my days.

But almost as quickly as it had come on, the need to be back home passed. It took only a fleeting thought of Violet's face, her high cheekbones, the skin stretched tight and thin over them, her eyes dancing, mouth skipping over words.

What was her story, I wondered? More than anything, perhaps, I wanted to know why someone so adamant that she was a painter had no paints and easel with her.

The cups dry, I put them back on the shelf, and made for the door, thinking about colour and pigment and bright green eyes.

Tomorrow, maybe, we could walk into the town we'd barely seen from the back of Mrs Kellow's wagon, and with a bit of luck there would be a shop there where I could buy the artist some supplies. My hands itched to pick up my tablet and click open an app, find the best deals, and order everything online for next day delivery.

But the internet and all its glories was seventy or more years away. Almost a lifetime. Despite myself, I climbed the stairs calculating how old I would be by the year I was born.

One hundred years. I'd be one hundred years old by the date of my birth. Although, I wondered as I paused outside Violet's room, even if I were to live that long, how it would be possible to be an old lady on the day you were to be born.

And if I went to the hospital where my mother had laboured to bring me into the world, would I be able to lean over the little bassinette and see myself a baby, wrapped tightly in a pink blanket?

I shook the thought away. It was an exercise in pointlessness to even consider such things. In the same way I gave up wondering if I was dreaming, if I were in fact simply in a coma dreaming – because all experience is subjective, isn't it? In the end, what is more real than that which we can see, feel, touch, taste, hear?

I put my hand to the doorknob to Violet's room, and the metal was cold against my fingertips. There was the sound of Violet's soft breathing from within the closed room and I dropped my hand from the door, never having intended to open it. I turned away and made for my own room, trying to shed questions and doubts as I went, determining simply to live where and how I found myself, minute by minute.

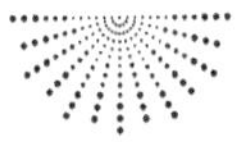

CHAPTER TEN

Over breakfast of hot tea and toast, made by yours truly, Violet was silent and brittle, spots of hectic colour high in her cheeks. But she ate a little before toying with her cigarette case and sipping at her tea.

'It's a lovely day,' I said. 'There's a nice bench outside if you'd like to sit in the sun for a while.' I'd explored the garden while waiting for her to rise.

Her gaze wandered over to me, searched my face for a moment, then settled back onto the table. I sat back down and gathered up her hands, chafed them between my own.

'Violet?' I asked. 'How are you feeling today?'

She looked at me again, and I couldn't tell what she was thinking. 'What is it?' I asked.

'Is it you?' she asked.

I cottoned on straight away. 'Yes,' I said.

'What if later it's not?' She blinked at me and her eyes were red from lack of sleep. 'What if I wake up tomorrow and you're here wondering why you're here, instead of making toast?'

I tried a joke. 'I hope you want me for more than my toast-making skills.'

She leaned suddenly against me, her head tucked in under my chin. 'Are you married, Fran?'

I allowed myself to stroke the dark hair tickling my neck. 'No,' I said.

She lifted her head and searched my eyes. 'Why is that?'

'I haven't found the right person, I guess.'

'Did you – do you – want to marry?'

I bit my lip, knowing that what she was asking was a different matter to how I could easily answer it. This was the moment when I needed to tell her that marriage in 2016 could mean a same-sex partnership – and that it was that which would be my preference.

But I hesitated, because I liked the warmth of her body leaning against me, the simplicity of the embrace.

She straightened, and this time her hand went to the cigarette case and opened it. She took a thin white cigarette out and lit it, breathing the smoke in and regaining something of yesterday's feistiness.

'Are you considering lying to me, Fran?' she asked. 'Does this question fall into the category under which you would think it appropriate to be *generally* a little loose with the truth?' Her eyes challenged me.

She tapped the cigarette on her saucer, dislodging a tiny pile of grey ash. 'It was a straightforward question, I would have thought.' The green eyes blinked at me. 'Did you have hopes of marrying? Were you looking for, hoping for, the right person? Not too difficult to answer, surely?'

It was impossible not to turn away from her. Getting up, I

fussed with a dishcloth, wiping crumbs from the table, then setting the cloth aside and sitting down again, in a different chair, further away.

'My friend Bronwyn was getting married,' I began, coming at it from an oblique angle.

Violet nodded, with a hint of impatience. 'So you said, but I was not asking about your friend, but about you.'

'Why?' I asked. 'Why do you want to know this?'

That made her look away, and a moment passed in which I knew she wouldn't answer.

'This is not such a straightforward question where I come from,' I said.

Her gaze fastened on me again, but she made no interruption.

I waved a hand. 'Here, when you ask a woman if she wants to get married, you are without a doubt asking if she wants to wed a man, have a family.'

She blinked.

'But it is not the same a hundred years in the future. A lot is not the same, but perhaps that one especially is different.'

I saw the glint of impatience in her eye again and took a breath, deciding just to get it over with. My mouth dried, but I ignored the dregs of my tea, of everything except those green eyes asking me questions.

'My best friend Bronwyn was marrying a woman called Louise.'

Her eyes widened, and she stared at me. Then she licked her lips. 'A woman?'

'Yes.'

She shook her head. 'It is impossible for a woman to

marry another woman.' She laughed. 'You will be telling me next that men have walked on the moon!'

I couldn't help my own laugh escaping my throat, dry as it was. 'They have. The first men to walk upon the surface of the moon did so in 1969.'

'You lie! You are teasing me now.'

I shook my head. 'No. The hundred years between now and when I fell off the ladder hanging lights for my best friend's wedding reception have seen a great deal of change.' I paused for breath. 'I'm reluctant to call all of it progress, but marriage equality certainly is.'

'Marriage equality? What is that?'

'A law banning discrimination against same-sex couples.' I searched through our conversations to one of the first we'd had. Violet's cigarette burned forgotten in her saucer. 'Your vicar could have had Miss Rottham's brother Robert after all.' It was difficult not to smile.

She was shaking her head, eyes round green pieces of glass. 'It is impossible.'

'The Queen herself signed off on it.' Perhaps I was enjoying myself a little too much now. But so far, I had the impression she wasn't objecting because she thought it so disgusting as to be unthinkable.

'There is another Queen?'

I nodded. 'Queen Elizabeth the second. She will be born ten years from now and will take the throne in 1952.'

Violet remembered her cigarette and pounced on it. 'I feel like I need a large dose of medicinal brandy!'

A quick look around the kitchen and I shook my head. 'I have to add that to my shopping list. Somehow I don't think Mrs Kellow deems it a suitable item for her pantry.'

That earned me a giggle, which a moment later was cut short.

'What?' I asked, seeing the look on her face and not knowing what it meant.

She narrowed her eyes, though whether at me, or against the smoke, I wasn't sure. 'There's something I'm still unclear on,' she said.

I raised my eyebrows.

'You never quite answered my question. Not quite at all.'

'Ah.' There was no point pretending I didn't know to which question she referred.

'Yes. Ah, indeed.' Those cat's eyes of hers blinked at me. 'I could make my own inferences from this conversation, but I'd prefer it if you could just tell me.' She blew smoke in my direction with a wry smile. 'So there is no chance of misunderstanding.'

It was almost impossible not to squirm in my seat under her gaze. I sat still though, and looked at her, then gave a self-conscious laugh.

'It is never easy coming out to someone new,' I said. 'The awkwardness just never really goes away.'

A pretty frown puckered between her brows. 'Coming out?'

'That's what we call it when we have to tell someone that we are homosexual.' It seemed the easiest way to say what I meant. 'Lesbian, in the case of women who are sexually attracted to other women.'

'And you are lesbian?' She didn't muck around with the questions although her tongue stumbled over the strange word.

'Yes.' I felt my neck heat under her gaze and it took a great deal of willpower not to lift a hand to the hot skin. Instead, I simply sat and looked at her.

After a moment, she nodded. 'At least now I know there is just as much a chance that you are suffering some strange and dreadful form of delusions and belong in the mental institution along with myself.' She stubbed out her cigarette. 'Although, there is surely no way anyone would make up such preposterous things.' She smiled at me. 'Would I be able to have another piece of toast, please?'

I must have looked at her with astonishment written large on my face because she shrugged, her turn to be self-conscious. 'I feel a little better,' she said.

'But why, exactly?' I got up while waiting for her answer. Of course she could have more toast. Her last piece lay mostly in shreds on her plate, the apricot jam sticky upon it.

Her gaze was clear, direct. 'It's absurd, perhaps, but I feel like I know you a little more now, and by somehow knowing you, I can keep you with me.'

I stared at her, half a loaf of bread in one hand. 'You want to keep me with you?'

'Yes,' she said, and her little smile was back, laughing at me. 'You are the most entertaining thing I've ever met.'

I whacked the bread down on the table and stood with my hands on my hips, shaking my head. 'I really do not know what to make of you,' I told her.

She shook her head, then touched a hand to the thick rope of hair that hung down her back. 'I've never met anyone who did,' she said. 'Perhaps it is part of my charm?'

It was my turn to shake my head, but I did it in feigned exasperation. Truthfully, I was glad there was a spark back in the eyes that had been worryingly red and glazed this morning when I greeted her as she came downstairs.

And if she didn't want to make further mention of my sexual orientation, then I'd only expected that. I was simply glad it wasn't going to come between us.

'You're looking at me strangely,' she said. 'While holding a knife.' She hid her smile behind a hand. 'I just wanted some more toast.'

Tension drained from my muscles and I took a deep breath, let it out with a smile of my own. 'Toast and jam coming up,' I said. 'Then perhaps you would like to go for a walk, if you are up to it?'

She nodded and reached for another cigarette. I wanted to put out a hand and press it to the case, stop her from having one, but I put it on the loaf of bread instead and sliced a piece to toast. We could discuss quitting the smokes when things were a little more settled.

'I'd like to go to the shops,' I said, thinking of my purse upstairs and the money the real Fran's mother had pressed into my gloved hand, with the hissed words that it was to last a month, and then she would wire more. I was also thinking of paints and brushes, canvas. Surely somewhere would sell them? 'We could walk along the beach.'

'Do you think there is an art gallery here?' she asked, perking up again. 'I mean, likely not, since we are so far away from everywhere decent...' She frowned, turning her silver lighter over in her hand. 'But perhaps, even so. I should like that.'

'We shall see,' I said, and spread home-churned butter over the toasted bread before adding a generous amount of jam and sliding it towards her. 'Maybe there is, or at least someone's art for sale, to take advantage of the tourists.'

Her mouth turned down, and glum. 'That's what we are, isn't it?'

'What?'

'Tourists. What a dreadful thing to end up being. A tourist in one's own life.'

'But you are only a tourist in this town,' I said. 'Which is completely different, and more of an adventure.'

She looked at me through narrowed, suspicious eyes. 'Are you always this optimistic?' she asked.

I had to think about it. 'Yes,' I decided. 'Yes, I think I am.'

'I don't know whether it suits you,' came her reply.

I moved behind her, put my hands on her head and kissed her crown. 'It suits me just fine,' I teased her. 'But it would look mighty peculiar on you.' With that I laughed and went to the door. 'Bring your toast,' I told her. 'Let's sit in the garden and decide what you will paint first when I buy you your new supplies.'

Stepping out into the new day's sunshine that spread across the lawn like a fresh tablecloth, I picked my way to the garden seat and smiled when I heard her step behind me.

'What did you just say?' she asked.

'I told you to bring your toast.' The sun was landing just right upon the bench, and although the seat could have done with a couple cushions, it was all right for now. I tucked my skirt in around my legs and looked ruefully at it. Perhaps I'd find a pair of riding breeches or something I could muck around in while at the cottage here. Better than the fiddly stockings I'd had to fuss around with for almost ten minutes while dressing that morning.

'No,' she said, arriving beside me. 'No that's not what you said.'

I squinted up at her. She stood with the rising sun behind her, a backlight that turned her hair to dark flames around her head.

'Yes, it is. I said to you to bring your toast to eat while we sit in the garden and decide what you will paint first.' I smiled at her. 'And here you are, with your toast, in the garden.' I patted the seat next to me and she sank down onto it as though her legs had given out. 'Do you think you would like to paint the sea? It's very difficult to capture, I think, but it would be marvellous in this light.' I looked around. 'The light is very fine here, don't you think?'

Her voice was more of a croak. 'I don't have any paints.'

'Or brushes, or canvas, or an easel. I know.' I turned to look at her face. 'I thought we'd go into town and get you some. There's bound to be a business that sells them.'

She reached out and grabbed my hand, holding it tightly, urgently. 'You would do that?'

'Of course.'

'But did my father not instruct your mother to tell you that I must not paint anymore?'

I looked at her in surprise. 'Why would he say that?' I shook my head. 'And if that was the case, as you say, then no – I missed that bulletin.' Turning my hand over, I gripped hers in return. 'How's that for lucky?'

Her head shook from side to side, slowly. 'I didn't think I would ever get to paint again,' she said.

That had me sitting up, leaning towards her. 'There are things I don't know yet, aren't there?' I said.

She nodded.

I thought quickly about it. 'Explain it succinctly, in one sentence. Then we can take it from there.'

Astonished, she gaped at me, then closed her mouth, considered my words, and opened it again. 'Art makes me want things that are bad for my health.'

'Art is what the soul craves,' I said, a frown on my face.

'Yes,' she said sadly, simply. 'And how I long for it.'

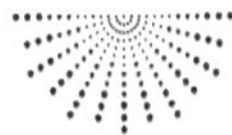

Violet wafted out into the garden dressed in bright yellow, a large hat pinned to her head.

'You look like you belong in a painting,' I told her.

She assessed her dress and smoothed a hand over the cotton. 'I'm afraid I rather like clothes,' she said.

'And bright colours.'

'Yes.' She looked around at the sea, sky, garden. 'It seemed to suit the situation in which we find ourselves.'

I smiled at her. 'You will be the loveliest looking woman in the town,' I said, meaning it. I wanted to pull her close and bury my face in the soft fabric like a bee collecting pollen.

'That is a terrible line of flattery,' she said, walking over to me and linking an arm through mine. 'No wonder you're still unmarried.'

'Huh. That explains a lot. I should stick to reciting poetry, then?'

'Oh my goodness yes, if you know any.'

I raised my head to the cornflower sky as we left the

garden and stepped out along the lane towards town. The sun felt like golden dust on my skin.

'I know a few,' I said. 'Comes with the territory of owning a bookshop, really.' I patted her thin hand. 'And I studied English Literature at university.'

Her eyes rounded. 'You went to university?'

'All my friends did,' I said.

'Even the women?'

'Especially the women, actually.'

She shook her head. 'So hard to believe.' A nudge, a gentle bump of hips. 'Recite a poem for me then.'

'Any particular topic?' I asked.

She laughed. 'Oh, now you're boasting. Be my guest and take your pick.'

I looked around at the day, sifting through the poems I kept in my memory, then I looked at her, at her fine, chiselled features, and decided. Nothing like the Romantics, when wooing a pretty woman.

'Lord Byron,' I told her, and went on to recite the poem.

> She walks in beauty, like the night
> Of cloudless climes and starry skies;
> And all that's best of dark and bright
> Meet in her aspect and her eyes;
> Thus mellowed to that tender light
> Which heaven to gaudy day denies.
>
> One shade the more, one ray the less,
> Had half impaired the nameless grace
> Which waves in every raven tress,

Or softly lightens o'er her face;
Where thoughts serenely sweet express,
How pure, how dear their dwelling-
        place.

And on that cheek, and o'er that brow,
So soft, so calm, yet eloquent,
The smiles that win, the tints that glow,
But tell of days in goodness spent,
A mind at peace with all below,
A heart whose love is innocent!

Violet was silent a moment after I was done, then turned to me and raised an eyebrow. 'What a shame my thoughts are neither serene nor innocent,' she said.

'They are not?' I was enjoying the gentle teasing.

'Decidedly not,' she affirmed. 'I do however have the raven tresses, and the first lines appeal to me a great deal.' She closed her eyes for a moment as we walked. 'She walks in beauty, like the night, of cloudless climes and starry skies.'

'And all that's best of dark and bright, meet in her aspect and her eyes,' I repeated. 'That suits you perfectly.'

Her eyes danced at me. 'Do you think so?'

'Indeed.'

She laughed. 'Are you flirting with me, Fran?'

I sniffed and tucked her arm more securely into mine. 'Certainly not,' I said.

Her laughter drifted out over the water, and we fell silent, walking in gentle companionship, taking in the view, the fresh summer warmth, and I breathed it all in, relishing the growing heat of the day from under my own straw hat, and breathing in too, the scent of Violet next to me. She smelled like an exotic lily and looked like a radiant sunflower.

'What are you thinking now?' she asked, catching me off guard.

I cleared my throat. 'Nothing very much,' I said.

'Oh no.' She shook her head. 'That is not the correct answer. I demand honesty from you.'

'Fine,' I said. 'But you have to be prepared for the consequences, if you are to ask things like that, and want a straight answer.'

'I am prepared. Now tell me what you were thinking.'

'I was thinking you smell like flowers.'

She looked at me. Tilted her head on the side. 'What sort of flowers?'

'Orchids, from an exotic night-blooming garden, taken straight out of a leather and gold-bound volume of Arabian tales.' Okay, so I elaborated a bit, but that's what poetry does to a person. It runs swift through the veins and raises a woman's temperature.

Hugging my arm tighter, I felt the soft sway of her walk beside me. 'I've never been out of England,' she said.

'I've always wanted to go to Italy,' I said. 'Or perhaps France. I was really hoping for the French Riviera, you know.'

She cocked her head to one side. 'We could take a small villa over there,' she said. 'On a hillside in Italy, perhaps, next door to an olive grove, where a handsome young man picks olives and loads them into wicker baskets carried by a donkey with extraordinarily large ears.'

I laughed. 'Why such large ears?'

She shrugged. 'That's just the way I see him. He has large ears.'

'And wiry grey fur. And every evening, we would pack up our paints and our books, and wander down to have an early dinner in the courtyard of an Italian café, where we would eat fresh pasta and bread and wash it down with rough red wine.'

'And we would be always warm, and full of sunshine and grapes and olives, and I would paint all morning, and then after a siesta, I would come to find you – what would you be doing?'

I thought about it. 'I would have another bookshop, of course, and it would be open in the afternoons, and you would come inside, blinking in the sudden dimness, and there would be an endearing smear of paint on your cheek, and every day it would be of another colour and I would try to guess what you were painting by the different smudges.'

We fell silent, only the sounds of our footsteps on the packed dirt of the road, and the cawing of a gull over the rustle of the sea.

'There is a war over there,' Violet said sadly, and her hand tightened on my arm. I smoothed a palm over it.

'Yes,' I said.

She looked at me. 'When does it end?'

I met her eyes.

'You will know,' she said, and I saw the delicate convulsion of her throat.

'1918,' I said. 'It goes for another two years.'

She was appalled. 'Another two years of war! There will be no men left.' She shivered despite the sunlight.

Silence fell again and stretched out like a cobweb over the day. We'd been laughing a minute ago.

'I should still like to go to Italy or France,' she said. 'I would like to be far away from here.'

'From here?'

She waved her hand at the day, the place. 'From dreary old England, with its long winters and its narrow, mechanical people, and its bland food, and its fathers who don't want their daughters anymore because we dare to think and dream and want!'

I stopped walking, forcing Violet to do the same. 'Tell me about your father,' I said. 'You obviously have issues with each other.'

Violet snorted, standing there in her pretty yellow dress. 'My father. You met him.'

'Not really,' I said. 'He barely said a word to me. I only know that he and my mother stayed closeted in the sitting room for a good long time.'

'Talking about me, of course,' Violet said, and then sighed, the fight going out of her. She turned and resumed walking, bringing me with her.

'My father believes I am unwell,' she said, turning up her face to the sun and blinking in the light. It brought out deep red highlights in her hair.

'Your health does seem a little precarious,' I ventured.

She ducked her head back down, tucking her chin to her chest. 'It is,' she said. 'But not in the way he thinks – at least not as bad as he thinks!'

'What does he think?' I asked, untucking her arm from mine and holding her hand instead.

The green eyes flickered in my direction then slid away

like the tide from the beach. I watched her chew upon her lip. 'It is a long story,' she said at last.

I gestured at the road ahead of us. 'It's a long walk.'

I heard her intake of breath and she blew it out in a puff of air.

'Well then,' she said, and her fingers were clasped upon mine. 'Here it is. Last year, I got tired of arguing with my father to allow me to go to The Slade…' She looked at me to check that I was familiar with the prestigious art school. I was. She nodded. 'And so, I packed up my things and went anyway. Found a tiny rat-infested room to rent and set about going to school.' Her eyes were round and serious. 'Oh Fran – so many wonderful artists have been through those doors – I just wanted to be one of them!'

'What happened?' I asked gently.

She looked miserable and mutinous at the same time. 'I didn't have enough money,' she said. 'I posed for a painter, but he couldn't pay enough, and my health suffered. There wasn't enough to eat, or anything else.' When she looked at me, her eyes were haunted. 'I started losing track of myself, Fran,' she said, her voice barely more than a whisper over the surf. 'Father found me and brought me home and hasn't trusted me to know my mind since.' She gazed out over the sea. 'We are here while he decides what can be done with me.'

'Done with you?'

'Yes. I am obviously not up to marrying and being a good wife, and what respectable man would want me anyway, when it comes out that I have been an artist's model and have all sorts of strange ideas?' She sniffed, and her mouth hung loosely around her words. 'So he is looking into alternative scenarios.' A damp sigh. 'In the meantime, I am to be kept away from painting, for my own good.' Violet looked at me, and her eyes were steady again. 'He tells me that what he is doing is looking out for me, that it is all for my own good.' The eyes wandered to look back at the sea. 'It's just that I do not believe him. Cannot believe him. Nothing he has ever done has been for my benefit. And my stepmother is of no help. She doesn't understand me. She hasn't enough imagination.'

'Can't you just continue to live at home? Or set up your own household?'

'I would rather die than continue living at home!' Violet blinked several times. 'And I am not trusted to manage my own household.'

Which explained, I guessed, my own presence here – and my mother's reluctance to agree to it in the first place, afraid that the task would take over my own life and keep me from doing the normal things expected of a woman by her generation. Marriage, family.

I didn't know how I felt about having a family, but marriage of the sort expected in 1916 was not for me.

Violet's hand had grown cold in mine, and her step slowed. I tucked her fingers back in the warmth of my elbow, drawing her closer as we walked, the road beginning a long shallow slide down to the bay.

'Do you miss your bookshop?' she suddenly asked.

I remembered my promise to be truthful. 'Yes.'

She was silent for a moment, then drew in a deep breath. 'I don't blame you,' she said. 'How marvellous it must be to be in charge of your own life in such a way, to have a business and a livelihood, and not be reliant on anyone except yourself.'

I said nothing. What was there to say?

'And your friends – you must miss them too.'

'Yes,' I said, because it was true. Squinting out from under the shadow of my hat, I wondered if Bronny had celebrated her wedding yet, and if they had held it at the bookshop. She had her own key to the business. I wondered what had happened to me there – had I fallen into a coma? Had I died? Simply vanished from sight?

'Are you all right?' Violet asked. 'I am sorry. I oughtn't to have brought up a subject painful for you. I am a fool – of course you would rather be home again, with your business and your friends.' She blinked and dipped her head so that her eyes were hidden.

I put an arm around her. 'It could be much worse,' I said.

She looked at me. 'How? You have been torn from every-thing you know!'

A shrug I hoped came off as disarming. 'I have you,' I said.

She snorted. 'I'm not entirely sure that is any consolation.'

Shaking my head, I squeezed her. 'Violet, don't say that. It is not who you are.'

'Who is it that I am?'

'You are the one who walks in beauty like the night, remember?'

She smiled.

CHAPTER TWELVE

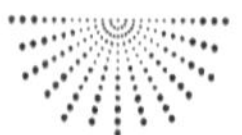

The town was disappointingly small. I had hoped we had landed in one of the larger tourist towns along the coast, but it was a hope in vain. When Violet's father had decided she needed rest away from everything and everyone, he had not taken his decision lightly.

'There is no one about,' Violet said, standing on the road above the beach. 'And what is that smell?'

'I believe it is fish,' I said.

She wrinkled her nose. 'Father has sent us to a fishing village?'

'Definitely not the Riviera,' I agreed. The spread of the beach lay to our left, and we could stroll there, perhaps, but to our right there was a jumble of fishing boats hoisted up upon the stones, men milling around unloading fish and dragging nets hither and thither.

Violet's shoulders sagged and when she looked at me there was hopelessness in her eyes. I touched her arm.

'Come,' I said. 'Let's walk and see what there is to see.'

'There are fish,' she said.

'And a little beach.'

'Certainly,' she agreed. 'Because one really wants to sit by the water with the stench of fish in their nose!'

I was disappointed as well, but I tugged her away back to the street where reluctantly she followed me across to survey the array of shops.

'Well look,' she said. 'This is even better. We have a butcher, a baker, and a candlestick maker.'

That did pretty much sum it up, to tell the truth. Although a candlestick maker would have been more interesting than the small grocers with their display of canned goods and flour bags in the window.

'There is a tea shop,' I said, pouncing upon the fact. 'Let's go and sit down for a while. It was a long walk.'

'For nothing,' Violet said, trailing behind me. 'There is not even a bookshop, let alone anywhere to get any sort of sketch book and pencil!'

There was no good answer. The door to the tea shop opened with the silver tinkling of a bell and raised my spirits a little. I dreamed of coffee but would settle for a good hot cup of strong tea. Maybe a cake. Comfort food. Good grief did I need comfort food.

Not even a bookshop.

Violet went straight to a small table under the window and sat down, hands limp in her lap. I ordered a pot of tea and a plate of small cakes, hoping as well to tempt Violet's appetite, although I didn't hold much hope of success.

She lifted her face to mine as I joined her, green eyes blinking in the dimness of the room.

'I will die if I have to stay here,' she whispered, her hand reaching out to grip mine. 'We can't possibly stay here for three whole months!'

I was tempted to agree. But was there any choice?

Violet hadn't finished. Her fingers tightened on my wrist. 'We're barely unpacked,' she said. 'I suggest we go back to the cottage, put back the few things we've taken from our bags, then board the next train.'

The tea came, and we both sat back while the woman placed it on the table between us, the interrupted conversation hanging in the air like a thick fug of smoke.

When she was gone, I shook my head. 'I'm not sure that is possible.'

Violet's hand shook as she poured the tea. 'We can't stay here,' she hissed. 'How can we possibly? We will go crazy!'

I leaned back on the hard chair and picked up my cup, absently sipping at the hot tea, thinking about what she'd said. Violet watched me like a dog expecting to be thrown a bone.

'I am already officially crazy enough,' she said pointedly.

I shook my head, and she put her tea cup down with a clatter on its saucer, then rose from her chair.

'Where are you going?' I asked, alarmed.

'Back to the cottage to pack.' She blinked at me. 'Come along. We're going to leave.'

'But…' I spluttered.

She shook her head. 'No. It is impossible. I cannot stay here; believe me that I tell you that very seriously. I cannot. I know myself, and this is not the place for me. I was willing to try my father's plan, because it was a reprieve, and time perhaps for him to change his mind about his larger ideas for me.' She swallowed. 'And I was also afraid of not doing what he requested, of what might come after it if I did not do so.' She drew breath. 'But everything is different now.'

'This is enough for you to change your mind about it?' I waved at the view through the narrow-paned window, then peered narrow-eyed at her. 'How is everything different now?'

She stood and folded her arms across her yellow breast. 'Everything is different because I have you.'

I didn't understand. 'Me?'

That got a decisive nod, and she was turning, walking over to the little counter and picking up a paper bag, bringing it back to the table and filling it with the cakes.

'We may as well take these with us,' she said. 'It is quite the hike back to the cottage.'

She was determined to go, I saw, and had no choice but to stand and follow her, the proprietor giving us odd looks as Violet pushed open the door and stepped through it on hard heels.

I hurried after her. She strode down the street and back up onto the rutted path that led back to the rented cottage. There was no speaking. Violet's hands were clenched rigid at her sides, the paper bag of cakes smacking against her dress as she moved. I let her have her silent fury at her father.

Her anger lasted the entire walk back to the cottage, but the silence did not. She turned to me, her face pale except for hasty red cheeks, and the breeze climbed up from the sea to toss about a couple unruly tendrils of hair.

'You can get us out of here,' she said.

'I can?' I wasn't sure how.

'Of course you can.' It was said with immense impatience,

as though it were all obvious. 'You are an independent woman! You are used to dealing with all manner of things.'

'Oh,' I said.

'We must choose where we want to go, and then we must simply go.'

'It doesn't sound that simple to me.'

A wild toss of her hat. 'Of course it is. This place is unsuitable; therefore we will go to a place that is.'

The cottage was visible in the near distance. We had walked fast, and I wished I had my comfortable pair of trainers for my poor feet.

'You father will not be pleased if we simply pick up and leave.'

'He does not get a say! Not this time! Not anymore!'

Violet stopped abruptly, and stood with her hand pressed to her chest, the colour sliding from her face as I watched.

'Violet, love – what is it?' I asked, going to her.

Her expression was a mixture of chagrin and pain. She tugged at her hat, tearing it from her head and pressing her arm to her forehead.

'I cannot think,' she said. 'This is all too much of a cruelty.'

'It is all right,' I soothed, placing a hand between her shoulder blades. 'Everything is going to be all right.'

She shook her head but seemed calmer, her eyes staring at me, then closing. She leaned against me. 'I'm sorry,' she said. 'I'm sorry. Everything is threatening to get muddled again.' Green eyes stared at me. 'You will help me, won't you Fran?'

How impossible it was to ignore that plea. I nodded, and took her hat, and the bag of cakes, and turned her gently in the direction of the cottage.

'I will,' I said simply. 'But let's get out of this wind and sun and have a rest while we think it all through.'

She nodded against my shoulder and walked docilely at my side the rest of the way to the cottage.

'Perhaps you should lie down for a little while,' I said as we threaded ourselves through the gate.

There was no answer, so I simply led her into the house and up the stairs to her room, which was the same in every detail to the one I had used the night before, apart from the clothes strewn about the furniture. I moved something lacy aside and patted the bed.

'Promise me,' she said, sitting down. 'That we will find somewhere else to stay.' Her eyes had taken on a feverish cast. 'I cannot do it, Fran. I simply cannot. You must not make me.'

I stared at her, not knowing what to say.

She stood up. 'What are you doing?' I asked, vague panic rippling under my skin.

But she only went to her trunk and lifted the lid. 'I want to give you something,' she said, sinking down onto her knees and pushing clothes and things aside.

'What?' I asked.

She countered with a question of her own. 'Do you have a pen?'

'Um,' I looked around, as though one might materialise. 'I guess so – in my room.' I stood. 'I'll get it.'

She nodded from the trunk, and I left to fetch a pen, wondering what it was she wanted to give me.

My own room was neater. I'd folded and put everything back in the trunk, although that was more a symptom of my discomfort of being here, rather than any inherent tidiness of character. There was a pen on the dresser, however, next to a notebook I'd found in the real Fran's room at home and packed to bring with me. I'd sat up a while after Violet had gone back to bed the night before and filled several pages of the book with clumsy handwriting marred by ink splotches from the unfamiliar fountain pen. But it had helped, to write everything down.

Pen in hand, I went back to Violet's room. From downstairs came sounds of movement and I guessed our cook had turned up, perhaps with the girl who would do the heavy work. I couldn't remember either of their names.

Violet was waiting for me, a rectangular board in her hands the size of an A4 piece of paper. She leapt on the pen and took it off to the dresser, not letting me see what she was up to. A moment later she was back, making me a present of the board.

I took it, and gazed down at it, feeling the colour drain from my own cheeks.

'Do you not like it?' she said anxiously.

That wasn't it. I liked it very much.

'It is exquisite,' I said over the lump in my throat.

CHAPTER THIRTEEN

I could feel Violet staring at me, her bottom lip caught nervously between her teeth, watching my reaction. But there was no helping it. I backed up and sank down onto the chair by the window.

'What is it? Do you hate it that much?'

Wordless, I shook my head. Swallowed. Found my voice.

'No,' Violet, that isn't it at all. I love it.' I did, and suddenly there were tears in my eyes and I stifled a sob. If I'd still thought this was a dream, I knew now beyond a doubt it wasn't any normal sort of one. This was real in ways I did not understand.

She was on her knees in front of me in a moment, her hand on my leg. I felt it there and grasped it in my hand. It was real, she was real, and I was sitting there with the painting she'd just given to me.

'What is it then? Fran? You must tell me what is wrong.'

I shook my head again. My cheeks were wet. Sniffing, I turned the painting over to see what she had written on the label stuck there.

Even though I already knew what I would see.

Blinking at the signature, I found my voice. 'Why did you sign it like that?' I croaked past my tears.

Her green eyes stared earnestly up at me. 'I didn't mean to offend you,' she said. 'It was harmless fun, I promise.' She reached for the painting. 'Here,' she said. 'Let me cross it out and sign it properly.'

I shook my head and did not let her take it. 'No.' My smile was watery, but genuine. 'I'm sorry,' I said. 'It's just a shock.'

She was perplexed. 'Why is that? It is only a painting.' She tilted her head and looked at it. 'Not even especially good. But I could not bring my bigger ones with me.' She coloured. 'And it is one of my favourites, even if it isn't exceptional.'

'It is very good,' I said. Unsurprisingly – now that I knew a little more of the artist – it was Expressionist in style, an emotional experience of the subject, rather than the reality. 'Is it a real place?' I asked.

'It's the walled garden at home,' Violet said, sitting down against my knee, her hand still touching me. 'My stepmother has let it grow over. It was a kitchen garden once, when my mother was still alive, but now it is a tangle.'

And a tangle held in by high walls was how she'd painted it. But it was beautiful too, the plants an overgrown riot of twisted limbs and thorns with the most exquisite burst of coloured flowers in the shadows. I was familiar with every brush stroke.

I turned it over again to see the signature. 'Vivi Madden.'

She shrugged against my leg. 'I'm sorry. I probably shouldn't have used your name. It was a whim.'

A whim that would stick. She would sign all her work

with that name. Oh god. I hadn't realised. Not for a moment. I just hadn't put it together.

Setting the painting aside for a moment, I bent forward and wrapped my arms around the woman on the floor, closing my eyes against her dark hair.

'Vivi is a combination of my first names,' she said. 'Violet Vivien.' She gave a delicate shrug and her breath was a tickle against my ears. 'I simply thought it would look good – like a real artist's signature.'

'It is a real artist's signature,' I told her.

'And you're not mad about me using your name?'

I shook my head. 'Not at all.'

She twisted in my arms. I hadn't let go of her and didn't want to. Her own arms snaked around me and I felt the warmth of her cheek against my own. It was soft, and I closed my eyes against the sensation of it. She pressed her lips to my cheek.

'Thank you,' she said.

'For what?'

'For being so moved over my little painting.'

I sat back, and she touched cool fingertips to my wet eyes. 'You're crying,' she said, and her voice held a touch of wonder.

'You are a marvellous artist,' I said. I meant it.

She tipped her head to the side and a sly and crooked grin spread across her features. 'You have heard of me?' She blinked. 'In the future, I mean. In two thousand and sixteen?' Her eyes shone.

I reached out and stroked her hair. The hat lay on the floor beside the trunk and she looked ravishingly beautiful sitting on the floor amidst discarded clothes and her yellow skirts.

'I'm afraid I paid more attention to books than I did paintings,' I said, and it was almost the truth.

Except when it came to Vivi Madden and her work. That I knew about. But I kept my mouth shut. I needed time to think about it. A glance at the painting and my head spun.

'You have not heard of me, then?' she asked with a playful pout.

I looked at her, and something in my expression made her sit straighter, turning serious. 'Remember your promise, Fran,' she said. 'You must not lie to me. I could not bear that.'

I had to touch her again. Fingers to her cheek, her hair. I looked at her and realised she was right. I had to tell her something and right now, or forever keep it to myself. And since this was no longer just a dream, the truth it had to be. Some of it, at least. Until I'd had more time to think.

'It is a shock,' I said. 'I'm sorry – it's just taking a while to sink in.' I shook my head. 'Everything is all so unbelievable.'

'So you have heard of me!' She jumped to her feet and picked up the painting. 'I knew it! I knew I would keep painting! There is just no way I cannot.' Turning to me, her eyes burned. 'Tell me,' she demanded.

'It is not quite what you think,' I said in an effort to calm her.

She plumped down unexpectedly in my lap, holding up the painting for us both to see. 'Tell me exactly what it is, then,' she said, and leaned back against my chest as though it were the most natural thing in the world.

There was a moment's quiet while I gathered my strewn thoughts, and I heard more sounds from the kitchen, reminding me incongruously that it was almost lunch time, and outside there was the gull again, and still the sea breathing in and out like an animal washed up upon the beach. I took a breath.

'My grandmother brought me up,' I said, and she lowered the painting to her lap. I licked my dry lips. 'My mother ran off with some fellow when I was young and left me with my grandmother.'

Her eyes were wide, horrified. 'How dreadful for you!' she said.

I shook my head. 'Not terribly. Things got better for me when I went to live with my grandmother.' I gave a wry smile. 'My mother was something of a... nomadic soul,' I said. 'Always on the move. My grandmother lived in a proper house and owned a bookshop.'

Her mouth curved in a smile. 'Tell me more,' she prompted. 'That is where you gained your love of literature?'

I almost giggled. My grandmother had sold books on the ancient mysteries of pyramids, and fortune telling, and reincarnation. Not exactly literature. But... 'Yes,' I said. 'I gained my love for books from working in her shop.' I smiled at the memory. 'She made me work there even when I was a little thing. Told me I was not too young to dust and stock a shelf.'

Violet put the painting aside and turned in my lap, wrapping her arms around me. 'That is a wonderful story,' she said. 'Where was your father?'

'He and my mother parted before I was even born. He married when I was little, and the idea that I would live with him never crossed anyone's mind.'

If it was possible, Violet's eyes were even wider. 'They

were unmarried when you were conceived? And there were no consequences?'

I shook my head. 'By the time I was born...' I grinned despite myself. 'In nineteen eighty-seven...'

She gaped at me. 'Nineteen eighty-seven!'

'Yes,' I said. 'Crazy, isn't it?'

'It is that, for certain!' and she laughed before settling back down. She rested her head against my shoulder. 'Tell me the rest.' A nod towards the painting. 'Not to be selfish, because I do really want to know all about you – but my curiosity burns me – tell me about what you know of my work.'

I avoided a direct lie and went back to the centre of the story. 'My grandmother owned a painting signed Vivi Madden.'

I got a smacking kiss on the cheek. 'I knew it!'

'She owned that exact painting,' I said, looking at her.

Her face straightened into seriousness for a moment and she put a hand over her mouth. 'Oh Fran,' she breathed. 'You know what that means, don't you?'

I wasn't sure, and it must have shown in my face. She put her hand on my chest instead, laid it on the breastbone at the base of my neck and stared at me, her eyes bright green.

'It means – of course – that you must have given it to her.'

I blinked at her.

'And that means – of course – that you stay here with me. That you do not go back to your own time, but instead stay here with me.'

Was she right? Too many thoughts swirled around in my mind.

Her face fell. 'Oh goodness, I'm sorry – I'm being so

insensitive. This news makes me very happy indeed, but it must come as a shock to you.' She took away her hand and grasped mine in it instead, held it in tightly-clasped fingers.

But her expression didn't stay crestfallen for long. A moment later a smiled danced over her lips and her eyes were sparkling.

'I'm sorry, Fran,' she said. 'I can't help it. To me, this is the best news I've had in a very long time.'

I almost stuttered. She had placed my hand against her own breastbone. 'It is?' I asked.

'Yes,' she said. 'I know it has only been a couple days, but already I am glad we have come together. Especially now that I know I will not wake in the morning to find you gone and someone else in your place! That is very important to me.'

I licked my lips again, staring at her. 'Would it make so much difference? The real Fran is probably quite lovely.'

She moved my hand and kissed my curled fingers. 'Probably. She was pleasant the few times I met her.' Her eyes were serious, the colour of deep green seas. 'But she is not you and it is you I want here with me.'

What happened then was unforgettable.

Still holding my hand, she leaned into me, sitting on my lap, and pressed her lips to mine. They were soft, and warm, and her breath between them was like golden nectar. Her lips lingered upon mine, and she put my hand to her cheek and made me stroke her, my fingers willingly threading themselves through her hair.

Her eyes were wide open for a long moment, then dropped closed and she breathed into me, sinking loose-limbed against my body and I did not stop her, I gathered my other arm around her back and pulled her tighter, my hand at her waist, her breast soft against my own.

And there was still the kiss, a touch, a nibbling, breathing brush of lips, a rush of sensation that had me forgetting all sense of everything except Violet in my lap, kissing my lips.

Until someone cleared their throat in the doorway.

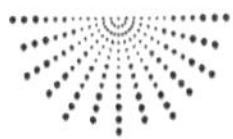

We broke apart in a rushing, blushing tangle, lungs heaving for air. There were no words in my head as I looked at the woman who stood in the doorway. Only the beating of blood between my ears.

'Who are you?' Violet asked. She was the first to speak.

'I'm Mrs Snell, I'm sure,' the woman told us, planting hands on thick hips.

'And who is that to be disturbing us?' Violet again. I was still quivering in the chair. Violet was on her feet, yellow dress crumpled.

'The cook,' came the woman's acerbic answer. 'Come to tell you your lunch is ready.' She watched us with sharp grey eyes. 'And your dinner, for that matter. You did not come to the kitchen to introduce yourselves, so I came to look for you.' She sniffed, letting us know in no uncertain terms what she thought of the position she'd found us in. I stood up.

'Thank you, Mrs Snell,' I said. 'My apologies for not coming to greet you. We'd had a long walk.'

That sniff again. This time it said the walk clearly hadn't been exertion enough to use all our energy.

The three of us stood where we were for a long moment, no one saying another word. I stole a glance at Violet and saw she was trembling.

'Will there be anything else, Mrs Snell?' I asked, hating the sound of my voice, the obvious dismissal in the tone, as though I'd known how to deal with servants all my life.

She looked at me for several incredibly long seconds before answering. 'No,' she said. 'As arranged, I do not serve you.'

I thought she probably meant that to have two different meanings but held her gaze. 'No,' I agreed, my voice even. 'Mrs Kellow did say.' She didn't drop her eyes. 'Thank you, however. The supper you left for us last night was very tasty.'

'I'll be off then,' she said. 'To visit Mrs Kellow, actually. Seeing as how she's my sister.'

I nodded. Waited.

She stared at me, then at Violet, back to me. Then turned on her heel and I heard her heavy, determined step on the stairs. If only I'd heard it when she'd been coming in the other direction.

'Shit,' I said. 'That was awkward.'

Violet stood where she'd landed, springing out of my lap. I reached out and touched her. She was rigid, her face pale. I forced her to look at me.

'Violet,' I said. 'Are you all right?' My heart was finally getting back to its regular rhythm. As long as I didn't think of what had just happened, neither the kiss, or the interruption, it might stay there.

Violet's lips were pressed together, bloodless. She shook her head. 'This is bad,' she whispered. 'This is very bad.'

I stared at her. There was no point pretending I did not know what she meant. It wasn't 2016, after all. None of our great strides in equality, as precarious as they felt in the tumult that was my own time, especially for those of us in America, were anything at all yet.

She squeezed her eyes shut, and pressed fisted hands to her temple. Moaned. 'Oh Fran, this is so bad.' Opening her eyes, she gazed unseeing at the room. 'You've no idea how bad this is.'

Stepping closer, I put my arms around her, peeling her clenched hands from her face. 'Shh,' I said. 'We will deal with it, okay? Everything will be all right.'

But she was shaking her head. I didn't know what to say, so I simply stood there for a moment, mind whirling.

She stepped out of my arms, looked wildly around the room, still shaking her head, then focusing on me again, and stilling herself for a moment.

'I don't regret it,' she said, features softening briefly before tightening up into fear again. 'I don't, Fran, I promise.' She even managed a smile. 'It was the best kiss I've had, and I even want another.' Her eyes widened in wonder as the thought hit her. 'I do. I want to kiss you again.' She closed her eyes. 'But this is bad.'

It was my turn to shake my head. 'I'll go talk to Mrs Kellow,' I said. 'Explain that it was nothing, that I was just comforting you.'

Violet laughed, a harsh, cawing sound, like the gulls outside over the waves. 'You'll have to talk to Mrs Kellow, that much is certain,' she said. 'But good luck convincing her that what the damned cook saw was anything innocent. It will be your word against her sister's – and her sister will be the one believed, I've no doubt whatsoever!'

She bent down and picked up a pile of clothes, went over to her open trunk and tipped them in. 'We have to leave now,' she said. 'There's no debating it anymore.'

I touched her arm. 'Slow down,' I said. 'Explain to me what you're thinking.' I looked at her. 'Please.'

Violet picked up another armful of clothes and sank suddenly down on the bed with them, as though the strength had drained from her legs.

'You're crying, darling,' I said, going to her and finding a handkerchief from the pile of fabric in her lap. I dabbed at her eyes with it and she looked at me.

'I am frightened,' she whispered. 'My father…'

'Your father?' I prompted, but a terrible knowledge settled in my stomach like a stone. A glance across the room showed me the painting, and there was a story to that painting, more than the one I'd just told, and it was a bad one.

I shook my head. There was so much talent in that painting. Violet had such a gift, especially considering she'd never had formal training. I didn't know if she'd ever, given the chance, achieve any fame or fortune from her painting – but it brought her an obvious joy, and I did not doubt for a moment that it was what she should be doing with her life.

But my grandmother had pointed to the picture when it had hung on our sitting room wall and told me a terrible story. For years after, I'd sat staring up at the painting and spun a dozen better endings to the artist's story. Better than the one my grandmother had told me, that had Vivi Madden dragged screaming into the dark mouth of an insane asylum, never again to see the light of day, strapped instead into a stained and tightly buckled straitjacket, left in ice water baths for hours at a time, thrown into moth-eaten padded rooms until her beautiful spirt was broken, and all that was left was the empty shell of her body to follow it, down into a murky, pictureless death.

Violet sat on the bed next to me, real, chest heaving as she stifled her sobs, a pile of lacy petticoats in her lap, her face pale and blotchy.

She looked at me. 'You are crying too.' And she took the handkerchief from me with a trembling hand and wiped at my hot tears, her own still wet on her cheeks. I caught her hand in mine. Held it tight.

'You are right,' I said. 'We have to leave.'

She looked at me, the rims of her eyes red. 'My father...' she tried again. 'He will lock me away when news of this reaches him.' Violet's tender throat convulsed. 'He has threatened to already, has sent me to see doctors, and I know he has half made up his mind that I belong there already. It is only your own mother, I think, who has stood between me and the sanatorium, and I love her for it, but it is temporary at best, and after today...' She screwed up the scrap of material and lace in her hands and stared at me in horror through her tears. 'It is certain.'

I put my arm around her, heart breaking. I knew she was right. I knew it would happen exactly that way. I leaned into her and breathed in the fragrance of her skin. Wild orchids, blooming in some dazed, dizzy dream.

'I don't belong in a lunatic asylum, Fran. I promise I don't.

I'm not crazy, not really. I would kill myself, left to rot in one of those places.'

Yes, she would. That was how the story had ended.

Her body, thin and full of painful bones just under the skin, was nevertheless warm in my arms, and I could not bear the thought that she would end her life in a mental hospital. She was too alive, too vibrant, too damned talented. She needed to live, to find a place where she could thrive, spend time with other artists, other like-minded people.

And she needed to be taken care of too. She needed a stable arm to lean on. I doubted there was a practical bone among those under that alabaster skin, and I didn't care. I was practical. I could recite poetry, and put on a good show, but what I did best was run things, organise things. Take care of things. Bronny had always teased me about it. Capability Fran, she called me.

I could take care of Violet. I was more than half in love with her anyway.

And I was the final nail in her coffin now, unless I did something. It would be my fault her father would have her committed. Mine.

She was looking at me, eyes wide. 'What are you think-ing?' she asked and clutched at my arm. 'You understand, don't you? I would die in a place like that – I really would.'

I leaned closer and pressed my lips to her forehead. 'I will not let that happen,' I said, and my voice was a hoarse whis-per. 'I promise.'

'That horrible woman will tell her sister,' Violet said, and she was shaking again. 'After they've sat with their nasty heads together, they will write to my father and tell him what they saw, and then my father will come and get me, and it will be the end of it.' She plucked at the dark skirt I wore. 'The end of me.'

I gathered her even closer. 'We will not let that happen.'

Our eyes met.

'Then we'd best move fast,' Violet said, through pale, bloodless lips.

CHAPTER FIFTEEN

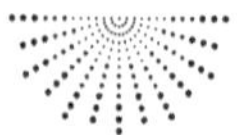

Violet crumbled the food between her fingers, but she ate some, and I ate more, knowing I would need my strength. It was tasteless.

We talked, for a while around in circles, then decided. With few options and a heavy heart, I agreed to the plan that seemed the simplest, the best.

That we had to run, there was no doubt. The spectre of the madhouse loomed over Violet's every move, the way she sat, ate, spoke. It was real, I knew it was real, and if we stayed where we were, she was doomed.

We ate, and I begged her to lie down and rest. I looked at her wan face pressed to the pillow.

'I won't be long,' I said. 'But with no telephone here, I see no choice.'

'I want to come with you,' she said, but I shook my head.

'It will be quicker if I go on my own.'

She closed her eyes. 'Hurry, then,' she said, and I nodded although she didn't see me.

'I will.'

'And lock the door. I don't want Mrs Kellow to come in.' She shrank down under the blankets and looking at her, I vowed there and then that I would never abandon her to this world that was so carelessly dangerous to her.

It was hard leaving her, even to do this one errand. She looked so small under the thick covers, her dark hair casting knotted shadows over her face. I wondered if she was strong enough for what would come next but threw the thought out. She just needed a rest.

Outside, the sun was still slanting its rays over sky and sea and land. I strode down the path, through the gate, and realised I'd forgotten my hat and gloves, and should turn back around to get them, knowing I needed to present a good face to the people I'd have to deal with. The fewer raised eyebrows, the better.

I hesitated on the road outside the cottage, looking to the left where Mrs Kellow had said she lived. She would be there, closeted with her sister, whispering and muttering under their breaths about the dreadful scene the cook had walked in on. If only I hadn't been so stupid! If only I hadn't encouraged Violet, if only it had really penetrated my thick head that someone else was in the house. And that it was damned well 1916!

But *if only* was no help. The deed was done. Violet had kissed me. I pressed my fingers to my lips and couldn't help the shiver at the memory. She had felt so good, so real, alive, delightful, I wanted more.

I shook my head. There couldn't be more. Look what trouble it had already caused. I paced several steps in the dust, debating.

Mrs Kellow was not the right choice. She would stand

there and stare at me with raisin eyes, then tell me that it was her moral obligation to inform Violet's father as to what had happened.

She would also simply do it faster if I went down there and told her we needed her wagon to move our trunks because we were leaving on the next train. Mr Farningham would get a letter in the very next post, if I did that. Maybe even a telephone call. There was no telephone in our rented cottage, but that did not mean Mrs Kellow didn't own one, and there would be one at the Post Office in the village for her to use if not.

We needed more time than that. I thought Mrs Kellow would choose a letter over a telephone call. Easier to put what had been seen down on paper, than attempt a conversation. In which case, she would probably spend all the rest of this day debating over the wording with her sister, and the letter wouldn't go until the next day's post.

Even so, that still meant that Violet's father could arrive on that evening's train. A stretch, but I couldn't count on him being later than that.

I stopped pacing. There wasn't time to fuss about going to the village to arrange transporting our trunks to the station. I barely knew who I would ask for such a thing anyway. This was not my home, or my time – I could spend a fruitless hour and come away empty handed.

For a long minute, I stood where I was, facing the ocean, the sun past 12 o'clock, on its long slide to the end of the day. I'd seen the timetable for the trains, there was one we could take this very afternoon, if we wanted to get clear of the place quickly.

We did, I decided. We needed to get out of here.

Violet had refused of course, to go back to her father's house, and she'd been almost as panicked when I suggested going back to mine and throwing ourselves on the mercy of Fran's mother.

Spinning on my heel, I turned back to the cottage, the decision made. The key slipped in my fingers and I struggled with it a moment before it turned, and the door swung open. I closed it behind me and took the steps at a run.

Violet, I'd thought, would be asleep, but when I appeared at her door, she was standing in the middle of the floor, folding her clothes. She turned and stared at me.

'Fran,' she said. 'What is it?' Even from the doorway, I could see the jump of the pulse in her neck.

I shook my head. 'I think we should take the next train,' I said. 'This afternoon. There is one at four.' I checked the clock that passed the minutes on the mantelpiece. 'It is two thirty now.'

She looked at me for a moment, then nodded. 'Very well,' she said. 'I couldn't rest anyway so am packing my things. Did you arrange transport for our trunks?'

'There is no time,' I explained. 'We would end up missing today's train, in the time it would take me to arrange that, and I think we need to keep ahead of things.'

Violet was not stupid. 'My father,' she said. 'We need to keep ahead of my father.'

'He could be here by tomorrow. Maybe not, but I'm not willing to take the risk.'

I saw Violet do the same calculation I had, then she nodded. 'What about our things?'

'We will take what we need most in our small bags. It won't be much, but...'

'But we will manage,' Violet said, and I sighed in relief.

'I know you like your pretty dresses,' I said, genuinely sorry.

'I like my freedom more,' she said, wryly.

Her tone made me smile at her. 'That's my girl,' I said, then stepped further into the room and picked up the painting. 'I am taking this,' I said.

She stared at me, then put down the dress she was holding and stepped up to me, reaching out a hand to touch my face.

'Fran,' she said.

I would have answered, but my voice seemed stuck somewhere about stomach level.

Then she was kissing me again, and the whole world tilted on its axis. When she stepped back, I stared at her.

'What was that for?' I managed.

She looked at me. 'To say thank you. And because I wanted to.'

'I like the last bit,' I croaked, and she smiled, face suddenly radiant.

'So do I,' she said. 'Now go pack your things. We've an adventure to go on.'

I stumbled back to my room on wooden legs, the painting tucked under my arm. An adventure. I supposed it was certainly that. Maybe I was dreaming, after all. Everything seemed surreal, moving so fast I could barely keep up.

But I packed my bag full of basics, and the feeling of cottons and linens under my fingertips made me sure again that this was all real in some way I didn't understand. I placed Violet's painting on top and stared down at it. How odd it was to see it here, after so many years of looking at it on my grandmother's wall.

Where it actually still was, my grandmother still in her house in Glastonbury, sitting on the stool behind the counter in her bookshop five mornings a week. She was seventy-five and spry with it.

Part of my mind went spinning off into questions of time and reality and all the arguments against what was happening. I shoved them aside. It made little sense, but then when you think about it – how much of the world do we really know?

I had one fear, and that was that the story my grandmother told me about Vivi Madden would come true, no matter what. Would she not otherwise have had a different tale to tell me?

I shook my head and closed the carpet bag over the painting. There were no answers for me. All I could do, was what I could – my best to make sure that Violet did not end up dying of slow suffocation, hung with her own bedsheet in a mental institution. I would either succeed or fail, but I would not do anything but try.

Who was to say I wasn't back in 1916 to do that exact thing?

'Fran?' Violet appeared fully dressed in my doorway, her bag in one hand, hat and gloves in the other.

'You look very smart,' I said. 'Perfect for travelling.' But I was thinking for a moment of the yellow dress, and how ravishing she'd looked in that.

She smiled at me. 'Thank you, Fran. I thought I'd go for practical, for once in my life. Blend in with the crowd, so to speak. It seemed wise.'

I nodded. 'Very wise.' She smoothed a hand over the dark green skirt and jacket, then gave me a twinkling smile.

'But I packed the yellow dress. I couldn't bear to leave it.'

There was no help but to laugh. 'Good,' I said. 'It's my favourite.' I blinked. 'When we get where we're going, I'll find a way to buy you dresses of every colour of the rainbow.'

She giggled. 'Paris is the capital for fashion,' she said. 'But I'll be content with just something to paint in, you know that.' Her expression turned dreamy. 'Paris,' she said. 'We can go there. I've always wanted to go there.' Her big green eyes blinked at me. 'Everyone knows it's where to be if you're an artist.' She bit at her lip. 'Better than London.'

'There is a war on,' I said. 'We need to give our destination some more thought.'

Violet shrugged. 'I've given it plenty of thought. We will be all right there.'

I wasn't going to argue. 'I guess we should go,' I said, and looked around to make sure I hadn't forgotten anything.

The damned hat was still on the bed and I picked it up, scowling at it.

'Here,' Violet said, coming over to take it out of my hands. 'Is it true no one wears hats anymore in your old time?'

In my old time. My past was now the future. That was mind-boggling. I bent my head.

'Only to keep warm, or to shade from the sun,' I said. 'Or at the races.' I thought about it. 'Or if you're going to a royal wedding or something, I suppose, but I've never had an invitation to one of those.'

She tacked the hat to my head with a long, lethal-looking pin. 'There,' she said, then stood back and looked me up and down.

I stood awkwardly under her gaze. I was still the same short, square woman I'd been before, which was something of a relief, but it did make me feel even more self-conscious in the long skirts and fashions, which were far more feminine that I was used to.

'What's wrong?' I asked.

'Nothing,' she said, and smiled. 'Nothing at all. You are perfect.'

'I am?'

She came over and tilted her head to kiss me on the cheek. 'Absolutely perfect. There's no other companion I want.'

'Good,' I grumbled, blushing. 'Because I'd hate to be stuck back here on my own.'

Her laugh led me down the stairs to the kitchen. 'We need each other, Fran Madden,' she said. 'That's all there is to it.' She set down her bags and went to the larder.

'What are you doing?' I asked.

'I'm going to wrap us up something to eat on the journey,' she said. 'It will take perhaps three hours to get to London, and I was thinking we might want to save the little money we have.'

She was right – and she was right about the other thing too. I did need her. As much as she needed me.

We were in this together, and standing there in the kitchen, watching her deftly wrap us up a meal, it really didn't feel too bad.

The danger was still there, the knowledge of what we were up against, but seeing her look up and smile at me, perhaps she had been right too about something else.

It was an adventure.

A damned scary one. But an adventure all the same. My heart pounded against my ribs. I picked up her bag.

'Ready to go?' I asked.

'Yes,' she said, slipping the food in a small basket and tucking her handbag in beside it. 'I'm ready.' Her eyes glowed at me. 'Are you?'

'Yes,' I said. 'Let's go and find a way to live.'

'Really live.'

I smiled at her.

CHAPTER SIXTEEN

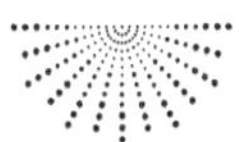

It had rained in London, and the city steamed and sweated around us. I stood on the platform, bag dangling from my hand, Violet pressed to my side, and felt as though the world had taken a slide sideways.

I recognised the station. I recognised almost everything, but over it all was a layer of difference that made me disoriented, that made my legs shake and quiver under me as though the ground was unsteady. It had been easy enough to ignore the odd sense of dislocation on the train, and even in the cottage, because they'd been so different.

But here, in the swelter of London in July, I couldn't ignore it. I had slipped into a twilight zone version of the world. The familiar warred with the strange.

'Are you all right?' Violet asked, clutching my elbow.

I swallowed and nodded. Then I answered. 'Not really.'

'What is it?'

There was a pressure on my chest more than the damp press of air in my lungs.

'Fran?' Violet's fingers dug into my flesh.

'I'm okay,' I said, and it was as much for my benefit as hers.

'But what is wrong? Besides it being terribly hot?'

I shook my head and whispered to her out of the corner of my mouth. 'Everything is so strange, Violet,' I said. 'It's the same, and yet it's so different.' I blinked at a cluster of young women moving past us under an arched roof I was reasonably familiar with. They though – they had stepped out of a vintage photograph, one that someone had painstakingly coloured. They did not belong in any world I was used to.

'There are an awful lot of soldiers,' Violet whispered. 'We are blocking the way.'

As we were. We'd seen soldiers, barely men, many of them, at other stations on our way here, but now they were everywhere, bustling about on mysterious business, calling and shouting to each other, standing in huddled groups. My heart knocked painfully against my chest for them. They were so young, and so many.

Violet tugged on my arm. 'Let's move,' she said. 'Those people over there are looking at us rather strangely. You simply stopped walking, you know, and now you're just staring around with your mouth hanging open.'

It was true. I was rooted to the spot, mouth open, gaping at the scene I'd landed in. I shuffled, bumped against Violet's basket, then nodded.

'You have to help me,' I whispered. 'Get me moving. I'm a little overwhelmed.'

There was a sharp pinch above my elbow, and I jumped, turning to Violet with wide eyes. 'What was that for?' I rubbed at the stinging skin.

She looked at me with sparkling eyes. 'You said to get you moving.'

'Yeah, by giving me a gentle push or something.'

That got nothing more than just a shrug and a wicked smile. I rolled my eyes at her and turned to find the nearest exit, started wading my way through the crowd, gaze skimming over everything, trying not to let it all short-circuit my brain again.

Beside me, Violet giggled. 'Worked though, didn't it?'

'Just as well we're not heading to that olive grove in Italy then, isn't it? You'd be whipping that poor big-eared donkey up and down that hill.'

'I would never hurt a harmless animal!' Her eyes were wide, horrified, then turned excited. 'Do you think we might get a dog when we get to Paris?' she asked. 'Just a little dog, a sweet pet to keep us company?' She jostled beside me as we walked. 'Do say we might.'

'We haven't even settled that Paris is a good idea yet.' I gestured at a soldier, standing on the platform looking at the timetable with shadows in his eyes. 'There's a war on, remember.'

'I'm not likely to forget, Fran,' came the acerbic reply. 'It's been going for two years.'

'Then you will agree with me that Paris might not be the best place for us.'

There was a moment's silence and we reached the exit, stepped onto the footpath and looked up at the squat and bleached sky above us.

'Well I'm not staying in London,' Violet said. 'Have you ever seen anything so dreary?' She shivered beside me despite the heat. 'This place is full of bad memories for me.' Her hand tightened on my arm. 'It haunts me.'

I nodded. London looked haunted to me as well, for different reasons, but I didn't expect Paris would be much of a choice either. Everywhere I looked, faces were pale, drawn. Out in the suburbs it might have been possible to pretend the world was not at war, but here, it was in every face I looked at, in the hunch of shoulders, and in the uniforms everywhere.

'We will see,' I said to Violet. 'We will speak to Fran's father, and see what happens.'

Violet moved off down the footpath, dragging me along with her. 'Your father,' she said. 'You have to act like he's your own father.'

'That's not going to be easy, you realise.'

She nodded, and stopped in front of a doorway, looking up at the building. 'This should do,' she said and reached to push the hotel door open. 'It looks cheap, at least.'

As long as it had a shower, I wouldn't complain. Then I realised that showers probably weren't invented yet, or some such nonsense, and my heart sank lower. Violet turned to look at me, her dark brows drawn together.

'You will manage,' she told me. 'We went over all I know about him on the train. We will do it again when we get to our room.'

I nodded and followed her over the doorstep and into the hotel. A dusty-looking woman greeted us from behind a desk.

'A room, please,' Violet said. 'For one night, perhaps two.'

The woman looked us over, then blinked, nostrils flaring

as though we smelled badly. Perhaps we did. It had been a long trip. But she turned to Violet.

'Which?' she asked.

'Which what?' Violet said.

A curl of lip joined the flared nostril. 'One night or two?'

'Oh,' Violet said, and I saw her sweep her own gaze over the woman, then turn her head and do the same to the interior of the reception room we stood in. 'One, please,' she said when she looked back at the woman.

There was a pause before the other woman said anything. 'One room, one night.'

'Yes,' Violet said, and I hid a smile. 'One room, one night, for my cousin and I.'

Another pause and I stood still and silent through it, then finally the woman turned and took a key from a row of hooks behind her. 'Third floor,' she said. 'That will be payment in advance, please.'

She named a price that seemed absurd to me, and I reached into my bag for the money, handed it over.

'One of you needs to sign the register,' she said, my money in her palm. Violet picked up the pen and signed, took the key, turned away.

'The lift's not working,' the woman called after her. 'You'll have to use the stairs.'

Violet didn't bother to respond, and I followed her lead. But I did glance at the registry book on the way past and smiled. There was that flourish of a signature again. Vivi Madden.

The room was as dusty as the woman had been, but I set my case down on the floor and sat on the bed with a sigh of relief. The bed, at least, was soft. I lay down on it. The day had been long, taxing. The pillow was soft too, and it smelt clean enough. I closed my eyes.

The bed moved beside me, and something warm filled up the space beside me. I opened my eyes to Violet's dark hair and pale skin, her green eyes glowing as they looked at me. She wriggled closer, moving her head to rest it on my shoulder, her arm lying over my chest and a proprietary knee over my own.

'Comfy?' I asked.

'Yes, thank you,' she said. 'And tired.' She yawned to prove her point.

And me – what did I do? I moved my arm to tuck her in closer to my side, then closed my eyes, the sound of her soft breathing in my ears. Perhaps I should have moved her gently onto her own bed, or done some other such thing, but she was a comfort lying there against me, and more than that, a delight too. I had landed in a sticky web, a tangle of time and circumstance I barely knew what to make of, but if there was one thing I could say for sure – it was that Violet meant something to me. I was attracted to her, I was falling in love with her, but more than that, I drifted off to sleep that day on that bed in the cheap hotel room, thinking that somehow, I was where I was meant to be. That maybe I'd fallen through time exactly because Violet needed me.

And because maybe I needed her too.

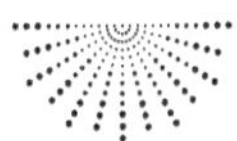

CHAPTER SEVENTEEN

We woke to a dark room and stiff limbs. Violet rolled off me, groaning, and I sat up, lifting my long hair from my neck. As soon as we were settled somewhere, I was going to cut off this great rope of thick hair.

'I'm starving,' Violet said. 'What time is it?'

'Where's the light switch, would be a better question,' I grumbled, remembering the lamp beside the bed and leaning past her to fumble for a switch.

The light was puny, but it still made us blink. Violet stretched and gazed around the room. 'We slept for hours, I think,' she said.

I was hot and sticky, and hungry too, desperate to wash, put on something clean, that wasn't travel-stained, and then sit down to a good meal.

'It is after eight,' Violet said, looking at the little watch she carried. 'No wonder I'm hungry.' She turned to me, grinning. 'Do you think they know we've run away yet?'

I shook my head at her. 'It's nothing to laugh about, you know.'

She rolled her eyes and plumped back down on the bed. 'But it's an adventure, and I know we're going to be all right now.' She leaned over and stroked a stay piece of hair back from my sweaty face. 'Thanks to you, Fran.'

I grabbed her hand and squeezed the fingers. 'Don't thank me too soon,' I said. 'We're not even half-way there yet.'

Violet shook her head, rising from the bed and stretching luxuriously in a way that said she had complete, if unfounded faith in me. She had taken her jacket off before lying down, and her white blouse was crumpled and twisted. I knew I was in trouble when I still found it totally adorable. Her hands reached toward the ceiling, then touched her head, pulling pins from her hair until it cascaded in an ebony stream down her back.

'Why are you looking at me like that?' she asked, and there was something in her voice – amusement, perhaps. I hadn't known she'd seen me.

I swallowed. 'Like what?' Feigning innocence has always been part of my modus operandi when the difficult questions were going down. Probably why I was still single at twenty-nine.

The smile that appeared on her face was lop-sided and knowing.

'Like you want to rain kisses upon me.'

Definitely a knowing smile.

Mouth dry, I fumbled for words. She took pity on me, and came closer, leaned over the bed.

'Don't worry,' she said, barely above a whisper, her face only inches from mine. 'It's not a bad thing.'

I wasn't sure any blood was making it to my brain. 'It's not?'

She shook her head. 'No.'

It took a moment to clear my throat and get the words out in something that was possibly the right order. 'Are you flirting with me?'

Her eyes widened, and even in the sickly light from the cheap lamp, they sparkled. 'I'm hungry,' she said.

I blinked at her. 'What?'

Straightening, she went over to the basket we'd brought with us on the train, and peered into it, then gave me a wicked look. 'I'm hungry,' she repeated. 'I'm hungry for you – for those kisses, but I think we need to eat.' Her smile widened. 'We might need our strength.'

'You are flirting with me.'

She dipped a hand into the basket and turned up with a large slice of pound cake in a cloth. Then she was back over sitting on the bed, holding up a golden morsel to me. I opened my mouth, barely thinking, and she popped it in. I wasn't sure I had enough saliva to chew it, but I needn't have worried. I was hungry, the cake was good, and Violet feeding me made the experience both nourishing and erotic. A disconcerting mixture.

She broke off another piece of cake and fed herself, little pink tongue licking up a stray crumb from her mouth. Her eyes never left mine.

'What are you doing?' I croaked.

Her eyebrows raised in a perfect look of righteous virtue. 'Whatever do you mean, Fran?' she asked, and this time used a delicate finger to wipe away a crumb from the corner of her mouth. I wasn't even sure there'd been a crumb there.

I shook my head.

Violet put the cake down and her face relaxed into a wide and easy smile. 'Oh Fran,' she said. 'How I love you already!'

'You do?'

Placing a palm on each side of my hot and plain face she delivered a smacking kiss on my lips. 'I do definitely very much,' she said. 'You are perfect.'

'Perfect?'

'Perfect,' she agreed, and let go of me. I wanted to snatch back her hands and replace them on my skin, but she was standing, stretching again. 'I'm going to go run us a bath.'

I blinked at her. 'A bath?'

She laughed. 'That is what I said.'

'We can have a bath?'

'I assume so. This is an hotel.' She looked around and wrinkled her nose. 'I think rather a poor one, but in case your father doesn't entertain our proposal very well tomorrow, it is, I suppose, wise to save our pennies.'

The reminder of tomorrow's job doused me in ice water. Violet must have seen my expression as she smiled kindly at me.

'You mustn't worry,' she said. 'It will all work out. One way or the other.' She paused with her hand on the door to the hallway outside. 'We went over everything about your father while we were on the train. How did you put it?'

'We did our homework,' I said, miserably.

'Yes. Exactly,' Violet said. 'Whatever that means. Your father is a good man – I know he will help us.'

I nodded because there was nothing else to do.

'Good girl.' I got a radiant smile. 'Now I'm going to go run the bath and very selfishly take the first turn.' She blew me a kiss. 'But I promise I won't stay in so long that the water goes cold.' She squinted suddenly at me, a smile playing around her lips. 'Unless you want to have your bath with me?'

I felt my own eyes widen. 'Have one with you?' I swallowed. 'At the same time?'

Her laugh was like the chimes of a golden bell. She pulled the bedroom door open and disappeared into the dimness of the hallway leaving me uncomfortably, my face burning, to imagine her leaning nude against me in the tub and covered in soapy bubbles.

The dining room was closing by the time we arrived downstairs, scrubbed clean – separately – and dressed in fresh, if crumpled clothes. For a brief moment, Violet was consumed with the idea of heading out to the Café Royal for dinner, and it's true – I was tempted, imagining who we might meet there, artists, writers – people I'd only read about, who lived in my world only in their enduring work and legends.

But I shook my head, convinced her not tonight. I was too nervous about what was on tomorrow's menu to relax and enjoy myself. Violet gazed at me with those large green eyes of hers for a moment, then nodded, and I was glad, because under the glittering excitement of her manner, she was pale and strained. What she needed – what we both needed, was something to eat, and an early night.

Violet turned her charms on the hotel staff instead, and charm she had aplenty when she put her mind to it. She flattered and cajoled them into making us a plate of sandwiches, even getting the dusty matron behind the reception desk to crack a decent smile. I watched in awe and a degree of pride, as Violet related effortlessly to everyone there. She had a way about her that was hard to resist. You couldn't help but smile at her obvious enthusiasm.

We sat at a small table for two in the corner of the dining room, a single lamp lighting things for us. A waiter brought sandwiches and hot tea for us and I thanked him profusely. The beef on the sandwiches was stringy, but the bread was fresh and cut thick. It was better than I'd expected at this time of night.

'You must not be nervous about tomorrow,' Violet said, looking earnestly at me, her pale fingers holding the white teacup.

I gave a short laugh. 'It's impossible not to be.'

She blinked. 'Don't be like that.' Leaning closer. 'I know you can do this.'

I wanted to throw my hands up in the air. 'I'm not even sure what I'm doing.'

Violet sat back and smiled at me. 'It's simple. You make your father an offer he can't refuse.'

I stared at her.

She shrugged delicate shoulders and I found myself looking at the hollow of her neck.

'What did you say?' I asked.

'Fran,' she chided. 'I asked you if you wanted to marry?'

'What?' For a moment I was completely nonplussed, forgetting where I was – forgetting *when* I was. Was she asking me to marry her?

I must have stared blankly at her face for a long moment, because finally she reached across the table and touched my arm. I felt the heat of her fingertips. Cleared my throat.

'You don't of course, we know that.' She spoke, and I watched her lips move. She was right, yes. I didn't want to marry, but the misunderstanding in my head had shaken me.

Because I was pretty sure I would have said yes, if she'd actually been asking.

And how crazy was that?

I touched my head, perhaps to make sure that it was my own, sitting on my own shoulders, that whatever else was going on, I was still me, could still count on being me.

My head, my shoulders, my mind – and apparently a heart that had gone its own way and fallen in love. Without blinking, without breathing, within the space of one beat and the next.

She frowned and then laughed. 'Fran, you're not listening to a word I'm saying.'

I shook my head. 'Of course I am.'

Those marvellous eyes looked heavenward. 'You are not. What was the last thing I said?'

I smiled. 'I've no idea.' I looked at her. 'I zoned out when you started talking about marriage.'

That got me an odd look. 'Zoned out?'

'Ah, was distracted.'

'Oh.' Her lips were perfect, red and full despite the thinness of her face. 'Zoned out. What a strange saying.'

'You've no idea,' I laughed.

Her perplexity was disarming. 'About what?'

'How very perfect you are.' It was out before I could stop it. 'I enjoy your company very much,' I added hastily.

Her smile was wide and delighted. 'You're the first person who's ever said that to me, Fran.' Her hand snaked across the table again and grasped mine. I held onto it. 'Thank you so much.'

I turned my back on Violet, giving her the privacy to change into her nightwear, and to hide my own blush as I peeled layers of fabric from my own square body, ducking my head into the white nightdress before my blush could spread over my shoulders and back and give me away.

But small hot hands touched my neck, brushing my hair aside and I felt her weight settle on the bed behind me.

'What are you doing?' I asked.

'Shh,' she said, and her breath was warm on the sensitive skin at the back of my neck. I had to close my eyes, swallow down the groan of desire that flared up.

It took me two attempts before I could say anything, and then I only managed her name.

'Violet.'

She kissed my neck, and I found myself bending forward, gasping for breath. 'What are you doing?'

'Looking…for…those…kisses…I…wanted,' she said, punctuating each word with a touch of her lips to my skin.

I struggled to turn around, the nightdress loose on my thighs. I hadn't managed to pull it down over my legs.

'Oh god, Violet,' I said, seeing her.

She rocked back on the bed, gaze fastened on me, lips parted, her chest visibly rising and falling with her breath.

'You don't have any clothes on.' My mouth dried up. Her dark hair spilled over shoulders that could have been carved from marble, such was their perfection.

And the rest of her. I moved my eyes back to her face, not daring to look. I snapped them closed. It was too much.

'What are you doing, Violet?' I asked, voice rasping against the back of my throat, eyes still squeezed shut.

She grasped my hand, and for a moment I thought I would hyperventilate when my palm landed on a firm, round breast.

'Violet,' I gasped. 'What are you doing?' I looked at her.

She had her own eyes closed, head tilted slightly back, a smile playing around her lips.

I wanted to kiss those lips.

I wanted to gather her close to me, press her hot skin against mine. She moved my hand over her breast, grazing the tight nipple.

I groaned. 'Violet. What on earth are you doing?' I wanted to close my own eyes again, but the lamp lit her from behind and her shape was so perfect, I was riveted by it. The tucked in waist, the gentle flare of her hips, the long line of her neck.

Her eyes flicked open and she looked at me, holding my gaze in her own, steady and unblinking. Then she swallowed, smiled, leaned closer until I could feel the heat from her bare skin in the air between us.

'Isn't this what you like?' she asked.

'I...I don't know what you mean.' My heart pounded so loudly I was afraid it would do itself some damage in there behind my ribs.

She wriggled forward an inch and rose onto her knees, sliding my hand down from breast to waist, holding it there. Holding herself only a breath away from me, and then stroking a hand over my cheek, she tangled her fingers in my hair, and closed the distance between us, and the softness of her breast lay against my cheek.

'Don't you want to make love to me, Fran?' she asked, and her voice was light as air, some sort of lilting song to the bass beat of my heart.

'What?' The squawked word parted my lips, grazing them against her, and I pressed them there, breathing in the scent of her, that wild orchid, Arabian nights perfume.

She moved, seemingly effortlessly and landed in my lap, a knee on either side of me, her beautiful, bare body in my arms.

'Don't you want me?' she teased, then grew serious, dipping her head down to stare in my eyes. 'I want you,' she said, and her voice told me it was true, husky with desire.

I nodded dumbly, and my hands moved on their own, stroking over hip and waist and wrapping themselves around her, feeling her ribs, but noticing more the silk of her skin. She shifted slightly, and her pelvis was snugly against mine, and she reached for my right hand, drawing it over her skin and up over her breast to her neck, her cheek, where she pressed it fast, then turned her head to touch her lips to my fingertips.

'Violet,' I said. 'I know we kissed earlier, but surely that was a mistake.' My body screamed a mute protest at the words spilling from my mouth.

Couldn't I, just for once, accept what was being offered?

'This isn't a game,' I added.

Her eyes widened. 'I am not playing,' she said, and trailed my fingers down the china skin of her throat. 'I am not so innocent, you know. I understand what I am doing. I know what I want.'

I blinked at her, feeling the heat from between her legs against my belly. She closed her eyes and rocked her hips, lips parted, then dropped her hands and tugged aside the cotton of my night dress. She was wet against me and I struggled for breath.

I just could not leave well enough alone. 'You want this?'

She nodded, eyes closed, lips damp from her tongue. 'When I lived in London,' she said, opening eyes the colours of jewels. 'I took a lover.' She blinked, tipped her head to the side. 'Or he took me, I do not know which is more correct.'

I gripped her hips, heaving hot air in and out of my lungs, trying to get oxygen to my starving brain. 'This is not quite the same,' I managed.

She smiled at me, bent down and pressed her lips to my forehead. 'No,' she agreed. 'It is you.'

'And a woman,' I spluttered.

The lips smiled against my skin. 'In the studio next to the one where I stayed sometimes, lived a woman. She was a painter.' Her breath was a hot storm against my face. My arms slid around her and I closed my own eyes against the excitement of spread thighs against me. Just the knowledge of the way she sat upon my lap had me in a growing haze of desire.

Violet lifted her head and I found my own lips against her skin, trailing kisses despite myself down the curve of breast bone, leaving them lingering against the growing swell of her breast. Her chest swelled against me as she took a deep breath, let it out in a low moan.

'She had a lover,' Violet said, and for a dizzy span of seconds I didn't know who she was talking about. I had not had a lover for…a long time.

Then I remembered the story she was telling me, and tried to listen properly, my arms hugging her to me now, cheek resting against the base of her throat. I was hanging onto her, poised on the edge.

Violet's voice was a throaty whisper, and she moved against me again, the tickle of the hair between her legs on my belly making me swallow.

'It was a woman, her lover. I watched them through the keyhole.'

I looked up at Violet in wide-eyed, blinking amazement. She smiled down at me.

'Yes,' she said. 'I watched them undress each other.' She closed her eyes, as though reliving it for a moment. 'I watched them touch each other.'

My mouth was a desert. 'You enjoyed it?'

'Seeing them?' A slow smile spread across her lips. 'Yes.' Green eyes snapped open to look at my upturned face. 'So you see, Fran. I am not such an innocent after all.' She dragged a fingernail down my cheek, neck, then ducked both hands down and before I knew exactly what she was doing, she was tugging on the nightgown I still wore.

'Please take it off, Fran,' she said. 'Please.'

I did, and then her skin was touching mine, her curves,

the dips and hollows of her body pressed against mine, and I held her tightly.

We sat like that for a long minute, and her arms were around me, her hair on my own shoulders, her fingers tight against my back.

'Lie down, Fran,' she said. 'Lie on the bed.'

I gazed at her with glazed eyes. Then did as she said, unable to take my hands from her as I followed her instructions. She smiled down at me, moving with me until I lay properly on the bed, and she knelt over me, bottom lip nipped between small white teeth.

'I don't know what to do next,' she said.

I half sat, reaching for her, but she pressed me back down with a smile.

'I should have said, I don't know where to start.' Her smile was wide, wicked, and it took my breath away.

'Wherever you want,' I gasped.

Her answering smile was even more teasing, and in a fluid, graceful move I could never have replicated in a million years, she stretched out beside me, taking my hand and tugging me over onto my side. I went willingly.

My hand, trapped under hers, cupped a breast, caught a nipple between fingers warming to their task, and then she was pulling it away, pressing my palm hard against her skin, taking it downwards, across soft belly, and still further.

'Touch me, Fran,' she said, her voice in my ear, her breath tickling the sensitive skin there. 'I want you to touch me.'

I'd done what I could. I'd made sure she knew what she was doing, what she was asking, and I relaxed against her with a sigh. There was nothing I wanted to do more than touch her.

Her knee landed on my hip and she drew my hand down between her legs, and I heard the sharp intake of her breath when my fingers touched her hot flesh. She was swollen, wet, and I felt a burst of pleasure so intense that if her hand had been on me, I would have come at the first touch.

Oh, but she was so warm, so slick, and she opened herself up to me with a wriggling groan, her breasts pushed against my own, her breath hot in my ear. I heard her whispering my name, and it all but undid me.

'Put your fingers inside me, Fran,' she said. 'I want you inside me.' She tipped her hips towards me and I slid one finger and then another inside her, my eyes falling shut as I did so, then snapping open to look at her.

She was watching me, her eyes wide and bright with pleasure, and a smile played around her parted lips.

'You are beautiful,' I told her, and she lifted her chin, her hand still on mine, and she pushed my fingers deeper, and I felt her muscles clamp around my fingers, then relax, and she was so wet, so warm, and it was impossible to think any further, all I could do was to move with the rocking of her hips, listening to the quickening of her breath, the pounding of my heart.

CHAPTER NINETEEN

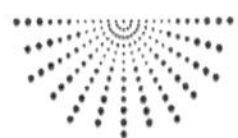

She came with a cry that was breathless with pleasure, her hand dropping its pressure against my own and clutching at me instead. I buried my face in her neck and went by touch, feeling her lock tight around my fingers, her body arching against mine, her hands gripping, scratching me, then finally, as the orgasm had shuddered through her, they held me, clung to me.

I listened to her relax against me, the sound of her voice a music of its own in my ear. I felt the curve of her lips in a smile and then she was shifting, moving back to look at me, and there was a wild joy in her eyes.

'So that is what makes a woman scream,' she said, laughing, and then she was hugging me tight, my fingers still inside her, her leg hooked around me, trapping my hand. I was okay with that. I loved the way she felt wrapped around me, the way I could feel the last lingering contractions of her muscles.

I kissed her, and she laughed again.

'What is funny?' I asked when she did not stop.

She shook her head. 'Nothing,' she said. 'Everything. I am overwhelmed!'

That had me moving, sliding my hand from her, wet fingers against her hips, pushing her back from me, looking down at her in concern.

'Are you all right?' I asked.

She nodded. 'Oh, Fran, I have never been better! Kiss me! I want to roll around on the bed kissing you. I don't want to stop!' She cupped both hands around my cheeks and pulled me to her lips. They were sweet, the kiss long and deep, and in another moment, I was all sensation, all desire again.

'Fran?' she asked, and I looked at those beautiful feline eyes. 'Can I ask you something?'

I managed a nod, then actual words. 'Anything.'

She nibbled on her lip and it was adorable, so I kissed her mouth while she did it. Then lifted my head again and waited. Her leg was wound around my hip again, and I was pinned against her, the curls between her legs damp against my thighs.

She licked her lips, looking up at me, hair spread in a dark halo around her flushed face.

'I would like to do more,' she said. 'Please may we do more?'

A movement, quick as a flash, and I was on my back, Violet leaning over me, her hair brushing against a nipple so hard it ached. I closed my eyes to catch my breath – her hair, like feathers of silk on my skin. When I opened my eyes again, she was watching me, a dawning smile on her face.

'That feels good?' she asked.

I groaned. Everything felt good. A nod.

She took the thick strand of hair and brushed it across the skin of my breasts, belly, neck, in a trail of erotic calligraphy.

As for me – gave myself over to the sheer, intense pleasure of it, of her – the way she crouched bending over me, her hair and breasts sweeping against my skin as she moved, planting kisses behind the feather touches, up over my own breasts, to neck, to that wonderful spot on the shoulder, up to my ear, and finally, when I was seeking her lips, they met mine and I lost myself in the taste of her.

She breathed words against my mouth and I opened my eyes.

'What did you say?' I asked. The words had been muffled.

'I said I saw them doing something.' She lifted her head and blinked at me.

My mind was a blank. 'Who?'

A smile sliding quickly from shy to sly. 'The neighbouring painter and her female lover.' Her lips were parted, and all down my body I could feel the heat of her.

I swallowed, not knowing where this was going, barely able to think at all, in fact.

'You want to try something you saw them doing?' That much penetrated my foggy brain.

She nodded. 'But I do not know if you will want it.'

I gazed up at her, running my hands down over the dip and flare of waist and hip. 'I'm pretty sure I would do anything you asked,' I replied. It was true. I was well past any sort of objection. My blood was running fast, skin screaming with the pleasure of being touched, head swimming with arousal. I wanted everything she did. I would do whatever it was. Twice, if possible.

She ducked her head down and whispered in my ear. Sat

back and looked at my face, eyes dilated in the dim light, gleaming. 'I don't exactly understand it,' she said. 'But it too made them scream.' She shivered, not from cold, but excitement.

Me, I just nodded, and she gave me a sudden, delighted grin. 'Fran,' she said. 'How I do love you!'

The words melted into me, and even if they were meant as flippantly as they were said, I relished them anyway and grinned back at her, laughing with her, and grabbing her bottom I urged her up.

She giggled and wriggled forward over me.

'This is the way you want to do it?' I asked.

She just nodded, and settled her knees either side of my head, holding herself just above me. I reached for her and tasted her.

She was beautiful, sweet to taste, somehow golden, like honey. I licked her lightly with my tongue, feeling her swollen and slick, and she gave a surprised, gasping moan, and I heard her hands land against the wall, heard the panting groan of her breath as I continued my delicate exploration, hands cupped to the delightful curve of her bottom.

I couldn't remember the last time I'd done this and didn't care to. The pleasure was in Violet, in holding my mouth to her, barely touching her so that she gasped and cried out for more, moving my tongue against her in low slow licks so that she squirmed against me, pushing my tongue inside her so that she called out and slammed an open palm against the wall.

'Oh Fran,' she cried. 'It feels so good!'

It did. Oh it really did. I lapped up the taste of her, her juices drenching my mouth, and still I could not get enough of her. She was beautiful, a pearl against my tongue, and I had never wanted anything more than I did to taste her at that moment, to be licking her, sucking her into my mouth, hearing her hot cries from above me.

She came again, her orgasm violent in its pleasure, and I kept my lips against her for a long moment before, thighs trembling, she sank down, hands dragging down the wallpaper, tumbling from me into a damp, panting tangle onto the bed beside me.

I found her eyes amidst dishevelled dark hair and smiled at the expression in them.

'You are so beautiful,' I said, smoothing a hand over her heaving ribs. 'You are the most beautiful creature I've ever met.'

She caught my hand and brought it to her lips, kissed the fingertips, then pulled me down to kiss my lips.

'I can taste myself on you,' she said.

I nodded.

'You like the taste?'

A smile. 'You taste like honey.'

She kissed me again, as if to see, then shook her head, laughing.

'You taste like honey to me,' I said, and she ran her fingers through the tangle of my own hair, pushing it back from my face, as I lay down beside me.

'Fran,' she whispered. 'The sensations were so strong.' She licked her lips. 'I've never felt anything like it.'

I smiled. 'You are wonderful.'

She laughed again. 'I am shaking.'

I sat up, tugging at her. 'Let's get under the covers,' I said. 'We will cool down fast after all that exertion.'

She clambered underneath the blankets with me and snuggled deep into my side. I tucked the covers around her shoulders and held her tight, dropping kisses in her hair, feeling a sweet, dazed euphoria.

'Fran?' she asked, after several minutes.

I looked down at her. 'Yes, Violet?'

She blinked at me. 'What about you?'

'What do you mean?'

She pursed her lips, thinking. 'I would like to touch you,' she said.

I almost couldn't answer, the sudden, swelling response from my body was overwhelming. Mute, I nodded.

'May I, then?' she asked.

I nodded again. 'I won't last long,' I croaked.

There was a small frown on her face. 'I do not know what you mean.'

'I won't be able to hold off coming,' I said, and felt my body heat with embarrassment. 'It's been a long time, since I've been with anyone…and you…'

'And I?'

'You are very exciting,' I finished.

'Coming?' she questioned, and I realised that despite the little bit of experience, there was far more she didn't know.

'Having an orgasm,' I said.

She bared her teeth in a wide smile. 'And the orgasm is the explosion?' she asked. 'When all the world ignites in wild colour and sensation?'

I grinned. 'That would be it.'

'I like those,' she said, settling her head back on my shoulder with a satisfied sigh. 'But I still want to touch you.'

Just the knowledge that she did was almost enough to undo me. Again the mute nod. 'Please,' I managed.

'I will likely fumble,' she warned. 'I do not know what it is I should exactly do.' The smile appeared back on her face again as she looked at me. 'But I want to learn.'

I nodded. 'You can learn on me.' My voice was hoarse. 'Have you never touched yourself?'

Her mouth fell open in surprise.

'Not even when you watched your neighbours?'

She shook her head. 'I did not know to.' Laughter again. 'I wish I had!'

She decided then it was enough talk, and in a moment, I was agreeing with her, all thoughts fleeing my head in favour of raw sensation. Her hand was smooth against my skin, finding a hard nipple and making it ache with her brushing touch. Then the hand was replaced with lips and she sucked my nipple into her mouth and I was arching against her, drowning in hot desire.

When her hand made its first, tentative touch between my legs, I cried out and clutched at her, fingers dragging over her back. She moved her lips to kiss me.

'Like this?' she whispered against me, her fingers dipping to stroke my throbbing clit.

'Oh god yes,' I moaned, unable to help myself. Her touch was everything I'd ever wanted and with my other hand, I touched her cheek, felt the contours of her face, her neck, cupped her breast, squeezed, feeling the warm, soft weight of it, and hearing her quickening breathing in my ear.

Her fingers gained confidence, exploring my slick depths. I was wet, desperate for her touch, legs spreading wider, inviting her fingers, gasping when they slid inside me.

'Is this all right?' she asked, and I was all I could do to nod, to cling to her. 'Yes,' she breathed then, against my cheek, and I felt her leg hook over mine again, and the hot wet press of her against my hip. Her moans joined mine, as she rocked herself against me, her fingers slipping in and out of me in a generous rhythm that had me calling out her name, the pleasure building.

'I am inside you, Fran,' I heard her whisper. 'And it almost feels like you are still inside me, as well.'

I was beyond responding. All was stars in my head, nebulae colliding. I clung to Violet and she to me, joined together in the most fundamental way, and when she cried out in my ear, her voice high-pitched with pleasure, my own moans joined her and we rocked together, her fingers buried deep inside me, her thumb moving against my clit, the friction building and building sending me straight into orbit, my orgasm crashing through me and washing me up a shuddering, jellified mess in her arms.

When I could finally open my eyes, she was staring at me, green eyes wide in the dim light.

'That was good?' she asked.

I nodded dumbly.

'Yes,' she agreed with a sigh, tucking her head onto the pillow beside mine. 'It was good.'

I pulled her close, every inch of me, inside and out, still humming. She turned over and I fit myself to her curves, wrapping my arms around her, tucking her bottom against me, enjoying her warm curves, the scent of her, orchids and sex, following me into the long slow drift of sleep.

CHAPTER TWENTY

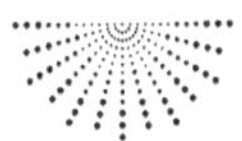

The morning dawned dreamless and hot. Even in the dim hotel room, it was warm and sticky, and it wasn't all due to the fact that I opened my eyes to arms full with Violet. I held still, one palm pressed against a soft breast, and tried to untangle my feelings.

'What are you thinking about?' Violet asked, squirming against me and stretching. 'You look terribly serious.'

'I'm not sure what I'm thinking,' I confessed.

She wiggled around in the narrow bed until we faced each other. A finger pressed itself against my lips. 'I'll tell you what you should be thinking.'

I smiled behind her finger. 'What's that, then?' I asked, kissing the digit against my lips.

She took her finger away and touched it to her own lips instead, as though transferring the kiss. The gesture made me smile wider, my heart a sentimental and swelling organ inside my bursting chest.

'You should be feeling the way I am,' she said.

'And how are you feeling?' I asked.

Violet pressed herself against me, and enticing mixture of softness and firmness. We fit together very well, although she was much smaller, except in height. I hugged her close.

'I feel marvellous,' she confided in my ear, then, as if a sort of punctuation, she nibbled on my ear, teeth grazing against me, driving me suddenly crazy.

'Oh my god,' I breathed. 'The things you do to me, Violet.'

'Good things?'

'Extremely.'

She laughed and launched herself upright, sitting in the bed stretching her fingertips towards the ceiling. 'I'm hungry,' she said.

I laughed too. 'That's how all this started,' I teased.

She looked at me and shook the waves of hair that bounced around her shoulders. 'No,' she said. 'We worked up this appetite of mine.' A sly smile. 'Perhaps we should do it all over again, so that I know it wasn't just a dream?'

I stroked my hand down her back and sighed. 'You are so very beautiful.' My fingers bumped over the knobs of her vertebrae. 'But if you've an appetite, we should get up and have breakfast. We need to fatten you up a little.'

She twisted around and poked me in the shoulder. 'All right,' she said. 'But we will play again, soon?'

I touched the fine skin on her collarbone, tracing my finger down it. 'It is play to you?'

She shook her thick hair from her shoulders and climbed from the bed. I watched her walk nude and long-limbed to search for clothes.

'Violet?' I said.

She shrugged, pulling on the garments that passed for underwear in 1916. 'It is play, and it is love, is it not?'

The answer didn't quite satisfy me, but I wasn't sure I could – or even should – articulate why. Instead I watched her in silence until she peered at me.

'Are you staying in bed all the day, Fran?' she asked.

'No,' I said. 'You are just such a pleasant thing to watch.'

That got a laugh, and a little twirling dance. A moment later she was over at the bed and pressing a kiss to my cheek.

'Darling Fran,' she whispered. 'You are precious to me.' Then she was up again, dancing across the room to search inside her case. 'Get up!' she called. 'I'm starving, and you have to visit your father after breakfast. Then we will be crossing the channel and heading to Paris!' She was back again, kissing me, and dancing away again, spirits high.

Groaning, I flopped onto my back and glared at the ceiling. For a delicious few minutes, I'd forgotten about what lay ahead of me. An interview with a man I had to pretend to know, to lay before him an outrageous plan I was already sure he wouldn't go for. But rolling back onto my side, I looked at Violet again.

Her hair was a dark storm of tangles around her shoulders, making her seem even more pale. There were dark smudges under her eyes, despite the dancing light in the green orbs. I thought of her – her impetuous spirit, her bubbling laughter, and that light in her eyes – I thought of it all trapped in a mental hospital, drugged, bound, broken, and I couldn't bear it. I pushed back the covers, knowing I would do anything to make sure that wasn't her fate. I could spend the rest of my life quietly loving her, giving her whatever she needed, to save her from the early, lonely death that awaited her.

I would do anything.

She danced over to me and put a hairbrush in my hand.

'What do you want me to do with this?' I asked stupidly, mind still elsewhere.

Her laughter was bright and real. 'Well I don't want you to spank me with it.' She laughed again, with one eyebrow raised. 'Will you brush my hair, please Fran?'

'I don't have any clothes on,' I said, gobsmacked over the spanking comment.

She giggled like a kid and pulled out the chair in front of the mirrored dresser. 'I don't mind,' she said. 'I love your body.'

That made me look down at myself in amazement. No one had ever told me they loved my body before. It was serviceable, I thought, square and sturdy, not beautiful, just perhaps honest. I reached for some clothes, anything near at hand.

But Violet was shaking her head. 'No, Fran, please don't.'

'What?'

Her smile at me in the mirror was mischievous. 'Don't put anything on. Come brush my hair.'

'What? Naked?'

She shook her head. 'Not naked. Nude. There's a difference.'

'No there's not,' I retorted. 'Both ways it's no clothes!'

Her eyes glowed in the mirror. 'Nudity is beautiful, natural.'

'And nakedness?'

She shrugged her delicate, bony shoulders, her slip loose about them. 'Nakedness is different, don't you think? Perhaps wishing it could hide itself?'

'Then that's exactly the right term,' I said. But I wasn't

reaching for my clothes. Instead, much to my own astonishment, I was walking the few steps across the room to Violet in front of the dresser. I touched her hair when I got there, and she smiled again.

'That is perfect,' she said. 'You are perfect.'

I shook my head, and when I lifted the hairbrush, my hand was shaking. She was looking at me in the mirror.

'I want to paint you,' she said, tipping her head on the side and examining my reflection. I loomed behind her, wide and white, a thatch of sandy hair visible between my legs.

'Paint me?' I asked, incredulous. 'Why on earth would you want to do that?'

She swivelled around in the chair until she was looking at me, not my reflection.

'Do you hate your body that much?' she asked, and there was curiosity in her voice. 'I think it is quite marvellous.'

'Don't be silly,' I said, eyes straying to the mirror despite myself. 'I don't hate it...'

'But?'

'Well, it's not beautiful. It just is.'

She touched warm fingertips to my belly and I shivered.

'This is the body that gave me such pleasure to touch last night,' she said. 'This is the body that has sat with me, walked with me, would carry me, if necessary.' She pressed her hand against my ribs, stroked the other over my hip and around to touch my bottom. Touched a kiss to the parting of my lips between my legs.

'Oh god,' I said.

Bright eyes looked up at me, a sudden glint in them. 'That excites you?' she asked.

'Oh god yes.' I couldn't deny it.

She slipped off the chair, and kissed me there again, on her knees in front of me. 'Open your legs wider,' she demanded, and me, hairbrush still grasped tightly in one hand, did as I was told. Her tongue darted out and licked me.

'I haven't washed,' I protested, still standing helplessly there.

She looked up at me again, eyes widening, then squinting at me in a sudden smile. She held up a finger. 'One moment, if it would make you more comfortable.'

Confused as to what she was talking about, I was rooted to the spot on trembling legs. My body had responded, even if my mind was blubbering around making objections.

Violet was on her feet, going to the washstand I'd noticed the night before. There was a jug and bowl there, and she tipped water from one to the other, and dipped in a cloth.

'It will be cold,' she said, coming back to kneel before me.

My brain was moving sluggishly, but it soon caught up when she pressed the wet cloth between my legs. She looked up at my gasped cry.

'I said it would be cold.' She bit her lip a moment. 'But I think it might be a little nice, too?'

My head was swimming and she moved the cloth against me, wiping gently with movements designed to clean, and perhaps, because it was happening this way, designed to arouse as well.

'That better?' she asked a minute later.

I nodded, no words on my tongue, and she tossed the cloth away, bending back to my thighs, one hand on each, thumbs pressing against me, spreading me open to her mouth, and her darting tongue.

I dropped the hairbrush, gripped the back of the chair

instead, holding onto it as the only way of staying upright as she licked and lapped at me, the back of her head dark against my white belly and thighs in the mirror. I couldn't drag my eyes away from the sight of both her and I. Moving up to see my face, my eyes were glazed, lips parted, and I stared at myself for a long moment, before dropping my gaze to heaving chest and tight nipples, and back to that dark head, moving against me as she licked me with her warm, wet tongue.

Then she dropped one of her hands and I felt her move it between her own thighs, felt her cry against me as she touched herself, and it was exciting almost beyond bearable, to know that she was touching herself, exploring the pleasures of her own body at the same time as she enjoyed mine.

I watched her in the mirror, feeling her movements, listening to her grunts of pleasure and my own, and gritted my teeth against my welling orgasm. I wanted her to come with me, and I could tell that she was close.

Her mouth tightened against me as she came, and her hand dug into my thigh, and I let myself go too, screaming out with the release, the head-rushing, dizzying, crazy joy of it.

Then I was stumbling backwards, the strength leaching from my legs, and I sat abruptly down on the bed with a bump. Violet, on her hands and knees, looked at me, and then we were laughing, both of us, Violet crawling towards me to be taken in my arms, so that we lay back on the bed, wrapped around each other, each other's thigh pressed tight between our legs, feeling the last quaking of our climaxes and squeezing our eyes shut, lips coming together blindly in kisses.

'See,' Violet whispered when we finally stilled. 'You are marvellous. I love every inch of you.'

It felt good with her wound around me like a sinuous cat. 'I think I might like seeing me through your eyes,' I admitted. 'You did enjoy that?' I had to check.

Her eyes widened. 'It was wonderful. I've never had such fun – I didn't even know it was possible to.' Snuggling closer, she burrowed into my arms and turned her face to the ceiling. 'My mother never spoke of sex.' Violet shuddered. 'She spoke of marriage, and a wife's duty – that's what she called it – but she spoke with thin lips and hard repulsion in her eyes, so I thought whatever happened between a husband and a wife must be a joyless thing.' A ghost of a smile crossed her face. 'Until I went to London.'

'Where you had a lover, did you not?' It was a hesitant question, but I asked anyway.

She inclined her head against my shoulder. 'Yes, but it confused me, rather than pleased.' Her eyes met mine, then looked away. 'It felt rather nice, the sex act, the second or third time, but it was nothing like the way you've made me feel.' Eyes widened again, and I couldn't help but feel a little swell of pride, no matter how undeserved. 'I used to watch those two women and wonder why they enjoyed it so much and I didn't.' A pause. 'I wanted to go ask them what they were doing that was so good, but then I would have to say I was spying on them.' Violet flung up a hand in a sudden gesture of impatience. 'Anyway, enough of that. I don't want to talk about it. It was a bad time for me. I got very sick.'

'Well that's not going to happen again,' I said.

She shook her head, looking at me with a wondering expression on her face. 'No,' she said. 'I don't think it's going to.' Her fingers touched my face. 'You make me feel alive and safe, all at the same time. How do you do it?'

'I don't know,' I answered. 'But I'm glad.'

She smiled at me. 'How do I make you feel?' she asked.

Looking down at her, I thought about it for a long moment, then swallowed.

'You make me feel marvellous,' I said. 'You make me feel like I could be something beautiful.'

Violet laughed and hugged me close. 'Oh Fran,' she said. 'You are already something beautiful!' She kissed me and the feel of her lips against mine was something like music to my senses.

She wiggled against me. 'Are you ready now?' she asked.

'Ready for what?'

'Getting up and going to see your father?'

I threw my head back and groaned. 'I'd rather do just about anything else.'

'But Fran,' Violet chided. 'Paris is waiting for us.'

I gazed at her, then nodded. Paris waited, and if not the city of light, then somewhere else I could keep her safe.

I kissed her again, making a silent promise.

CHAPTER TWENTY-ONE

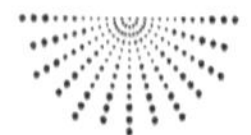

We almost missed breakfast, by the time we'd bathed and dressed, and made our way downstairs, Violet giggling, wearing her yellow dress again, and me blushing furiously at the thought of facing anyone who might have heard our cries through the thin walls.

'Are you all right?' Violet asked, leaning over the dining table to touch my hand, her face creased in concern.

I put down my piece of toast and thought about her question. 'Well,' I said at last. 'It depends entirely on which part of today I think about.'

Her smile was impish, and she was glowing. Happiness, and dare I say it – sexual satisfaction – became her enormously.

'Think about this morning,' she suggested.

'Then this is the most wonderful day ever lived,' I said in all sincerity, looking at her over the breakfast things. Her hair was pinned back to look as though it had been bobbed, an expert thing she'd managed in front of the mirror, without me, this time. Then she'd done mine, tut tutting over the knot

I'd been resorting to tie the thick pony tail of my own hair into.

'Fran?' Violet's voice brought me back to the table and her clear eyes laughing at me.

'I'm sorry,' I said. 'What did you say?'

'I asked when you wanted to go see your father?' Her glorious eyes still danced, but the question was serious.

I sighed. 'I think I ought to get it over and done with, don't you think?'

She nodded. 'The sooner we book passage to France, the safer we will be.' Her hand tightened on her cup. 'I cannot let my father catch up with us. Regardless of whether yours agrees to help us or not, we are going.' She sat straighter. 'Today.'

It was not a question, but I nodded anyway. I hadn't forgotten the spectre of the sanatorium. It would follow us all the way to France, and probably lodge with us there for a considerable time.

Unless of course, I could convince Fran's father to help us. It seemed a long shot to me, but Violet thought there was a chance he'd come through for us, so I was willing to try.

We needed money, that was the issue. It was all very well to run away to a new life, but somehow that new life needed to be funded. I wasn't afraid of work, but I was in a strange place, in a different age. It would take a while for me to get properly oriented. If Fran's father could even just give us a little money, it would give me the breathing space I needed.

Fran's father. We left the dining room, my breakfast mostly uneaten, and went straight out into the new day. Violet took my arm and patted it with her other hand and I was glad again of customs which let women walk arm in arm in friendship.

'I wish he was expecting me,' I said, as we made our way to Whitehall. 'I'd feel better if he was expecting me.'

'There wasn't time,' Violet said. 'I expect we could have telephoned his office, but there hasn't really been time for that either – and also, I'm afraid if we did that, we'd just be put off. At least if you turn up there, it will be harder for him to ignore you.'

My heart sank like a stone. This was an impossible task. We were being stupid. I knew nothing about this man, and here I was about to walk into the War Office, cast about helplessly in its miles of corridors, looking for a man I wasn't even going to recognise when I found him. I wanted to turn tail and find another way.

Any other way.

The building loomed in front of us, huge, ornate, sold just a few months ago in 2016 to be turned into an hotel and luxury apartments. Standing here though a hundred years earlier, it would be a hive of activity, with the movements and supply of the army directed from inside its 1000 or so rooms.

Somewhere in there also, was a man whose rank I didn't know – because Violet didn't – and whose actual job I was a little hazy on too.

'Are you sure you don't know what department he works in?' I asked now, staring up at the ornate façade, feeling my mouth dry up like a vanishing oasis in the desert.

Violet cocked her head to the side, standing close to me, her hand tight upon my arm. I could tell she was a little intimidated by the thought of going inside that building as well. Which she wasn't actually going to do, because this was one job complicated enough already. We'd already decided she would sit this one out – if I managed to actually find the man I was supposed to be related to.

'Directorate of Military Intelligence,' she said. Then said something in a low voice I didn't quite catch.

'What did you say?' I asked, turning to look at her, feeling my heart catch suddenly in my chest. 'What did you say?'

A very pale Violet looked at me, her eyes dark. She took a breath. 'I was afraid to tell you before.'

I shook my head, unable to form words, struggling for them. 'No,' I said finally. 'Repeat what you said just before. Word for word.'

She dropped her gaze. 'My father works there too.'

A glance at the building across the street. 'He works in the War Office?'

'Yes.'

'In the same department?'

A bleak nod.

'And you're only just telling me this now?'

Her eyes met mine. 'I was afraid you would refuse to go, if I told you before now.'

I stared at her. For a long minute. 'What happened to the openness and honesty that was so important to you?' I asked. 'Or does that only go one way?'

She shook her head, tears springing to her eyes. 'No, Fran, please don't think of it like that. I was afraid, that was all.' She wrapped her arms around herself and stared at me with haunted eyes. 'He terrifies me. My father. He terrifies me with what he can do. We have to get away.'

It was my turn to shake my head. 'But what if I run into

him in there? That would just make everything worse. A lot worse.'

Her nod was miserable. 'But you know now, so you can avoid him.'

'Only if I'm exceptionally lucky.' I groaned. 'I've never been exceptionally lucky, Violet.'

'I am sorry,' she said, hanging her head. 'I was just very afraid.'

She wasn't lying. I could tell in the way she stood there on the footpath, hugging herself, her slight frame shaking in the muggy warmth of the morning. I nodded.

'Okay,' I said.

Her eyes lifted to mine. 'Okay?'

I touched her shoulder because I had to. I wanted to do more, to wrap my arms around her, but we were standing in the street.

'Okay. So I'm going to go in there and get it over with. Who knows, maybe I'll get lucky for the first time in my life.'

Violet was pained. 'Please don't speak like that, Fran,' she said.

Squeezing my eyes shut for a moment, I nodded. 'I'm sorry,' I said. 'It's just a bit stressful.'

'I'm sorry I kept it from you.' Violet moved closer.

I nodded. 'I guess I understand why you did.'

She shook her head. 'I don't think you can but thank you for trying to.'

I stared at her, sensing there was a great deal she wasn't telling me, that perhaps there was a great deal more to her relationship with her father than she could easily say. It made me even more uneasy for her.

I smoothed my fingers over her hand and tucked it in the crook of my arm. 'We're going to be all right, I promise.'

She looked at me, all big wide eyes. 'Are you sure?'

I was determined. 'Yes. Even if this doesn't pan out, we'll come up with something,' I said. 'So let's find you somewhere to sit and have a cup of tea while I do this thing, okay?'

Violet nodded, and I wanted to take her in my arms and kiss her as she stood there vulnerable and uncertain. But we were standing on the footpath, people all around, so all I could do was pat her hand again.

'You look beautiful in your yellow dress,' I whispered.

She shook her head. 'I shouldn't have worn it.'

'Why ever not?'

Her pale hand gestured at the throngs of people. 'Look at them,' she said. 'I am out of place. They are all the same colour as the war, and here I am, like some silly strumpet who realises nothing.'

I didn't like her speaking of herself like that, even if she did have the tiniest point. Around us, even though it was summer, there were soldiers in their drab uniforms, and the women were subdued, favouring dark fabrics, sober in expression as well as dress. Violet was, in fact, gaining some strange looks as we stood there on the kerb.

'Come along, love,' I said. 'I think you are beautiful, and soon we will be in a place where you will shine like the sun.'

It might have sounded like romantic nonsense, but I'd never meant anything more in my life. I led her down the street to a tea shop and pushed the door open, ushering her inside.

'I'll be back as quickly as I can,' I said. 'But now that I've had a chance to be completely freaked out by the sight of the

War Office actually being used as a War Office, I'm concerned I may be gone a few hours.' It would probably take that long just to find the right department.

Violet was looking at me with one eyebrow raised. 'Freaked out?'

I let myself grin. 'I guess I better not say anything like that in front of dear old dad, am I right?'

She nodded. 'Most definitely. I've no idea what it means – although I can guess – but it doesn't seem at all appropriate.' A smile spread across her face. 'You are awfully entertaining, though. And very kind.'

'Love you too, babe,' I said, slipping into 21st century-speak just for effect.

Her eyes widened, then narrowed in a beaming smile. 'I love you as well, Fran,' she said, and touched my hand.

The gesture, the words, spoken in a low, confidential tone, made me pause. I'd been flippant, but Violet wasn't. I wanted to sit down, my legs suddenly boneless.

'You take my breath away,' I said and stared at her.

Someone cleared their throat behind me, and I looked hastily around, moving out of the way so a gloriously bearded gentleman could give me an odd look and move past.

I turned back to Violet with a sigh. 'Do you remember the way back to the hotel?' I asked.

She nodded. 'Yes. I did used to live in London, Fran,' she chided.

Of course. I'd forgotten that for a moment. It made me frown, and I bit my lip on what threatened to come out of my mouth. She shook her head.

'You needn't worry. I won't be slipping away back to my old haunts,' she said, reading my mind, or perhaps just my face. 'I shall settle here and drink a pot of tea and try not to worry about you. Then, if you are not returned, I shall go back to the hotel and in an extra effort not to worry, I shall busy myself remembering all our delicious activities of last night and this morning.' Her smile was wicked, deliberately lascivious, and I almost groaned.

'You little vixen,' I said to her, the stood, and drew in a deep breath, nodding. 'All right then. I'll go do this thing.' I didn't want to look too closely at Violet, because I might not have been able to stop myself from kissing her.

'Soon,' I said, and she nodded.

'I'll be waiting.' Something about the way she said it had me faint again, and it really was time to move. A nod, a smile, and I was pushing my way from the shop, bumping into people's tables and excusing myself in what was probably a terribly uncoordinated dash from the place, Violet looking at me the whole time with her wide, green eyes.

Once outside, however, I sobered up quick, the War Office casting its shadow over the road, bearing down on me as I crossed the road on shaky legs towards it.

Passing through the entrance was like being swallowed whole into the mouth of a great beast. Or perhaps machine was a better analogy. The great British War Machine. I could almost hear the grinding of gears and the gnashing of sharp-toothed pinions.

My heels tapped on the floor as I walked, like some sort of Morse Code, and I reached out and touched a surreptitious hand to one wall, steadying myself. Then stopped walking altogether and bent over slightly, drawing in deep, slow breaths trying to calm down, get my heart to stop doing the damned jitterbug in my chest.

My mind screamed at me. I was not equipped for this. I was a shopkeeper, for heaven's sakes. I bought books, stocked shelves, sold books. I employed someone to bake muffins. Excellent, delicious muffins, but even so, being discerning about baked goods did not qualify me to enter these halls.

'May I help you?'

I spun around so quickly, I almost went arse over heels, and wouldn't have that been a fine thing? As it was, it took all my willpower not to bolt past the young woman in uniform and rush the doors like a maniac.

'You look a little lost,' she said, smiling at me, polite sympathy written all over her face. 'Are you sure you're in the right building? We don't get many people in off the street.'

I was certain they didn't. It wasn't a department store, after all. But she was being awfully nice, so I swallowed down a lump of fear and plastered a sickly smile on my face.

'I'm afraid I'm looking for my father,' I said, trying to copy the cadence of Violet's speech.

The woman's eyebrows rose towards her hairline. 'Oh,' she said. 'Is he expecting you?'

Nope. He wasn't.

I shook my head. 'No, he isn't.' Another deep breath and I finally managed to stand without the support of the wall. 'But it is very important that I see him.' I tried the smile again. 'I've come specially to speak to him. There's ah, some urgent family business I need to consult him on.'

That much, at least, was true. And that relaxed me. I could get through this. I would only be telling the truth, after all. I could do that. There was no part of this I had to make up.

Except for recognising him in the first place.

Surprise turned to concern on the woman's face and I watched it with gratitude.

'Let me see if we can find your father for you then, shall we?' She walked a few steps and waited for me to follow him. I did. With alacrity.

'What is your name?' she asked.

I cleared my throat. 'Fran Madden,' I said. 'Um, Francesca Madden, that is.'

'And your father is?'

This part I would have to wing. Violet hadn't known what rank the man held. Just his name.

'Reginald Madden,' I said, then added helpfully, 'he's in the Directorate of Intelligence.'

Her eyes widened, but her steps didn't slow. 'Well,' she said. 'That's quite a hike but I'll be happy to take you to his secretary, and she can see if he's available.' I got a sympathetic smile. 'It really would have been better to telephone first and make an appointment.'

I nodded. 'Even if he is my own father,' I said.

'Yes, I'm afraid so.' She tap tapped down the corridor to a staircase. 'Because he is also a very busy man.'

Which I now knew, was why he hadn't been at home with his wife and daughters.

I was too nervous to do anything to pass the time apart from sitting hunched over, hiding my face and hoping like hell that I wouldn't come face to face with Violet's father. Part of me wanted to be furious with her for not telling me he worked in this building – in this very department – but every time I blinked I could see the fear on her face, and when I thought of the fate she was trying to escape, I knew it was impossible to blame her. I would probably have done the same. I tugged my hat lower over my face and tried to imagine myself invisible.

Finally, there were voices in the room I was waiting outside, and I tried to compose my face into some sort of intelligent expression. Or at least one that didn't look completely terrified.

Taking a deep breath, I reminded myself that I was twenty-nine years old, had seen things this man hadn't even dreamed of, and that the worst thing that could happen was...

Was that Violet would end up dying in a mental institution.

'Fran, what on earth are you doing here?'

I stood up fast and stuttered. 'Father?'

He hooked me by the elbow and scooted me in through the door, past the severe woman typing at a solitary desk, through another doorway and into his office. It was dim, utilitarian, and his desk was piled high with papers. The stark black word *confidential* stared at me from most of them. He saw me looking and went around to sit in the chair behind his desk, sweeping up the papers into a pile and setting it to the side.

'Fran,' he said. 'Sit down.'

I sat. Gripped the arms of the chair.

He shook his head, and I looked at him, realising that his face was the masculine version of my own. Including a neat and rather dashing moustache. His stare though, was unnerving.

He lit a cigarette and frowned at me. 'Fran, aren't you supposed to be ensconced somewhere on the coast?'

I cleared my throat. 'Yes,' I said, and waited for more words to follow that one. They didn't come.

He lifted his eyebrows. 'And the reason you are not is...?'

Christ. Straight to the point. I resisted the urge to clear my throat again and simply looked him in the eye instead.

'It wasn't suitable,' I said. 'At all.'

Now he squinted at me.

'And I'm afraid we ran into a bit of a...situation.'

The eyebrows raised again. 'Does your mother know where you are?'

I shook my head.

'When did you speak to her last?'

Now I looked down at my hands, tied in a tight knot on my lap. 'When we left the house to catch the train,' I said.

There was a moment of silence, then he shook his head and smiled at me. I probably gaped at him in return, the smile was so unexpected.

'Fran, my girl, you'd better start at the beginning.'

Where was the beginning? I took a deep breath. 'Violet,' I said.

'Ah. Violet.' He flicked ash from his cigarette and blue smoke wound its way to the high ceiling. There looked to be a lot of it already up there. 'I thought the story might begin with Violet Farningham.' Fran's father – my father, for all intents and purposes – leaned back in his chair again. 'What has she done this time?'

Shit. I didn't know where to start.

'Come on, Fran. Spit it out. You know I didn't approve of you looking after that girl in the first place. I thought it would be nothing but trouble for you.'

I was shaking my head before he even stopped speaking. 'No,' I said. 'It's not like that at all. I like Violet very much.' I cast around for the right words. 'She and I made friends straight away.'

'Her father tells me she is unwell.'

I dug a thumbnail into my palm. 'No Father, I don't believe she really is. Not in the way he says. She's passionate, intelligent, and a very talented artist.'

His eyebrows made it nearly all the way to the ceiling as well. 'But that is not what her own father has to say.'

'Well, I'm afraid I don't know Mr Farningham very well at all, but I do know his own daughter is terrified of him, and that is wrong whichever way you want to look at it.' I sat still and let my words hang in the air.

Reginald Madden stared at me for a long moment through a cloud of cigarette smoke. 'Well. Leaving aside that question for a moment, you've not explained why you are here in my office, instead of enjoying a holiday at the seaside. I was under the impression from your mother that you were looking forward to it very much.'

'I was looking forward to it very much,' I said. I'm sure it was even true for the Fran whose place I had taken. The twin lifelines on my palm itched, and I rubbed at them with a thumb.

Fran's father – my father – stubbed out his cigarette and contemplated me. 'I think you'd better tell me then, why you are in London, instead of where you are supposed to be.' He blinked silvery blue eyes at me. 'Where is Violet?'

I found myself not wanting to say. In fact, I had the strongest sense that this was a grave mistake altogether. I did not know this man well enough – I did not know him at all. Violet barely knew him, only believed him to be fair-minded on the basis of brief meetings when she was young. My palm itched again, and a headache spread tentacle fingers up under the knot of my hair.

'She is still at the cottage,' I lied.

He shook his head. 'Then I'm afraid I don't understand. What is this situation you have run into? Why are you here? It is a journey of several hours to come to London. If you needed anything, why did you not simply contact your mother?'

I had to think of some answers for him, and I had to do it quickly and convincingly. I stuttered over a smile.

'You're right,' I said, and took a deep breath. 'I feel silly now; I have overreacted. This is my first time out in the world, and I am being silly, running to you at the first hint of something going wrong.'

There was a knock at the door and I cringed in my seat, dreading the opening door revealing Violet's father there. My father looked up at the interruption and said the exact words I hoped not to hear.

'Ah, Isaac, how convenient of you to turn up right this minute.'

The immediate footsteps coming closer sent chills up my spine and I stood up, pushing the chair backwards so that it scraped against the floor. I turned to my father.

'I'm so sorry to have bothered you, father,' I said. 'It was silly of me to come here and waste your precious time.'

'Francesca?' It was Violet's father, his voice deep and suspicious. 'What are you doing here? Where is Violet?'

I turned to face him, barely able to look into his granite eyes. Sucking in a breath, I stuck a shaky smile on my face and shook my head. 'Mr Farningham,' I said. 'Violet is still at the cottage. We realised once there, that we'd gone unprepared in our packing, so I volunteered to come up here to do a little shopping to make our stay more comfortable.'

Both men stared at me.

I looked from one to the other. 'We had not realised that there would be so few shops in the village.' I tilted my head and struck a tone of embarrassed confidence. 'I'm afraid I cannot enjoy the cottage and garden so well without a few things to keep my hands from being idle.' I hoped I didn't sound as big a dick as I felt. 'Books,' I said hastily. 'And some sewing, I thought.'

'Violet is not to be allowed to paint,' Mr Farningham interrupted me. 'That was one of the terms of agreement with your mother.'

'Oh, I realise that,' I said. 'But there are many things we can occupy ourselves with, only I could not buy any of the necessary things where we were staying.'

My father shook his head. 'You are not explaining why London, then, Fran. Surely you could have made your necessary purchases at a closer town.'

My blush wasn't forced. I was red in the face because two very scary looking men were staring at me with deep frowns. Violet's father particularly, made me uncomfortable and I had to wonder exactly what it had been like growing up in a household ruled by him. Not fun. It can't have been fun at all.

I turned to Fran's father and made my voice apologetic, embarrassed. 'I'm afraid Mother didn't give me enough money for extras such as we desperately need.' I added a pained smile. 'And it's been a long while since I saw you, Father, I thought it would be nice to visit you, as well as achieve something practical.' The story limped into being and I couldn't help my own wince at it.

My father though, he looked at me and laughed. 'Isaac, can you believe the nerve of my daughter?' he asked. 'She comes here asking for money!'

'And to see you, Father,' I said. 'But it was silly, you are right. I'm so sorry.' It galled me to be sucking up to this man, and I straightened. 'Please do not bother yourself over this. I will make the purchases I can, and head back to the cottage again.'

'You were not supposed to leave Violet alone,' Mr Farningham said.

I shook my head. 'Oh, Mr Farningham, I didn't.' I smiled at him. 'Mrs Kellow is a lovely woman, and she is sitting with Violet for the afternoon.' I made my smile even warmer. 'I believe they were going to bake a cake together for our supper.' Inside, I would have been rolling my eyes, if I weren't so frightened. They'd have to take red hot pokers to me for me to tell either of them that Violet was waiting across the road for me.

'You mentioned a situation you found yourselves in, Fran,' my father said. 'What was that?'

'My trunk went missing,' I said, thinking at lightning speed. 'Someone took the wrong one when they got off the train, and I have theirs, and they have mine.' I swallowed. 'So I have no clothes, either.'

Violet's father stood shaking his head. 'Reggie,' he said. 'Give the girl some money for new clothes and things, so she can get back to looking after Violet.' He narrowed his eyes at me. 'When I told your mother that I didn't want Violet left on her own, I did not intend for you to absent yourself in favour of a stranger. Do you understand me?'

I nodded, heart pounding. 'Yes sir,' I said. 'I'm very sorry. It won't happen again.'

He sniffed and transferred his attention to my father. 'We've a meeting with the Brigadier, Reggie, if you remember. We don't have time for this.'

My father was already digging out his wallet and sifting through the contents. He nodded and then shoved his wallet back in his pocket and bent to his desk. 'I've no cash on me, Fran. If you take this note to Mr Parsons at the bank on the corner, he will see you get what you need.' Straightening, he handed me a hastily scrawled note and I took it in a shaking hand. 'And for heaven's sakes, next time you have a crisis, use your head and get your mother to deal with it.' Impatiently, he gestured at Violet's father. 'We have more important things to do.'

I nodded and squeaked my thanks. Clutching the note in a sweaty hand, I backed away from the desk and scuttled backwards to the door, saying my goodbyes. They went unnoticed however, as both men ignored me, bending over a folder on the desk, my abortion of a visit dismissed from their minds.

CHAPTER TWENTY-THREE

The War Office sat at my back like a large ship as I escaped and crossed the road to the tea rooms, hoping that Violet was still there. I didn't know how long I'd been, but it was a couple hours, and I was shaking like a child and deathly afraid that her father would spot her wandering the street.

She waved to me as soon as I rattled the door open, and I saw her wide smile and wiggling fingers with a loosening of tight bands around my chest that told me I was in trouble in this direction as well. Not simply from a pair of very scary fathers, but that for the first time in my life I might really be falling in love, and no amount of telling myself it was too quick, too fast, could make it otherwise.

I slid onto the chair next to hers. 'I am so glad you're still here,' I whispered, voice husky with my realisation, and I touched a hand to her thigh because I couldn't bear not to touch her at all.

She smiled at me and leaned closer. 'I had to wait for you,' she said. 'You are doing all of this for the both of us, after all.

The least I could do was to wait for you.' She touched her fingertips to my hand. 'But you are dreadfully pale. Did it not go well?'

I shook my head. 'It went about as badly as it possibly could have.'

The colour drained from Violet's face, and her hand clutched at mine. 'What happened?' she hissed, then looked around as though her father was about to come charging through the door, straightjacket in hand. Her expression made my heart lurch painfully.

'I'll tell you about it on the way back to the hotel,' I said. 'I think it would be best if we got going right now, though. Would that be okay?' The note from my father burned in my purse, and I knew I'd have to visit that bank, but I wanted Violet safely back out of sight in the hotel.

I opened the door to the tea rooms and peered all around at the people on the footpath, crossing the road. Violet crowded behind me at my back.

'What are you looking for?' she asked, her voice thin and frightened.

'Your father,' I said. 'But I'm just being over-cautious, because I know he was on his way to a meeting when I left, and that it's almost completely certain he won't be out here.'

The door closed behind us, and Violet bumped along behind me as we sidled down the street, desperate to lose sight of the big building of the War Office, me calculating in my head how long it had taken to retrace my steps out of the place, and how long his meeting was likely to last...

'We're safe,' I breathed. 'But I need to get you back to the hotel.'

'What happened?' Violet hurried along beside me, her yellow dress standing out like a sore thumb.

'Let's just say, it didn't go well,' I said, turning the corner and finally leaving that dreadful building behind. We walked another few steps, then I stopped and turned to Violet, putting my hands to her shoulders. 'It didn't go well in there,' I said. 'But we are going to be all right, you hear?'

She nodded, her skin so white I could see the tracery of blue veins under her skin.

I smiled at her, my heart slowing now we were out of sight of the War Office, and I thought of the note in my pocket.

'Why are you smiling?' Violet asked.

'Because even though that was a disaster, it wasn't a complete disaster.' I wanted to kiss her but just looked instead. 'Come on. Let's get you back to the hotel, and then I have an appointment at the bank.'

'Bank?'

'Yes.' We turned another corner. 'I got in to see my father, after a bit of a wait, but it was obvious within a couple minutes that I couldn't tell him anything near the truth.' I paused, gathered my thoughts. 'It wouldn't have meant anything to him that the village where we were staying was the dullest, least suitable place on earth.' I found Violet's hand and gave her fingers a reassuring squeeze.

'And then your father opened the door and walked into the room.' I shook my head. 'Just like that,' I said. 'He just appeared like it was a bad dream.'

Violet put her hand to her mouth. 'What did you do?'

'Thought on my feet faster than I've ever done before,' I said. 'I told them that you were still at the cottage, and that I'd come to London because the village where we were staying didn't have any of the things we needed to keep ourselves occupied for three months.'

Her eyes widened as we swept along the street. 'What did they say to that?'

I shook my head. 'It wasn't enough, so I made up a story about losing my luggage, someone else taking my trunk by mistake and so I needed money for more clothes.'

I wiped my forehead. It was damp. 'They were busy,' I said. 'Distracted, which is the only reason they accepted my story.' I dug in my purse and handed Violet the note my father had given me.

She stopped walking to peer at it, then lifted round eyes to me. 'This is an...'

'Authorisation to give me money,' I said.

'But what amount?' Violet asked, looking back at the paper again. 'It doesn't say an amount.'

I shook my head. 'He was in too much of a hurry.'

Her eyes grew even wider. 'Then you must go to this man at the bank before your father realises what he has done and calls to say you're to have no more than a couple pounds.'

I wanted to kiss her again. 'Yes,' I said instead.

Violet looked down the road. 'I will go the rest of the way to the hotel on my own. It would be silly for you to accompany me, then turn around and come straight back. You must go directly to the bank.'

'Your father and mine were going into a meeting when I left,' I said.

'Well hopefully it will go on for a while.' She looked down at the note again, then handed it to me. 'How much will you ask for?'

'How much do you think I could get away with?' I didn't know much about how much was a lot in 1916.

'Twenty pounds,' she said promptly. 'If you were to get that much, we would have enough to keep ourselves for a couple months.'

I tucked the note back in my purse again. 'That's what I'll do, then,' I said.

Violet reached out and took my hands. 'Thank you,' she said, and her eyes were shining again. 'I do feel safe with you. I know that we will be all right.'

I nodded. 'I'll always do my best, Violet,' I said. 'You can count on me for that.'

Swiftly, almost too fast for me to know it had happened, she leaned forward and kissed me on the cheek. Then she dropped my hands and was moving away. 'Thank you, Fran,' she said. 'And hurry back.'

I would. I'd go and get us some more money, then hurry back to the hotel, and we would make the plan for the next step of this wild journey that now felt a lot more serious than before.

Retracing my steps, I thought of my bookshop in Bath, but it felt terribly far away. Instead, the ghost woman from my dreams lurked under my thoughts, and a vague vision of a bookshop in France, Violet stepping through the door with a smudge of paint on her cheek, her face lit up with a smile.

Who was the woman from my dreams? I wondered on it as I hurried back down the street to the War Office. Perhaps she was Violet, I thought. That might make sense. As much as any of this did.

Stopping at the intersection, I looked around for the bank on the corner Fran's father had spoken of. I could feel the footpath under my shoes, I could feel the close heat of the day pressing against me, and all around me pedestrians jostled and murmured.

It was all real. As real as it needed to be, anyway. And back at the hotel, Violet would be waiting for me.

There was a bank on almost every corner I could see. Digging out the note, I looked at it again, but it didn't say which one to go to.

On a sigh, I knew I'd have to try them all. And quickly.

CHAPTER TWENTY-FOUR

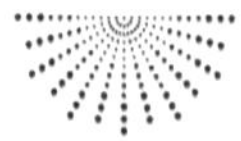

'I am Mr Parsons,' the short, slight man said, peering at me over his spectacles. 'What may I do for you?'

I held out the note. 'My father gave me this to give to you. He said that you would help.'

The man blinked myopically at the scrawled note then raised his eyebrows at me. 'Come this way please, Miss Madden, and we will see to it that you have exactly what you need.'

I gave him a completely genuine smile of relief. The Madden name obviously carried some weight with this gentleman. 'I'm supposed to be on holiday with my cousin,' I told him, taking the offered seat at a wide desk. He sat down on the other side and opened a drawer, removing something that looked an awful lot like a withdrawal form. I hoped to hell it was.

'I'm afraid there was a dreadful mix-up with my belongings, and I'm left with nothing,' I elaborated.

'Nothing?'

'Neither clothing, nor...' I paused. 'Personal items.' I gave

him a deliberately embarrassed smile. 'My father has generously instructed me to replace everything I need. And to
make some extra purchases.' I sat up straighter and leaned
forward, the smile on my face now confiding and excited.
'We're staying at the seaside – for the sake of my cousin's
health, but there is not a great deal there for us to do. I'm
thinking we will need books, and sewing materials...' I tried
to think of other random things a woman would have
wanted to keep herself occupied in these times. 'Knitting,' I
said. 'I want to buy a quantity of wool – we'll busy ourselves
knitting socks and undershirts for the soldiers. It's the least
we can do, don't you think?'

Poor Mr Parsons was nodding under my barrage of information. 'Quite,' he said. 'Very admirable of you both.' He
picked up a pen. 'I will fill out this form on your behalf, and
we will make a withdrawal to cover your expenses.' He wrote
in a couple of the lines on the form, then picked up the note
to frown at it.

I swallowed. This was the important bit. Tucking my
hands into my lap, I concentrated on appearing completely
relaxed.

'Your father has neglected to state an amount,' Mr Parsons
said.

'We agreed on twenty pounds,' I said, relieved not to hear
my voice quaver at the number. 'We will be renting the
cottage for the entirety of the summer.' I put a smile in my
voice. 'Three months – are we not very lucky, Mr Parsons?'

He looked up at me, face creased. 'It is a large sum for a
lady to carry.'

I took a gamble and sat up straighter. 'I've much to
purchase, Mr Parsons, and my father would not like to see

me go without the things we need. This holiday is his own treat for me, and I know he wishes me to have the most enjoyable time in the midst of this darkest of years.'

The banker looked at me for a moment, then dropped his eyes to the form and took up his pen again. 'If you will wait here a moment, Miss Madden, I will see to this.' He pushed back his chair, nodded briefly, then walked away, form and pen in hand.

I watched him cross the marble floor, then speak briefly to a female clerk who nodded and glanced across the room at me. I turned quickly in my seat and dug my fingernails into my palms, imagining that behind me, there was a telephone being picked up, and a voice asking to speak with Reginald Madden regarding the enormous sum of money his daughter was asking for.

Bending forward, I sucked in a breath. It was warm in the bank. Too warm.

'Are you all right, Miss Madden?' a female voice asked.

I swivelled around in my seat and took in the face of the clerk looking at me with raised eyebrows. I gave her a sickly smile.

'I'm fine,' I said. 'It's just very close in here.'

'Oh yes,' she said, straightening. 'It's an awful month to be stuck in the city.' She held out an envelope. 'But you are going to the seaside, I hear. Mr Parsons asked me to give you this. I'm afraid he had to take an important telephone call.'

I felt myself go pale. 'It…it wasn't my father, was it?'

Her eyes widened. 'No, Miss Madden, I don't believe so.' A tiny crease of concern appeared between her eyes. 'Are you sure you're all right?'

'Yes,' I said, taking the envelope still held out to me. 'Thank you, it's nothing that a nice cup of tea won't solve.'

The concern turned sympathetic. 'There's a very nice tea rooms directly across the road. I go there almost every day.'

I stood up and my smile was genuine. 'That's very kind of you. Thank you very much.'

She nodded. 'You're very welcome, Miss Madden. Have a nice day.'

I was out of the bank moments later, trying not to run. A reckless dart across the road, then down the street, around the corner and finally I dared slow and look at the envelope.

Twenty pounds. It was all there, in handy dandy five-pound notes. I counted it twice, then leaned against the brick wall behind me and wiped the sweat from my brow. Then I stood back up on legs that definitely weren't the steadiest, and I turned myself towards the nearest bus to the hotel room, and Violet.

She was pacing back and forth in the small reception, and when I closed the door from the street behind me, she launched herself at me.

'Fran,' she hissed. 'I had to sign out of our room or pay for another night.' One hand clutched at my shoulder, the other made a sweeping gesture behind her, and I saw our bags in a pile by the reception desk. The woman behind the desk had regained her frosty scowl from the first time we'd met her.

'At least you were able to wait inside,' I said.

Violet rolled her eyes. 'I was lucky they let me pack our things. We should have been out an hour before I got back, apparently.'

I nodded. 'Okay, well then, let's leave, shall we?' I noticed she'd also taken the opportunity to change out of the bright yellow dress.

We walked over to our bags and bent to them. 'Did you get it?' Violet asked in a whisper.

'Yes,' I said. 'Unbelievably, I did.'

'The whole amount? Twenty pounds?'

'The whole amount,' I agreed.

She straightened, staring at me. 'Oh my goodness,' she said. 'We really can do this.' Her eyes grew wider still. 'I'm going to be safe,' she whispered, almost unbelieving. 'It's really true, isn't it? I'm going to be safe?'

'Yes,' I answered. 'Yes, we are going to make sure of it.'

She was dazed, following me out of the hotel and onto the street shaking her head. 'Tell me this isn't a dream, Fran,' she said.

I laughed. 'Do you want me to pinch you?'

That got her giggling, and a moment later, she had dropped her bag on the footpath and was bent over cackling madly.

'Violet?' I asked. 'You're not going to go all hysterical on me, are you?' I was kidding. Sort of. She looked a little wild.

But I got a shake of the head, and then there were arms flung around my neck and she was hugging me tight.

'Oh Fran, thank you!' she said in my ear. 'Thank you so, so much.'

'Violet,' I said, not knowing whether to tug her from me, or squeeze her to me. 'I didn't really do anything.'

That had her standing back, looking at me with wet eyes. She shook her head. 'Fran,' she said. 'You did everything. Without you, I don't know what would happen to me.' Her face darkened. 'Well, actually I do.'

'Don't think of it,' I said quickly. 'Come on, the adventure is just getting going. And we need to move quickly.'

Violet picked up her bags and stared expectantly at me. 'I'm ready,' she said. 'How do we get to Paris?'

I looked back at her, my own bags back in my hands. It was a good question, and I hadn't had much time to think about how it could be done in 1916, in the midst of a war.

But I had been having one nagging thought since I'd backed out of that room in the War Office. I took a deep breath.

'Violet,' I said, standing on the path outside the hotel, London hot and restless around us. 'I don't think we should go to Paris.'

She stared at me with blank eyes.

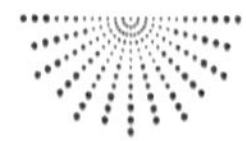

'What?' she asked, and blinked.

I glanced around. 'We need to get off the street,' I said. 'Let's go sit down somewhere and talk.'

She shook her head. 'But Fran, Paris.' I could almost see her dig her heels in. 'You promised we could go to Paris. And you know why. You know what it is I need. That I will not do well without the things it has to offer – and it is what you need too! Both of us will suffocate if we are forced to live a normal, everyday life!' Her face took on a pinched look, the eyes darkening with hurt.

It was my turn to shake my head. 'No, Violet. I promise I'm not saying we should stay here or go anywhere that will not give you – us – the things we need. Please give me the chance to explain. Please.'

Her expression was unreadable for a moment, then she nodded. 'Of course,' she said. 'Of course, I am sorry, Fran. You just startled me. Of course you must explain, and I promise I will listen.' She narrowed her eyes at me. 'But it had better be good.'

I nodded. 'I'll explain. And it will be good, I think.' A quick look around the street. 'Let's go to the railway station, find somewhere to sit down for a moment.' Maybe we could have that cup of tea the bank clerk had suggested. My mouth was dry.

We walked the short distance to the station, found ourselves a cup of tea and a place to sit. I balanced the cup and saucer on my knee, aware of Violet's dark gaze on me.

'Are you all right, Fran?' she asked.

I tried not to shake my head. 'The morning is catching up with me, I think,' I said. I was exhausted. 'I'll be all right in a few minutes.'

'I can't believe you got the money,' Violet whispered. 'And such an amount!'

It was hard to believe, that was for sure. 'If they hadn't been so distracted, your father and Fran's, I don't think we would have been near so lucky,' I said. 'They just wanted me out of there.'

Violet hunched down in her seat. 'My father was really there?'

'In the flesh,' I said, and looked at her, grimacing. 'He's an intimidating man.'

She nodded. 'Yes. And always very distant to us children.'

'You have brothers and sisters?' I'd never thought of it before. Violet always seemed so self-contained. 'You've never mentioned any.'

'My step-mother had a child two years ago. His name is Roger.'

'A half-brother.' I took a sip of my tea, tilted my head. 'You never mention your mother either.'

Violet gazed out over the busy station plaza. 'My mother died a few years ago. She had tuberculosis.'

I reached for her hand. 'I'm so sorry.'

She shrugged. 'It was difficult, yes, but some time ago now.'

There was a lot more I wanted to know, but now wasn't the time for questions. Not those ones, anyway.

'About Paris,' I said.

Violet turned in her seat and looked at me. 'Yes,' she said. 'About Paris.'

I cleared my throat. It would be best to just lay it out. A deep breath and I was as ready as I would ever be. 'I saw evidence on Fran's father's desk that he regularly travels to and from Paris.'

She stared at me.

'Your father may do the same, for all we know.' I cleared my throat again. 'I think we would be too easy to find in Paris.'

She shook her head. 'How? It is a large city.'

'It is,' I agreed. 'But the area where we would want to live and socialise is fairly small.' I'd already dug through my mind for everything I knew about artists in Paris during this period. 'Montparnasse, where we would want to be – where most of the artists are – is relatively small. We would stand out…'

'We will stand out wherever we go.'

'True,' I said. 'But not everywhere will our fathers be looking for us.' I tried a different tack. 'Have you ever mentioned wanting to go to Paris, be an artist there?'

'Of course,' Violet answered. 'It's what I've always wanted

to do.' She stared at me, then put a hand across her mouth. 'Oh no.'

'I think it's probably the first place they'll look, once they've decided we're not in London.'

She shook her head. 'But I don't want to go anywhere else. Where else could we go?'

I'd already thought about it. A little. 'Do you remember, Violet, when we were just getting to know each other?'

A smile quirked at her lips and I rolled my eyes. 'Not getting to know each other like *that*,' I said, remembering in a burst of hot pleasure her skin against mine, the taste of her on my tongue.

It took a deep breath to bring me back. 'Okay,' I said, resisting the urge to find some of her skin and touch it with electric fingertips. 'The donkey.'

She blinked at me. 'The donkey?'

'Yes, the donkey. It had big ears, remember?'

Violet gave a laugh and shook her head. 'We were telling stories,' she said. 'What does our big-eared donkey have to do with anything?'

'We were making up stories, sure, but we were imagining how we'd like to live.'

An impatient shake of her head. 'There is fighting in Italy,' she said. 'It seems an imprudent idea.'

I licked my lips. 'Not Italy.'

'Where then?'

'The French Riviera. Just like we also talked about. Your studio, my bookshop, remember?'

'I remember.' She paused. 'Where? Exactly?'

My mouth was dry again. I took a quick sip of tea. 'I

thought of it on the way back to the hotel, Violet. It's the perfect place.'

'Where, for heaven's sakes?'

'Nice,' I said.

She squinted at me. 'I do not really know anything about Nice.'

'It's lovely there,' I told her, remembering the visit I'd made in 2005. 'Not only that though – it is quite the place for artists and writers.' I took another breath. 'Especially over the next few years.'

Violet sat straighter. 'Who?' she asked.

'Ah, Matisse has a studio there, he lives there for the rest of his life, in fact. Picasso. Chagall.' I smiled at her. 'And as for writers, several will come and go from the place, although you won't recognise their names yet. F. Scott Fitzgerald. Hemingway.' I winced. 'Not that I'm entirely sure I would want to hang out with those two, but still, it stands even so – the towns along the coast there are definitely places to be if you're an artist.'

Her eyes were shining. 'And the likelihood of being found?'

I shook my head. 'Slim, I think.'

'Slim.' She nodded. 'Not as good as none, but perhaps the best that we can hope for.'

'Yes. I think if we are found at all, it will take some time to track us down there.' I hoped to god I wasn't being naïve, because that's what we'd both been up to this minute.

'And,' I continued, 'if they do find us, then it will be after we've had time to get settled. I'll have work, we'll be supporting ourselves.'

Violet nodded vigorously. 'There will be no need for my

father to drag me off home to a hospital. We will have proved we can look after ourselves.'

Yes. That was exactly the idea.

I'd searched around my mind on the bus back to the hotel for another answer. That perhaps there was somewhere in this country that we could go, but whichever way I looked at it, fleeing to France was the best idea. Further away, and ah, more liberal when it came to unconventional living relation-ships. Radclyffe Hall had agreed with me, along with count-less other English 'inverts' of this and earlier times.

It was the best idea.

Violet was rattling her cup. 'When do we go?' she asked. 'Surely it is better to go straight away?'

'Yes, but I don't think we should go from Dover either.'

She slumped back down in her seat. 'Why not?' she said, then answered her own question. 'Our fathers.'

'Yes. But we can take a ferry from Folkestone to Boulogne instead. Or at least I hope we can.'

'What does that mean – you hope we can?'

'I don't know much about ease of travel in this particular year.'

A smile spread over her face. 'But you do know about artists and writers – and we will figure out the rest, just you wait and see.' She reached for my hand and squeezed my fingers under the table, where no one could see. Her eyes held my gaze, their emerald light brightening everything about the moment.

'I want to kiss you,' I whispered.

A smile appeared on her face and it was beautiful, wicked, and tired all at the same time. She really was the most magical combination of things.

'I would like to do a great deal more than kiss you,' she said, her voice low, lashes shadowing her cheeks as she lowered her gaze to sweep over all of me.

'Oh my goodness,' I said. 'You take my breath away.'

Her smile widened. 'And you mine. I have not felt this way before.'

I wanted to press a hand to my thumping heart. 'You like it, I hope.'

She laughed, throaty and low and I found myself looking at her neck, slender, pale, and I wanted to press my lips to the tiny pulse jumping there.

'I like it very much indeed,' she said. 'I think I may never want to give it up, now that I've found what makes me feel this way.'

For a moment, I blinked at her, replaying her words in my head. 'Tell me,' I said. 'Is it being with another woman that makes you feel this way, or is it...'

'You,' she said.

'Me,' I finished.

'You,' she repeated.

Throat tight, I couldn't help asking more. 'How can you be sure? It's all happened so fast.'

She tilted her head to the side. It was very appealing. 'How can anyone be absolutely sure of anything? I am going by what my heart is telling me.'

I was stupid, dense. 'What is it telling you?'

Her fingers linked with mine and she held my hand tight. 'It is telling me that you and I have come together for a reason, and that reason needs to be fully explored.'

'Fully?' I could feel my cheeks heat.

'Very,' she said, then let go of my hand and stood,

smoothing her skirt. 'Now, are we at the right train station for Boulogne?'

I stumbled, changing gears, but caught up. It wasn't the place for such a private conversation anyway. We were attracting looks as it was – a gentleman on a bench beside us was looking more often at Violet than at his newspaper. I found it hard to blame him. She was fascinatingly beautiful.

'Fran?' Her smile turned tentative. 'Fran, are you not well?'

'I'm fine,' I said, shaking my head. 'Sorry, I was just wool-gathering.' I tried to remember what she'd been saying. Something about trains. 'Ah, I'm afraid I don't know where we should take the train from to get to Folkestone. We always fly where I come from.'

It had slipped from my mouth without any thought, but when I saw her eyes widen, I backtracked and went over what I'd said.

'You fly?' She blinked. 'How do you do that?'

'We have passenger planes.'

'Aeroplanes?'

'Yes. Planes and automobiles – that's how everyone gets around.' I spread my arms a moment. 'Big aeroplanes too, carrying three or four hundred passengers.'

Violet stared at me, shaking her head. 'Impossible,' she said.

'Nope. 'Fraid not.'

'Astonishing.' Her frown turned into a wide grin. 'The things you have yet to tell me. And the questions I have!'

I smiled back at her. 'Well, we've a long trip ahead of us. You'll have plenty of time to quiz me all you like.'

'It is a very long trip, I think,' she said, bending down to pick up her bags.

'Yes, from Paris to Nice anyway, I imagine.'

'Then not only will we get plenty of opportunity to discuss the many matters that are on my mind, but we will get a sleeper car as well, yes?'

I glanced at the man hiding unsuccessfully behind his newspaper. His eyes slid quickly from Violet to the newsprint in front of him, leaving me wondering how much of our conversation he'd been able to overhear.

'Come on, Violet,' I said. 'Let's go see about this train. The day is getting on, and I don't really want to spend another night in London. Not if it can be helped.'

The French Riviera beckoned. An apartment, a studio, the dim bookshop of my imagination. A smudge of paint on Violet's cheek.

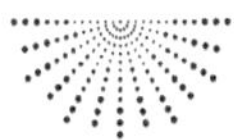

'I am exhausted,' Violet said, sinking down onto the seat while I drew closed the compartment door. The noise of the other passengers receded, and the train lurched under our feet. A whistle blew.

'Tell me a story,' Violet said, pulling me down onto the worn cushion next to me and leaning into me in a way that made me blink down at her, at her small round head with its knot of dark hair, at the pale skin that looked like it had never seen the sun, the dark lashes casting blue shadows on her cheeks.

'A story?' I said stupidly, my mind thinking only of her. She looked up at me and I was hypnotised by the kaleidoscope patterns of her irises.

'Yes,' she said, and snuggled even closer. 'Tell me about your life.' The train jolted and there was the whistle again. We were pulling out of the station, leaving London behind us. I had little idea of what lay ahead.

'My life?'

She rolled her eyes. 'Yes, your life. You can't very well tell me about anyone else's, can you?' Her lips curved into a smile. 'Well, I suppose that's not strictly true – you know a little of me, for instance. Me and my painting.' She fell silent, gazing out of the window at the city falling away behind us as though a strong breeze was blowing it from our lives, and I hoped to god she wasn't going to quiz me on the extent of my knowledge of her. But we'd changed her story, hadn't we? Derailed that path of her life. She was on a brand new one now. With me.

But she smiled again and looked at me. 'Tell me about a completely normal, average day in your life.'

I had to stop myself from repeating her words. Then did it anyway. 'A completely normal, average day in my life? That's not very interesting.'

She shook her head. 'You forget that it is.' Sat up, looking seriously at me. 'Let me tell you what my completely normal, average day looks like, and maybe then you will see why I ask.'

I could do nothing but gaze at her.

'I wake early, usually from a poor night's sleep, but I don't rise until 8 in the morning because the fewer hours I have to spend in the company of my family, the better. I dress myself, and head down to breakfast, where my step-mother is already at the table eating a plate full of food and reading her mail. There is never any mail for me, so I butter a piece of toast and pour a cup of tea. There is enough food served for me to have more than two pieces of toast, but my appetite is not great, so I imagine most of it goes to waste. I don't know what is done with it, actually.'

She shrugged and during her pause the train clattered upon the tracks, taking her further and further – irreversibly further – from the life she described. 'We don't have a large staff, but there is a cook and kitchen maid, and others. I do not cook for myself, I do not make my own bed, I get up and eat toast, and spend the rest of the day trying to find something with which to fill my time. My step-mother does not like me to go visiting her friends with her, and I am no longer allowed to set up my easel and paint, so I do nothing.'

'Nothing?'

'I sit in the garden. I look at the flowers, the trees, the sky, the light slanting across the lawn. I paint pictures in my mind, and then eventually it is time to go back to bed and another day is blessedly over.'

She raised her eyebrows at me, then sat back down against me, leaning against my chest and pulling my arm around her. 'So I would very much like to hear about one of your own days.' We swayed together with the movement of the train. For a moment there were voices outside our compartment door, and shadows behind the glass, but they moved on before we could draw apart.

'Well,' I said, then floundered for a moment, still locked in the bleak retelling of her days. I cleared my throat. 'I'm a bit busier than that, yes.'

'Tell me,' she demanded, and I could see the ghost of her reflection in the window, superimposed over the passing scenery, the slight curve to her lips.

'Coffee,' I said. 'That's what gets me out of bed.' I shrug. 'And the alarm clock, but there's coffee in the kitchen, and it's where I head first. I drink it sitting at my kitchen table, scrolling through Facebook, and the news sites, catching up with whatever has happened overnight around the world.'

A frown replaced the smile. 'What is a Facebook? And what do you mean by news sites? Do you mean a newspaper?'

How to explain? 'Sort of like a newspaper.' I tightened my arms around her. 'We have something called the Internet, and it is…' It was harder to explain than I'd anticipated. 'It's a way of sharing information electronically, I guess is the easiest way of putting it. And we read the information on screens – interactive screens, like a book we can comment on and help write.'

'I do not understand.'

I shook my head. It was like that old joke of trying to explain an elephant to a blind man. Pursing my lips, I tried to find a way. 'We have things called eReaders,' I tried again.

'What are they?'

'They are electronic books. About the size of a regular book, but they are just a device with a screen – no pages. You touch the screen, and the text of whatever book you want to read appears. And we have other screens that don't show just books, but newspapers, magazines, and social groups like the one called Facebook, where everyone has a special page where they write things about themselves and share it with everyone else who has a device. And wants to look.'

Violet was still frowning. 'It sounds very odd,' she said. 'Something like magic. I do not even know what you mean by electronic. Is it run by electricity?'

I could smell the coal the train ran on, the hot steam huffing and puffing overhead, and everything from my old life seemed a million miles away. 'I guess it is pretty odd. They're called computers, these devices, and we carry them everywhere, and they are able to access just about all the information in the world – or so it seems.' Her eyes widened, and I laughed. 'But everyone's favourite thing to do with them is to take photos of themselves and share them with everyone else.'

That had her shaking her head. 'I do not understand, Fran.'

'Nor do I half the time,' I said. 'Let's just say that we don't have to go down the street and buy a newspaper anymore. We can click a button or touch a screen and the information appears.'

'What else do you do?' she asked, moving on uncomfortably.

'Coffee, then shower, dress, head downstairs to the shop. Cynthia arrives – she does the baking and looks after the coffee for the customers.'

'Does everyone drink coffee?'

'And tea, but Haven is famous for its coffee and muffins.'

'I thought you sold books?'

'We do. But I also sell my customers something to eat and drink while they browse the shelves. The longer I can get them to stay in the shop, the greater the chance they will come back, and buy while they are there.'

Violet's eyes were wide. 'When we open our bookshop, shall we do the same thing? It sounds very nice.'

I smiled at her and hugged her. 'I think so too,' I said. 'And we can have part of the shop as an art gallery. That would be brilliant.'

Her smile was wider than her eyes, the train curving around a corner and bumping her against my breasts. 'I would like that. People will come from all up and down the Riviera to our bookshop and gallery. They will drink tea and coffee and eat – what was it?'

'Muffins.'

'I do not know what they are either!'

I laughed. 'I will bake you some when we are settled.'

'I will look forward to it. Are they a type of cake?'

'Similar to a cupcake but more bread-like. Less sweet.'

Violet moved and kissed me on the cheek. 'I want to try them,' she said. 'Those and many other things! Everything!' She gestured expansively.

'Everything?' I teased.

'Yes,' she said emphatically. 'Look how much we have already done together – there must be much more.' She was looking at me now, her eyes twinkling.

'Are you…' the question petered out.

'Talking of our love-making?'

Yes. 'Yes,' I said. 'I guess so.'

A smacking kiss on the lips, then another, that lingered, set all my bones and muscles melting.

'Yes,' she whispered. 'I want to do everything, learn everything, with you.'

I couldn't help it. 'But we've only just met.'

She leaned back, surprise obvious in her eyes. 'What do you mean?'

I felt stupid, but it was too late. 'I mean, we've only known each other for a number of days. What…what…'

'I don't understand,' she said. 'We might only have known each other a short time – but think of all we have shared in that time.' Her eyes were confused. 'Think of all we have shared!'

I felt doubly stupid. 'But…'

'But what?'

'But, well…' I stared at her, tongue tied in knots. She

stared at me.

'Fran,' she said. 'Please just say what is on your mind. I cannot read what is there without you telling me.'

It burst forth from me like a bung from a hole. 'We haven't known each other long. I am afraid...' The burst of pressure dried up.

'Afraid of what?' She sat next to me now, straight-backed and serious, examining my reddening face. I saw the moment understanding dawned in her eyes.

'Oh,' she said. 'I see.' She looked away a moment, then back at me with a frown. 'Why are you afraid of that?'

'Of what?' I squeaked stupidly.

She shook her head. 'That it is the experience I desire, not you?'

She was even more astute than I'd given her credit for. Touching a hand to my hair, she stroked the hot skin of my cheek.

'Oh Fran,' she said. 'I knew during our first conversation that you were interesting.' A smile. 'Do you remember telling me I had to quit smoking the cigarettes?' There was another shadow outside the door and I hoped it wasn't the ticket collector. Not yet.

I did remember. A nod.

'Have you noticed that I have done so?'

Oh shit. I hadn't until now. I strained to remember the last time I'd seen her smoke and couldn't.

She was grinning at me. 'Poor Fran,' she said, stroking my hair again. 'So many things to worry about – including me.' She laughed. 'But you do not have to worry about me not wanting you.'

I was lost for words. She'd stopped smoking because I'd

told her it was bad?

'By our second conversation, I knew you were fascinating.' Violet edged closer and I felt her warm breath on mine. 'During the night we spent at the cottage, I realised just how special you were. And that you made me feel such real confidence. I've never felt truly that I can have the life I need, until now.'

I wanted to catch her fingers in mine and kiss them, but I was paralysed by the intensity of her feline gaze.

'By the next day I was feeling other things also.' She moved her hand to indicate her body. 'A fascination with you that wasn't entirely of the mind.' She slid closer still, so that our thighs pressed together, and she was almost in my lap.

'Imagine how it was then to discover that you might share those feelings? Those desires?'

I swallowed. She'd been attracted to me from the start?

'And then we kissed.' A fingertip touched my lip. 'You remember the kiss, surely?' Her voice teased. I nodded, helpless, everything fading away until there was only Violet there in front of me, the sound of her voice, the touch of her finger, the whisper of her breath.

'Good. I want you to always remember that kiss. Myself, I will be an old woman and still think of it, still feel the ghost of it upon my lips. How it set me on fire, all of me.'

Her lips brushed against mine and I gasped at the touch.

'Then of course, there was the night we just spent together.' Her words were a whispered kiss of their own. 'How could you believe that was just a passion for experience and not also for you? I gave myself to you. And took you for myself.'

Violet leaned back, and I swayed in my seat. 'It is not just a wild thirst for life that makes my heart beat so loudly when I am around you,' she said, touching a hand to her chest.

'It is desire for you, Fran. For you and everything that you are.' Her hand grasped my own and pressed it to her heart, her body hot beneath the fabric of her blouse.

She smiled. 'It may only have been days that we have known each other, but my darling, love can happen in the space between one heart beat and the next.'

CHAPTER TWENTY-SEVEN

We arrived in Folkestone in a haze of fatigue that the fresh wind from the sea did little to dispel. It was late in the day, we were grimy from travel, and there was no ferry to Boulogne until the next morning. It was, quite frankly a relief. I was tired of travel. Tired of trains, the noise of them, the incessant clatter on the tracks, and the swaying back and forth between the dining cab and our compartment whenever we wanted a cup of tea. Violet too, standing now on the platform with her bag in hand looked in desperate need of a rest.

Which we found in a dark stone inn on a street that wound back from the harbour as though turning in on itself. But the food was good, the landlady motherly, and the beds clean. We shared a room again, ushered in through the low doorway like a pair of schoolgirls, the landlady fussing around us to plump the pillows and crack the window open to the smell of wind and salt. She smiled and tutted and all but tucked Violet into the large bed we were expected to share and had no objection to doing so. We'd told her we were cousins, which I suppose was true in its own weird way, and Violet told her that we were on the way to help our other aunt run her war orphanage, which was, of course, utter rubbish, but the landlady lapped it up with glittering, avid eyes. I can still to this day feel my utter confusion at such a far-fetched story being believed.

But believed we were, and coddled into our room, assured that if we needed for anything, then the generous lady would be more than pleased to help. She left the room and we sat on the bed, our hands seeking each other's out, the fingers entwining. With little conversation, we went and washed, used the bathroom, undressed, and slid in between sheets cool and soft on our skin, there to wind ourselves around each other, sharing limbs heavy with fatigue.

And yet, as the moon rose above the waves of the channel to peer in through our window, I could not find any rest. I dozed, dreamed of the ghostly woman who haunted my dreams. She stood behind me, one hand reaching out to touch me – never had she been this close before – but every time I turned around to confront her, she slid away into the shadows and I was left chilled and uncomfortable.

The window was still cracked open and through it came the late-night sounds of the sea stirring against pilings, smacking against the stained sides of old boats, and holding hushed conversations with the wind.

I spent the rest of the night in feverish calculations. Mrs Kellow would have written her letter by now. Fran's, the real Fran's, father would have discovered the stolen twenty pounds by now. And indeed, it was stolen. There in the bed I blanched at the thought of what I'd done and gotten away with. Then I rolled over onto my side and looked at the dark and pale of Violet lying on the pillow next to me. Her skin looked like wax in the moonlight, hair like molasses. She breathed quietly, and as I watched, her eyes under their pale lids moved from side to side. She was dreaming, and I wondered what she dreamed of. Did she have a ghost haunting her as well? I wondered if she were my ghost, and if she dreamed that I was hers.

Lying in the bed, I shook my head. She was haunted by someone, all right, but he didn't stalk her in her dreams. Her father was real, flesh and blood, and we were running from him, from the fact that if we didn't run, he would see Violet in an institution.

That's why we took the twenty pounds. That's why we boarded the ferry for France later the next morning, huddled together for the interminable crossing, my mind conjuring vague accounts of German submarines sinking passenger ships, planes with bombs howling overhead.

But in the end, the crossing was unremarkable and then we were standing at last on wobbling legs in France. Violet lifted her face to the sky, closing her eyes and breathing deep of the French air as though it tasted of freedom.

Which for her, it did.

Then there was another train trip, and Paris welcomed Violet's shining, upturned gaze like she had come home.

'Can't we just stay a couple days, Fran?' she asked. I turned away from the woman in the ticket office to look at her. 'Just a couple days,' she repeated. 'A quick look around. It seems wrong to come all this way, and then leave without seeing anything.'

The woman waiting for my money cleared her throat. Spoke rapidly at me. I dredged up my schoolgirl French and answered her, sliding our new francs across to her, all the while shaking my head.

'We'll come back soon, Violet,' I said. 'We can visit as often as we like once we're settled. It's only a train ride, look.' I held up the tickets to Violet, then picked up my bag. A man in a uniform shouldered past me to purchase his own ticket.

Violet sighed. 'I know you're right,' she said, and tucked an arm in mine. 'It just seems such a shame.' But then she smiled. 'You got us a sleeper car, didn't you?'

I laughed, looking around for the correct platform. We'd exchanged our pound notes for francs, eaten lunch sitting in watery sunshine at a café just outside the station, where to my exquisite delight, I had been able to enjoy a cup of coffee, secretly deciding that once we were settled, it would be a staple in our pantry. There were some things it just wasn't fair to go without.

'Yes, we have a sleeper car,' I said. 'Which is just as well, because it will be a long journey.'

'Which is just as well because it will be a long journey and I am wishing to lie beside you,' Violet said in a low voice meant only for my ears.

'Oh Violet,' I groaned. 'Why do you have to say these things in public?'

'Because we do not yet have anywhere private,' Violet answered. 'I will be very glad when this travelling is over.'

As would I. It was exhausting, and not just because of the actual travelling. My dim calculations of the night before echoed between my ears. Our families would know what had happened at the cottage. They would know of the kiss. They would have our trunks, they would know we had left.

Our fathers would know I had lied to them. Which I did not regret for a moment, but which still made me look around warily.

'Your head will swivel right off, if you keep doing that,' Violet said, watching me. 'What are you looking for?'

I shook my swivelly head. 'Nothing,' I sighed.

'Fran.' Her voice held a warning, and those magnificent green eyes narrowed themselves at me.

'I'm being paranoid, I think,' I said. 'Pay no mind and let's just find our platform.' There was another soldier at the ticket kiosk. He wore a British uniform.

I shook my head. The man was the wrong height. Violet's father was tall, Fran's shorter, square like me. I took a few steps then stopped.

'What are you thinking, Fran?' Violet asked, not budging. Then she looked around too, her eyes suddenly wide. 'You don't think?' She sighed. 'They will know everything by now, won't they?'

I nodded. What else was there to do? It was the truth.

'But they couldn't possibly be here already. I mean, my father – he couldn't be here yet.' She turned to me and hugged herself, her carpet bag banging against her knees. I took it from her.

'I don't think so,' I said, but I had seen the documents in Reggie Madden's office. The one talking about a flight to Paris. A flight. An aeroplane. If they'd hopped on one of those, they could be here even now, could have been here ahead of us.

'You are not sure.'

I shook my head. 'I will just be glad to get there, that is all.'

She stared at me for a moment longer, then nodded, took her bag back from me and looked around the train station. 'There,' she said, glancing down at the tickets in my hand. 'Our platform.'

We waited in a tight knot of two for the train to pull in, which it did in a vast cloud of steam and the stink of coal. I barely blinked at it. How fast we become used to things. How quickly we sew together the fabric of our reality with whatever resources are available to us. It had been less than a week, and already I no longer bothered to marvel over the sights and sounds and smells so different to the world I was used to.

But then, I was caught up in a drama, complete with captivating damsel in distress and villainous pursuer. I was falling in love, and I was part of something in a way that, dare I admit it, I had secretly always wanted to be.

This was what it was to risk everything for love.

Our compartment was stamped on our ticket, and we fumbled our way through the cars until we found it. Third car down, middle of three compartments. The dining car was next behind ours.

We stashed our bags, and pulled the door closed, muffling the sounds of the passengers and the station, sitting silently and woodenly next to each other, hands tightly clasped, waiting for the whistle that would signal our departure. Only then would we feel able to relax.

'Thank goodness,' Violet said when it sounded. 'I will be so very glad to get to Nice.' She turned her gaze to me. 'They won't find us there,' she said. 'Not straight away. We will have time to establish ourselves, and then there will be no argument. My father will not be able to make me go home. I will be all right.' She leaned into me. 'I couldn't be doing this without you, Fran,' she said.

It was true, but I didn't want to dwell on it. We weren't safe yet. I wouldn't feel safe until we were in Nice. Until then, the painting in my bag was a spectre of what still might be. Until we were well-established in our new life, I would not be entirely convinced that Violet's disastrous life-course was completely derailed. I took a deep breath.

'We will be there by morning,' I said, sliding an arm around her bony shoulders. 'And we will find somewhere to stay, and I will go out and look for work straight away. I won't even wait a day.'

She looked at me, the train bumping us into each other as it gathered steam and clattered out of the station. We did not even look to the window to see Paris.

'What sort of work?' she asked. 'I can look for work too.'

That made me shift uncomfortably. I did not want her to have to work. I wanted to look after her. Protect her. Let her be the artist she really was. 'I want you to paint,' I said. 'That's your job.'

'But we will need money,' she said.

'We have some. And I will bring in what else we need.' I hugged her. 'Besides,' I said, believing it, 'soon you will be selling your work, and earning more than me.'

She laughed, a low, sweet sound. 'You are too good to me, Fran,' she said. 'Whatever did I do to deserve you?'

I laughed as well, my spirits lifting. 'It will all work out,' I said. 'How could it not? We are on a grand adventure!'

Violet nodded. 'One last night of travelling, then we are

free, and I need never worry again. We will paint, and sell books, and meet other artists, and *live*.'

We could do it too, I knew we could. Away from our families, from England, it was no pipe dream, but a real life we could have. I gazed at her and pressed hot lips to her cool cheek, felt her shift more comfortably into my side.

I closed my eyes and allowed myself to relax.

We could do this. Hell, we were doing this.

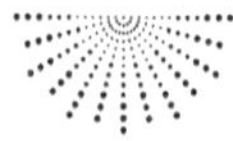

Not even ten minutes of peace and everything exploded into chaos. Maybe if we hadn't been so tired, if we hadn't already been travelling so long, then things might have gone differently, but sitting here now reliving it, I can only say – what happened, happened, and I still can find no blame in my heart for any of us.

A sharp rap on our compartment door, and we both startled, having spent the last five minutes in silence together, pressed together in nervous weariness upon the train seat, lulled almost into a stupor by the mechanical clattering and swaying.

Violet sprang out of my arms and we both looked toward the door, no time to notice anything except the door being wrenched open and a glowering face attached to clenched fists.

'Father!'

A frozen heartbeat, then the three of us were standing, crowded into the compartment, the ticket collector doing his best to squeeze in behind Violet's father, determined not to miss a minute of the unfolding drama with the English Officer and his daughter.

I don't know how long we all simply stared at each other. It could have been mere seconds; it could have been minutes. It felt like hours, stretched in horror out in the thin air between us.

'Father,' Violet repeated, her voice a strangled squeak again. 'How did you find us?'

He advanced a tight step upon her, and she backed away, sidled around away from him, an impossible task in the compartment. For a moment, his eyes flickered toward me, and my mouth dried up, my heart stalling.

His eyes were black with fury, his body rigid with it. He wore a uniform, and I knew that was how he'd found us – tracking us from one place to another. It would be easy for a man in his line of work, military intelligence the perfect priming for tracing two runaway women.

He shook his head. 'What on earth do you think you're doing, Violet?'

Her hair fell from the pins, she shook her head so vigorously. She opened her mouth, but no words came out.

'You had a perfectly nice place to stay on the coast,' he continued, leaning forward over Violet. 'Your stepmother is beside herself!'

Violet shook her head again. 'I couldn't stay,' she defied him, throat bouncing as she swallowed. 'I know what was waiting for me after our nice little holiday!' Her voice was horrified, clogged with sudden tears. The conductor leaned forward behind her father, and I wanted suddenly to smack him in the face for looking at Violet like that, like her pain was his unexpected entertainment for the day.

'Leave her alone,' I said, not even knowing I'd been going to speak.

Violet's father shifted his gaze to me, and it landed on me like it had actual weight. For a moment my legs threatened to buckle under the anger in it, but I straightened instead, remembering who I really was – a strong, independent woman used to fending off the anger of men.

I shook my head at him. 'Violet is old enough to decide where she wishes to go.' My voice, although I shook inside, was calm, unwavering.

'You,' he said, pointing a finger at me. 'You have much to answer for. Your mother assured me you would be a responsible and reliable companion for Violet, and yet here you are, stealing money from your father, inciting your cousin to flee across the Channel.' It was his turn to shake his head. 'What did you intend to do with her when you got to wherever you're going?' The ticket collector's eyes widened, and he almost rubbed his hands together in glee.

'I will repay my father the money, once I have found work.'

Isaac Farningham gazed at me, then laughed, a dirty, ugly sound. 'Work?' he said. 'When have you ever done a day's work in your life?' He flicked a contemptuous glance at his daughter. 'And Violet here – you realise how unwell she is?' His eyes narrowed back at me. 'But you are just as sick as she, aren't you? Now there was a revelation, a most disgusting state of affairs described to us by a complete stranger!'

I sucked in a breath, stood as tall as I could. 'It is no sickness,' I said. 'And we are both of age to determine our own fate, and if we do no longer wish to be under your thumb, then there is nothing you can do about it.' I held his gaze, and it was no effort, because his fury was matched now by my own. Especially as I could feel Violet trembling beside me. I reached out and touched my fingers to her hand. It was cold, a tight bunch of her skirt clenched in it.

Her father stared at me in silence for a full minute, and I glared back at him until he tipped his head back and laughed. It was a loud and harsh sound.

'Listen to you,' he said. 'What is wrong with you? You are nothing, a woman…Do you not realise you have no power against me?' He turned back to Violet again, dismissing me, leaving me rigid and impotent.

'Violet,' he said. 'We'll be getting off at the next stop, and you will be coming back to England with me.'

'I'll not leave Fran,' she said, and I touched her hand again. She let go of her skirt and held my fingers instead. 'I am not going anywhere with you,' she told him, chin tilted upwards.

He lunged for her then, mouth twisted in a snarl, arm shooting out to grab her by the shoulder.

He was fast.

But Violet was faster.

She had to shove the ticket collector aside to get out the door, and shove him she did, the nasty little man spinning into her father, tangling them both together for a precious moment that allowed Violet to escape. She was out of the compartment in a flash, heading along the corridor of the train in a mad dash towards the end of the car.

Her father growled, sprang forward, elbowing the other man aside, dashing after Violet, a harsh cry on his lips.

I followed right behind and we all ran after her, and she was at the end of the car, wrenching open the door, flinging herself out onto the step, jumping the gap to the next car, pulling the door wide, disappearing inside the next car, swallowed up by the dimness.

The noise of the train was deafening, and the wind battered at me as I made the leap behind Violet's father, his incoherent cry batted away by the rush of air between the carriages. Then he was dashing after her and I was following, my mouth open around screamed words that I couldn't hear over the rush of wind, the pounding of my heart.

What was Violet trying to do? I didn't know – she was going to run out of train, leaping as she was from one car to the next. Soon she'd hit the engine and it would be the end of the line. But I followed her, making the jump over the gap between one shuddering car and the next, because there was nothing else to do, and I would not let her be alone when her father caught up with her and I knew she ran with the impetus of a frightened animal, her headlong flight an instinctual thing, the frenzied bolting of a desperate fox with the hounds after it.

Then it happened, and even as I think about it from the great distance of time, I can see it as if in slow-motion, the way he lunged for her as she made the leap across to the last car, and I can hear the sudden, sharp whistle from the train as though it was warning us, and I can hear his grunt from in front of me, hear it somehow over the whistle, over the shriek of the wind, over the excited shouting of the ticket collector who slammed into my back a moment later when Violet's father in his pristine uniform, the sharp-pressed creases like knifepoints in the trousers, misjudged his lunging leap and lost his footing, his strangled cry forcing everything else out from my ears as he twisted and crashed down into the gap between the car where Violet turned and stood, horror on her face, and the car where I looked across at her for a moment before reaching with suddenly numb fingers to fumble for a grip on his jacketed shoulders.

I could not get any such grip, and a second later he was gone, dragged through the gap and under the train as though it was nothing, as though the metal monster we rode on didn't notice his passing at all, or took it as its due.

Violet screamed, and kept screaming, and behind me the old man in his railways uniform babbled incoherent French in my ear. As for me, I had no air in my chest, and try as I might there didn't seem to be any available to breathe either. Time wrapped itself in a bubble of horror, stretching out and taking on the iridescent gleam of blood spilled.

It snapped, and the train was moving full speed again, Violet was screaming, the man behind me babbling, and there was the rush of air on my face, and I gulped at it, swallowing it, breathing it deep into the slack sacs under my ribs, and then I jumped the gap, grabbing onto the doorway of the final car, Violet falling into my arms, and I was pushing her inside, looking up near the ceiling and finding the emergency rope. I yanked on it with fingers still feeling the fabric of the man's uniform sliding away from under them. The whistle blew again, a high shriek at the sky, railing at the faceless clouds, and then the train was shuddering, and the shrieking was from the wheels against the rails, the harsh scraping of metal against metal and I pressed Violet against the wall of the lurching car and wrapped my arms around her, muffling her screams in my shoulder.

CHAPTER TWENTY-NINE

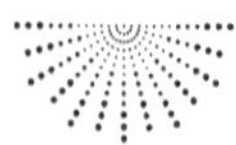

'Good God, Fran, what the hell were the two of you thinking?'

I stood silent, pressed against the wall of the sitting room we were in. Outside the door I knew the police captain lurked, and probably his wife as well. The walls were thin enough that they wouldn't even have to press their ears to the door. I knew this from overhearing the conversation between Fran's father and the *gendarme* not ten minutes earlier.

Fran's father – not mine, I could feel no connection to him – stopped his pacing to stare at me, finally, his eyes meeting mine. He shook his head.

'I don't understand a bit of it,' he said, and I wanted to press a hand to my breast, thankful that his voice was several crucial decibels quieter.

'We were on our way to Nice,' I said.

'What the hell for?'

'To live.'

He closed his eyes. Shook his head again. 'This is such a

mess.' Eyes snapped open. 'Do you know exactly how much of a mess this is? Isaac is dead. Dead. Do you realise?'

'I'm well aware of it,' I replied, glad for the wall pressed against my back. 'I was there when it happened.'

More headshaking. 'That I know! You and Violet are facing charges of murder, for heaven's sakes.'

'No we're not.' I'd heard his conversation with the French policeman. I'd had my own with him. 'The ticket collector saw it all.'

Reginald Madden deflated, sank into an armchair and rubbed his hands over his cheeks. I looked at him. He'd shaved in a hurry before leaving London. He'd missed a patch just under his ear.

'You're both bloody lucky – and I'm not going to apologise for my language. I say it again, Fran – what the hell were the two of you thinking?'

'He was going to put Violet in a mental hospital,' I said.

'So your mother has told me.' He dropped his hands and looked at me. His eyes were bloodshot. 'What made you think that wasn't the right place for her?' He shook his head. 'She's obviously unwell.'

'She just saw her father sucked under a train,' I said.

Fran's father narrowed his eyes at me. I leaned my head back against the wall and waited.

He shook his head, ran a hand through his hair, which already stood up at several shocked angles from his conversation with the police.

'And what's this about a letter from the woman where you are supposed to be staying?'

I shrugged.

'No. Your mother told me about that too. It was sent to her, after all. She called me on the telephone and read it to me.'

'And to Violet's father, obviously.'

'As indeed she should have. It only confirmed his opinion of his daughter's illness.'

I resisted the desire to look up at the ceiling. Violet lay in a bed in the room above us, asleep. Sedated. Courtesy of the town's doctor, who had been summoned after we'd been brought here from the police station.

'It is no illness to fall in love,' I said, looking straight at the man. I didn't expect him to believe me and I didn't care. Violet's father was dead. The babbling ticket collector had continued his babbling at the police station, but fortunately he'd backed up my assertion that Isaac Farningham had slipped and fell, not been pushed. In which case, Violet and I were exonerated of any official suspicion.

'It is,' Reginald Madden said, and I drew my mind back to the conversation. 'It is, and it is a crime!'

I shook my head. 'No, it is not a crime. Not between women.' I looked around the room, hoping I'd be able to go shortly, back upstairs to check on Violet. 'And especially not here in France. Which is one reason we came here.'

His face was red, but I spoke again before he had a chance to.

'We are both over age,' I said. 'Old enough to determine what we wish to do with our lives, to live where and how we like.' I drew breath and gave him one concession. 'I'm sorry about the subterfuge to get money, but it was my only choice since I would never have gained your permission.' My gaze was steady. 'Once this interview is over, and Violet is awake, she and I will continue on our way to Nice. There we will find somewhere to live, and I will find work. We have a dream, and that dream is to be together, and independent. Violet wishes to paint – it is what she needs to be happy – and I, I will find work, and one day I wish to open my own shop…'

He spluttered. 'A shop?'

I shrugged and turned my gaze around the room. 'A bookshop, with space for a small art gallery.'

I felt him stare at me. 'I do not know you,' he said slowly. 'You've changed, and I do not recognise this person you've become.' A weighted pause. 'You have given it this much thought?'

My eyes returned to him. 'Yes,' I said simply.

'This is decided, is it?'

It seemed a stupid question and I was tired. We'd been hours at the police station, and then hours more here, the police man's wife constantly watching us. I wanted some peace, some privacy. I wanted to hold Violet and tell her it was all going to be okay.

'Yes,' I said. 'You don't, I imagine, envision me coming home, do you?' I blinked at him. 'What would Mother do with me? I will never change. She would never be able to marry me off, even if the scandal from this ever fades.'

I had him there, I knew that. 'And as for Violet,' I said. 'Her father is dead, and that leaves her with only a stepmother, who has no interest in her. There is literally no one to care what she does.'

I shifted and stood up properly. 'Except me,' I said. 'And I have told you our plans.'

Madden was staring at me and I looked back, waiting for

whatever would come next, but waiting more for the moment to leave the room and return to Violet. I wondered when the next train to Nice would be. The next day, most likely. Although, I supposed, standing there, that we could go back to Paris now, if we chose. There would be no one to come looking for us – one man was dead, and the other sat in a chair staring at me.

Inwardly, I shook my head. I would talk it over with Violet, but I leant still toward Nice. I wanted its warmth and sea breezes, its artists and writers. It would be an easier place to live, at least in this time.

'I want to leave now, if there's nothing more.' I said finally, tired of waiting.

He shook his head at me. 'This is really it? This is really what you want? What about your mother, your sister?'

His questions made me sigh. 'Mother won't be pleased to see me, not after this.' I thought of the child. 'Marigold, I will miss. But she will always be welcome to visit us.' My lips quirked in a smile and the man supposed to be my father stared at me.

'You think this is funny?' he demanded.

'Not at all,' I answered. 'The farthest thing from funny, actually. It has been a distressing and tiring day and I am greatly looking forward to it being over.'

Reginald Madden, also in his uniform, stared hard at me for a long moment, then got abruptly up and stalked to the door, laid his hand on the knob.

'Your mother will be so upset,' he said, and those were parting words because a moment later the door was wrenched open and he disappeared through it, scattering the police captain and his wife.

I breathed out, leaning against the wall again for a moment, and realised finally how loudly my heart knocked against my ribs. And I had a headache. I rubbed at my temples, sighed, then stood, walked to the door and out of the room.

The hallway was empty, voices drifting through to me from the front of the house. I ignored them in favour of the stairs, taking them two at a time, my skirts swishing about my legs, shoes clattering on the bare floorboards.

I stood in the doorway and Violet looked at me from the bed.

'I thought you were sleeping,' I said.

'No.' She was sitting on the edge of the bed in her underclothes, purple shadows around her eyes. She reached out her hands to me.

I moved into the room and took them, sitting down beside her on the rumpled sheets. She gripped my fingers and stared at me.

'We have to go,' she said. 'We can't stay here. Your father will drag us back to England, and I won't go.' Her wide eyes blinked at me. 'I just won't.'

Shaking my head, I lifted her hands and kissed her pale fingers. 'You don't – and won't – have to,' I said.

Her lips parted, and she gaped at me. 'What?'

It was my turn to squeeze her hands. I could hear the smile in my own voice when I answered. 'We're not going back to England, Violet – not unless you want to live there...'

'I don't want to live there!' She stared at me in the dim light from the window. Outside the wind blustered at the glass and the sun was clouded. Violet shook her head. 'We can go to Nice?'

I nodded. 'Or Paris, if you prefer.'

Our hands interlocked. 'But how?' she asked.

I smoothed my thumb over hers. 'Violet, the one person who could perhaps have stopped us is dead.'

'My father,' she said, her eyes steady enough on mine, but her throat convulsing as she swallowed. 'What about yours?'

'What can he do?' I lifted my shoulders. 'I am too old for him to have any legal say over my movements, and he knows full well the scandal that would greet our return, if he were able to insist on us going back. We would never live it down, and it would hurt them considerably.' I glanced toward the bedroom door. 'I've no doubt that he's on damage control duty right now.' I slid an arm around Violet and pulled her close. 'The best thing for everyone, is if you and I continue on our way, and we all know it.'

'To Nice,' she said, and her lips moved against my ear. 'I want to continue on to Nice.'

'Not Paris?'

She shook her head and her hair tickled my cheek. 'No. Nice sounds perfect,' she said. 'You made it sound perfect.'

I looked at her. 'I'm glad. It's where I want to go.' A kiss on her cheek. 'Much warmer.'

'Further away from the Front.'

'That too,' I agreed.

'And there are artists there or will be.' Violet's eyes seemed less bruised already, and there was a little colour in her cheeks.

'Yes,' I said. 'Artists, writers, everything we need.'

She leaned against me, a small, sad smile on her face. Then it was gone, and she turned to me, serious. 'You won't ever leave me, will you Fran?'

I was astounded. 'What do you mean?'

'I won't wake up one morning and you'll be gone, will I?' she asked. Looking down, she took my hands again and rubbed at the twin lifelines on my palms, then lifted her eyes to mine. 'I couldn't bear to lose you, Fran.'

I returned her gaze, then looked down at my hands. Even in the dimness, the double lines there were visible. The only thing I couldn't see was their true meaning.

'No,' I said. 'No, you won't wake up to find me gone.'

'But how do you know that?' Her green eyes blinked at me. 'How can you know that?'

I didn't know that. I didn't know anything. The spectre of her question rose in front of me like a dim shadow stepping from the corner.

I cleared my throat. 'I don't know how this works,' I said. 'I don't know anything about it at all because it's all been an impossibility.' She gazed at me, the colour leaching from her face again. 'But,' I said, leaning forward to press a finger against her lips. 'I believe I'm here for a reason.' I did, that much was true. 'And I love you, and the reason is you, loving you.'

She sank against me, her head against my shoulder. We sat like that in silence for a few minutes, although thoughts swirled around in my mind in a maelstrom of questions I didn't have any answers to.

'How about you get some more sleep, Violet?' I asked at last. 'It's been a terrible couple of days.'

She nodded against me, and I moved to tug the covers back over her. Her thin hand grabbed my wrist.

'Will you stay with me?' she asked.

'I need to go see about the train,' I told her. 'There may be one leaving this evening.'

Violet let go. 'But you'll come straight back?'

'Always,' I said, and meant it.

As much as I could.

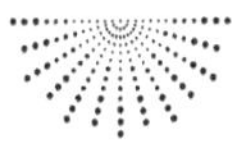

The police captain took us in his car back to the station, and bought our tickets himself, placing them in my hand on the platform, before nodding to us and turning on his heel. Appropriately dark clouds gathered on the horizon and brooded over us.

'Your father left no message, Fran?' Violet asked.

I shook my head. 'No. Madame Bernard told me he got into his car and drove away without a word.' I tried a smile for Violet, who had risen silent and pale from her nap and dressed in her dark green travelling suit. I'd watched her put a hand on the yellow fabric of her dress, then push it aside. She'd feel like wearing it again, I promised myself.

I found the thread of our conversation again, clearing my throat. 'I didn't expect him to leave anything for me. When he walked out of the room today, I knew I'd likely never see him again. I think there's a good chance we'll never hear from him again either. Or Fran's mother.'

'And my father will never haunt me again.' Her eyes

widened as she realised what she'd said. 'I mean he'll never be a danger to me.'

I linked her arm through mine and put my hand over hers. 'I know what you meant,' I said. 'And he'll do neither. He's no danger, and he'll not haunt us either.'

A hesitant, uncertain smile spread across her face and she turned watery eyes towards mine. 'We are on our own, Fran,' she said.

'Yes.' The train pulled into the station, filling the air with billowing clouds of steam.

We resumed our journey across France with an odd euphoria that came and went. We were free, even though I knew that when we closed our eyes, Violet's father took his slow-motion fall from the train again, but we were still free, and nothing could alter that fact. Violet tucked herself up beside me on the train and chattered, then fell silent, then chattered again. I couldn't stop looking at her, feeling the warmth of her pressed close against me, listening to the sound of her voice, content even in the sound of her inter-mittent silence.

When dusk spread deepening darkness outside the windows of the train, we pulled the blinds and locked the door, turning to each other with serious eyes, and we undressed each other in a silence bordering on sacred.

We slid into the lower bunk, pressing close to each other in its narrow space. Violet's hitching breath against my lips was still sweet and I couldn't do anything but kiss her, my hands running themselves over her bare skin, following the flow of her curves. She was warm silk beneath my palms.

Violet's hands fluttered and smoothed against me,

touching me on the cheek, the neck, breast, reaching for me, dipping fingers into my wetness, making me gasp, making me pull her against myself, burying my face in the thick dark cloud of her hair, exploring her with my own fingers, kissing her gasping lips.

We touched each other, lying skin to skin as the train swayed underneath us. It bore us along through the night and we moved with it, rhythmic and synchronised, her breath mixed with mine, her hands upon me, and mine upon her, the softness of her breast against mine, her legs entwined with mine. We built together towards climax, moving as one delirious creature as pleasure overcame us, swept along the tracks in our narrow bed, the darkness as warm and deep as velvet around us, wrapping us in the bliss we were the architects of, our mounting cries in each other's ears.

We woke early, and dressed silently in the half-light, reaching out to touch each other as we did so, little touches, as though a moment was too long to go without the feel of the other's hand against our own.

Then we were ready, bags again at our feet, and the train gave a shrieking whistle to announce its arrival, the whooshing squeal of its brakes making us reach for each other, hands clasping, eyes meeting, then looking again towards the door. The train stopped, and we picked up our bags, opened the compartment door, and left the panelled cocoon to step out onto the platform in Nice.

Violet's smile was wide and sudden. 'We're here,' she said, moving away from the train, dropping her bag and turning in a slow spin, head flung back, a pin coming loose from her dark hair and spilling a stray curl onto her shoulder. She'd pulled the yellow dress out of her bag, giving me a determined, defiant look as she did so. I had simply smiled and helped her into it.

I wanted to go over to her and pick her up, spin her around faster in my arms so that she laughed out loud, a sound I coveted more than any other. So I did exactly that, and Violet's laughter was low and strong in my ear before I put her down and squeezed her hands. A watching porter clapped his hands and laughed too, before asking if he could get our bags.

Violet answered him, her French fluent, her teenaged lessons in it thorough. There were two high spots of colour on her cheeks and she gave him a suddenly giddy smile and told him we had no bags except those at our feet. Then she asked which way was the sea. He pointed and told her, and we took up our things and followed the direction of his finger and the sleepy smell of a sea basking in summertime bliss.

'It's so beautiful,' Violet breathed, standing on the promenade, gazing down at the calm water.

'Yes,' I said, gazing in turn at her. 'Very beautiful.'

She caught my look and laughed at me. 'Silly thing,' she cried. 'I was talking about the water!'

'It is lovely too,' I conceded.

Another laugh, and she linked her arm through mine, and we took up our bags again.

'Where shall we stay?' she asked. 'Do you know a place?'

It would have to be somewhere cheap. 'Let's try the old city,' I said. 'There's bound to be somewhere suitable.'

She nodded, and I could feel an excitement thrumming

beneath the surface of her skin, flowing through her very veins.

'I will be able to buy the supplies for paints here, won't I?' she said as though just realising this. 'And canvases.'

'And an easel. They will be our first purchases.'

Violet laughed and leaned into me, the sea lapping and purring at our backs, the dark things that had happened forgotten for the moment. A young woman passed in the opposite direction and caught Violet's smile, giving us one of her own.

'Perhaps not the first, Fran,' Violet said. 'We need a room, and food.'

I shrugged. 'Details,' I said. 'We are here so that you can paint, so paint you shall.'

We had walked away from the beach, up into the tangle of narrow streets of old Nice, which didn't look quite as old, I supposed, as it had the last time I'd seen it.

'Look,' Violet said, tugging on my arm and leading me across the street into the shade of a tall building. 'It's empty.' She stopped in front of the shop windows and leaned close, cupping hands around her face to peer in. 'Look, Fran. It's empty.'

'Yes,' I said. 'It's an empty shop, but I don't think it will make a good place to stay. We need a proper apartment.'

Stepping back, Violet shaded her eyes and gazed upwards at the upper story, and the little balcony jutting out over the street.

'The plant in the pot on that balcony is dead,' she said.

I squinted up at it. 'That's a shame, I guess.'

Violet rolled her eyes at me and picked up her bags again. 'Come on.' She stepped quickly along the footpath.

'What are you doing?' I asked, following her.

'Looking for the door.'

'What for? We need a boarding house or something, not an empty shop.'

But Violet just shook her head and a moment later pounced on a door, tugged at it, then stepped back and frowned when it refused to open.

'Violet?' I said.

She didn't answer, crossing the street instead and disappearing inside the shop opposite. I followed, quickening my own pace when I realised I smelled coffee through the door she'd just disappeared into.

'Violet?' I repeated, stepping inside the dim, fragrant interior.

She stood by the counter and turned a smiling face at me. 'Would you like a coffee, Fran?' she asked.

More than anything. 'Yes, please,' I said, and she nodded.

'Find a seat, I'll get us something to eat too.' She reached for her purse, into which we'd emptied half our money, and turned her back on me to speak to the old man behind the counter in a low mumble of foreign words.

I sat in a chair beside the window, grateful to set my bag down. We'd have something to eat, then find a small hotel or boarding house and get settled in. I was looking around through the window, wondering what sort of job I'd be able to find, when Violet arrived at the table in a breezy flurry of skirts.

'I've got us a place,' she said, sitting down and grinning at me.

'What?'

Her smile was wide, triumphant. 'I've found us a place to live,' she said. 'And I've found you your shop.'

'What?'

Violet giggled. 'Are you always going to make me repeat everything I say?'

'Until the day I die,' I said. 'Now can you tell me what's going on? Please?'

She rubbed her hands together and leaned over the small table. 'Coffee's on the way,' she said. 'And fresh rolls.'

My mouth watered. 'Yum,' I said, then decided I couldn't afford to be distracted. 'Now tell me.'

Her grin was wickedly gleeful. 'Across the road is an empty shop.' She gave an elegant shrug. 'Empty except for fittings, I suppose.'

I nodded.

'Above said empty shop is an empty *appartement*.' She blinked. 'Well, it's a furnished flat, which is good, because we don't have a bed, or anything else.'

I nodded again, eyes narrowing.

'And so, my dearest Fran, shop and flat are ours.'

My eyes were now so narrowed I squinted at her. 'What?' I said.

'Ours,' she repeated. 'Flat. Shop.'

I tried sifting around in my brain for appropriate words but couldn't find any. 'What?' I repeated.

Violet looked at me, folding her arms and raising her eyebrows. 'Must I say it a seventh or eighth time?'

It took all my will not to splutter, and even then, it didn't quite work. 'What the hell, Violet? A flat? A shop? How did you even have time to organise that?'

She gave me a smug smile. 'There was plenty of time while you were gazing dreamily out the window.' More serious now. 'Besides, Monsieur Dubois there is very keen to find suitable tenants and had had little hope of finding ones while the war was on, so you see it is ours.'

'But we've no money!'

Violet unhooked her arms and slid her hands across the table, taking hold of my own. 'My father just died, Fran,' she said.

I stared blankly at her. I knew that. My fingertips tingled. I could still feel the rub of his jacket against them.

Her hands were cool and dry. 'I am in his will.'

'What?' I winced. I sounded like an idiot saying that over and over.

Violet took a deep breath. 'My mother had a little money. When she died, it went to my father, but she made him promise that some of it at least would still come to me, if he were to marry again.'

I gazed at her.

She squeezed my hands. 'I'm saying, Fran, that soon I'm going to have a little money. Enough money to start up your bookshop.'

All the saliva in my mouth dried up.

'What do you say?' Violet asked.

I sucked in a breath. 'Our bookshop,' I croaked.

'With a little gallery in it for my paintings,' she said.

My voice was still full of grit. 'And every day you'll come down to see me in the shop.'

She smiled. 'And I'll have smudges of paint on my cheek.'

'And I'll try to guess what you've been painting by what colour the smudges are.'

Violet nodded, and I grasped her hands tightly. 'Am I dreaming?' I asked.

She shook her head. 'No.'

'Then how did this happen?'

'I don't know,' she said. 'I don't know at all.'

CHAPTER THIRTY-ONE

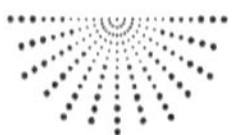

I stood in the middle of the room and sneezed.

'*Je m'excuse, Madamoiselle,*' Monsieur Dubois said. *I apologise.* 'It needs a little cleaning.'

'But it is perfect, isn't it, Fran?' Violet asked, turning to me with green eyes kindling in the gloom from the dirty windows.

'What sort of shop was it before it closed?' I asked the man who owned both this building and his own shop. I liked that there was coffee right across the street, and the rolls had been superb.

Violet looked at me and pulled a face, pretending to pout. I shook my head at her, trying not to get too excited, turning back to examine the long, wide room. It was hard to tamp down a sense of excitement though – already I could see exactly how I would set up the space, providing that I could get the shelving and things I needed.

'Fran has owned businesses before, Monsieur Dubois,' Violet said.

He looked at me with bushy eyebrows raised and I could read the astonishment in his rheumy old eyes.

'My grandmother owned a bookshop,' I explained – and why not? It was true. 'I practically grew up in it.' The windows, although filthy, were pleasingly tall and narrow along one wall. I nodded at them.

Monsieur Dubois waved his arms at the room. 'It was Madame Martin's shop.' He searched for the words in English. 'She sold the pretty things for dresses.' He rubbed his gnarled fingers together as though feeling the fine weight of silken fabric.

'But that is lovely!' Violet exclaimed.

'Ah, but the lady, she got old, and there was no one to take over her shop.' Dubois's crestfallen look was almost comical. 'Hers was the apartment upstairs also.'

'It has been empty a long while,' I observed, looking at the thick layer of grime. The large tables where once Madame Martin had measured and cut fabric would make beautiful displays for books and art prints.

Violet was looking at me, a decided gleam in her eyes. I returned her gaze, biting my lip to keep from showing my growing excitement.

'Perhaps you could show us upstairs, Monsieur?' Violet asked after a moment, letting me off the hook.

The old man nodded and pointed to a door at the back of the shop. 'This leads also to the upstairs to the apartment.'

We followed him, Violet reaching behind her back with her hand. I put mine in it and we walked up the stairs fingers entwined.

It took Violet only moments to fall in love with the flat. *Appartement.* I watched her eyes widen as they took in the large windows through which the sun slanted like a golden benediction. The floor space was the same as downstairs, but here had been divided into living and sleeping areas. Monsieur Dubois had been right – there was even a bed, and I looked at it, wondering if the esteemed Madame Martin had died upon it. But dusty as it was, the mattress was unstained, and the room warm and pleasant.

'There is a small room for another bed,' M. Dubois said in apologetic English, and Violet nodded.

'It would be absolutely fine,' she assured him although I could see that she was already sizing up the second room for a studio. It was small but filled with light. I watched her lips curve in a smile.

And it hit me – here I was, looking over a flat in France with Violet. Downstairs was a space I was seriously considering converting into a bookshop, as though everything was normal, as though I belonged in Nice in 1916.

Violet sidled up to me, touched my elbow. 'Fran?' she said. 'Is everything all right?'

I looked at her and made myself smile. A nod. I wanted to belong here, with this woman who was staring at me, a slight, delightful frown between her dark brows.

'Are you sure?' she whispered. 'You're looking awfully strange.'

Another nod. 'I want this,' I said. Her eyes blinked at me. 'I mean it,' I said. 'I really want this.'

I smiled at her, then turned to look out the window at the balcony. There was the terracotta pot with the dead flower in it. I wondered what we would plant there. Something vibrant, I decided. Something colourful, that glowed in this golden light the way Violet did.

My palm itched, and I rubbed at it, hearing Violet's voice behind me, speaking in French, talking numbers, details, too rapidly for me to follow without careful attention. Instead I stood in a narrow band of sunshine and didn't want to move. I didn't want to have to go back down those stairs and find somewhere else to live. Right here was good. Right here was Nice, with Violet.

I stood there for a long time, seeing this place here, and far away another bookshop with a flat above it. The two places wavered in front of me, and for a long moment, I couldn't tell which was more real.

There was a touch at my elbow and I started.

'Fran? Are you all right? What is wrong?' Violet peered at me, cat's eyes worried. I sucked in a deep breath and promptly sneezed, then laughed.

It was all right. I was definitely here, standing here with Violet.

'Well?' I asked.

She looked at me a moment longer, then her expression turned smug. 'Well what?' she asked.

'It, it seems too good, is this real, I mean really our new home?'

'Do you want it to be?'

Monsieur Dubois was gone. I put my arms around Violet and drew her into my side. 'Yes,' I said. 'I do.'

Her smile was wide and delighted. She hugged me tight. 'Then it is ours – Monsieur Dubois was very happy to rent it to us at an extremely reasonable rate.'

'The flat and the shop?'

She nodded. 'Both.'

I looked out the window, seeing the ocean in the distance,

the colour of turquoise. 'You can paint the sea, Violet,' I said.

She tipped her head on the side, gazing out the window as well. 'I can paint anything I want,' she said, and there was wonder as well as joy in her voice.

'Oh my goodness,' I said. 'There is so much to do!'

That made her laugh and skip away to spread her arms to the room. 'First, I think – a lot of cleaning. Monsieur Dubois is sending his daughter up with cleaning supplies, and linen for the bed.'

I shook my head, amazed. 'Today?' I asked.

'Now.'

My head spun, and I laughed. 'We've really landed on our feet.' I sobered. 'And we can afford it? Because I will go out and get a job right here and now, to tide us over, you know that, don't you?'

Violet practically wriggled with excitement. 'We can afford it. Monsieur Dubois and I made a deal.'

I frowned at her. 'What sort of deal?'

She danced a few steps on the wooden floor, shimmying in a golden pillar of disturbed dust, then laughing. 'I am going to serve tea and coffee and croissants for him for three hours, four days a week, and that will pay the rent for the flat and the shop until it is up and running.'

I gaped at her, my mouth falling open.

Then she was beside me, her thin fingers plucking at my sleeve. 'Oh Fran,' she said. 'Don't look like that! It is perfect – he says his shop is popular for artists – which means I will get to meet them.' She let go of me and spun back into the middle of the room. 'I can't believe our luck – it's like it's really meant to be, Fran! Don't you think it will be perfect? Artists and writers already go to buy their breakfasts and such right there – and we will have our bookshop right across the road where they won't be able to resist coming in!'

I was dazed. 'We can sell art supplies too,' I said, my voice rusty with shock.

'And we can display pieces of everyone's work right there in the shop too!'

'I need to sit down.'

Violet laughed, and pounced on me, leading me to a blue sofa and sitting me down, then placing herself neatly in my lap, arms around my neck, her face next to mine, flushed but serious.

'It is all turning out wonderfully,' she whispered. 'I only ever dreamed of this, Fran, and then you came along and it is happening. It is really happening.'

I could only nod.

She shifted and rested against me. 'When my father dropped me off at your house, so we could go to the seaside – for the sake of my health – I little realised I would end up here, like this.'

'I'm glad we have,' I croaked.

'Oh, so am I,' Violet said. 'Things were looking bleak indeed before this.'

She didn't need to elaborate. The hospital. The few, desperate paintings they allowed her to do, then the long, final descent into despair. I held her close, buried my face in her hair.

'Are you sure you're all right, Fran?' she asked.

I made myself nod. It wasn't quite the truth though. A creeping fear had burrowed in under my skin and was spreading to every nerve ending as we spoke. I sucked in a long breath.

'Yes,' I breathed. 'I'm okay, and everything is perfect.'

Everything was perfect – Violet warm and happy in my arms, the plush velvet sofa we sat on, the sun blushing at the window, and through the door, a bed that we would soon share every night, our new shop waiting for us downstairs.

Everything was perfect. I would have a bookshop, again, like I always wanted.

I was in love.

There was only one question that nagged at me.

How long would it last?

Because perhaps it really was all a dream.

CHAPTER THIRTY-TWO

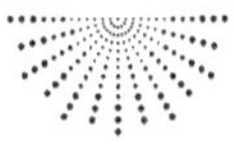

Or perhaps, if I was not dreaming, then what if I was still to wake up, back in the twenty-first century, my own time, my mission here completed?

After all, I pondered compulsively as we scrubbed and swept and dusted all that afternoon, here was Violet, safely in France, away from her family, her father in fact dead, and she no longer suffered under the spectre of that mental hospital. If I were that small girl again, sitting on my grandmother's ottoman in front of the fire, staring up at the painting on the wall, it would not be a story of grim tragedy she would tell me. Not anymore. Now it would be the story of a passionate and determined young woman who escaped to live a life of art and freedom in France during the First World War.

'My love,' Violet said, coming up to me, her hair escaping in dark and unruly curls from the scarf she had tied it back with. 'You have not been yourself all day.'

I wiped my forehead with my wrist, glad of the breeze which stirred the warm air in the room with the smell of salt.

'I'm all right,' I said.

She stared at me for a long moment, her eyes holding too many questions for me to meet their gaze for long.

'I don't know if I believe you,' she said. 'You are keeping something from me, I am sure of it.'

I closed my eyes for a moment, then snapped them open and led Violet to the sofa. It had been beaten within an inch of its velvet life, the dust rising from it in plumes, and we settled in its lovely depths, Violet not taking her gaze from me.

'There is something bothering you,' she said, and her voice wavered. 'Remember your promise.'

Not to keep secrets from her. Not to tell her lies.

I sighed. Held her hands in mine, stroked her long, thin fingers.

'You have to tell me,' she said, and there was a brittle line of worry in her voice now.

'You'll think me silly,' I said, lowering my gaze to her hands.

They held my own, the fingers surprisingly strong. 'I shouldn't think so,' she said, and her voice had softened.

I laughed, a short, broken sound. 'I'm feeling a little super-stitious,' I told her.

Her eyebrows arched toward the colourful scarf she'd found in one of the drawers in the bedroom, pouncing on it with a cry of delight.

'Superstitious?' she asked. 'Explain.'

I waved a hand at the room, them tucked it back into Violet's. It was the one with the twin lifelines. 'All this,' I said.

Her gaze followed mine to take in the dimensions of the

sitting room, the French doors leading out to the little balcony, the furniture Mme Martin had left behind, now gleaming and dust-free.

'It is beautiful, is it not?' she breathed.

'Yes,' I answered. 'It is.' Then I looked at her. 'And you – you are perfect, and I've never been this happy.' My heart felt suddenly so full I could barely breathe. 'It's true,' I said. 'I have everything I've ever wanted and more than I could have ever imagined.'

She looked at me in silence for a moment, then nodded. 'I understand,' she said, then pressed a hand to her own breast. 'It overflows here,' she said. 'And spills everywhere – my skin tingles, my palms itch.' She laughed. 'And it is impossible but to ask yourself – what have I done to deserve this much happiness?' Her hands moved to cup my face and her lips touched mine in a warm and tender kiss.

'But we do deserve this, Fran,' she said. 'Look at what we have done to get to this place.'

'Rather a lot,' I confessed.

Her grin was delighted. 'We took our lives into our own hands, our destinies. We came here because we knew it would feed us, and we were brave and courageous, and we deserve this so very much, Fran.'

I put my arms around her and drew her towards me, kissing her smiling mouth and breathing in the warmth of her skin. Then sneezed. Again.

Violet laughed. 'We need to finish here, then wash, and go in search of something to eat. I am starving.' Her eyes gleamed at me. 'Oh Fran – is this not the most exciting thing ever to happen to you?'

The whole week fell into that category, and I could hardly believe it had only been that long. A week. Bronny would be married, and me – what had happened to me, there?

A soft fingertip touched the tissue-thin skin under my eye. 'There are shadows here, Fran,' Violet said.

'I am afraid,' I said, then stared at her in horror at my words. I hadn't meant to say them.

But her beautiful mouth curved into a smile. 'Because you wish to stay here with me?'

There was a lump in my throat words couldn't get past. I nodded.

She leaned against me. 'I too, have had this thought.' She blinked at the room, which was dimmed with late afternoon shadows.

'You have?'

'Of course.' She chewed on a lip for a moment, and watching her, I wanted to stop the sharp teeth, kiss it instead. 'I would have died if I'd been forced into a sanatorium, Fran. There is no point saying otherwise.' Her eyes, when they turned to look back at me, were dark, as shadowed as the room. 'I might have struggled on for a short time, in the hopes of being let out, but then I would have taken my own life.' She shook her head. 'I could not have lived like that. I would rather have died.' Her hand crept to her mouth and she chewed for a moment on a finger. 'I tried to tell my father so, but he took it as all the more evidence that I was unwell.' Her hand fell away, and she smiled up at me. 'Although it was that conversation that brought me the summer with you.'

I didn't know what to say.

'So,' she said, and I watched the pulse in her pale neck

jump under the skin. 'You have essentially saved my life. Perhaps your job here is done, I have had that thought.'

'You have?' The question came out strangled.

'Yes, but I do not believe it to be true.'

'You don't?'

She sighed against me, her body melting against mine. How well we fit together, her and I. Never had anyone felt so right against me.

'I do not,' she said, and she looked up at me, her eyes large, round, serious. 'Because you want to be here. I think we must all get choices – just like we made the choice to be brave and come here – and you want to stay here with me, that is the choice you make.' She straightened slightly. 'Isn't it?'

I nodded, my life in Bath, in 2016 never seeming more distant as it did at that moment. 'I want to stay here with you,' I said.

She leaned back, a satisfied smile on her face, and took my right hand in hers, her thumb smoothing over the twin life-lines. 'That is your choice, and you have made it.'

I nodded, and let her statement stand, even while I wondered if it could possibly be that easy. Her hand tightened on mine.

'Besides, Fran,' she said, and those big eyes were looking at me again. 'It wouldn't be all right if you went back. *I wouldn't be all right.*'

I looked at her in silence.

'You saved my life, it is true, but for me truly to live, I need you at my side.' She wriggled somehow closer, as if to illustrate her words.

'And I need to be there,' I said. 'If I'm to truly live.'

We looked at each other for a quiet moment, then Violet smiled.

'Good,' she said. 'Now let us wash and change and venture out into our new home town and see if we can find something to eat. I've such an appetite!' She leapt up from the sofa and held out a hand to me.

I took it gladly.

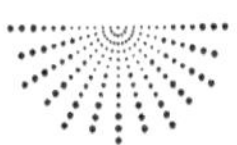

CHAPTER THIRTY-THREE

I thrashed myself awake to moonlight peering in the window at me, and for a moment I didn't know where I was.

Then I saw Violet lying next to me and exhaled in relief, pushing myself up to lean against the head of the bed, the cotton sheets twisted and damp from my dreaming.

Smoothing back my hair, I sucked in a deep breath of briny air from the open window and determined never to close my eyes again. Not to sleep, not ever.

She had been in my dream again. Her – the ghost who would not leave me alone. I had been walking in a strange town, its ancient walls high around me, my feet leading me through a warren of narrow streets. Like all the dreams she'd favoured me in, it was night, dark with no glimmer of a friendly moon like the one I'd woken to, the one who spun silver into Violet's dark hair beside me, made my breath calm, allowed me to swallow down the scream I'd woken to.

Usually when I'd dreamed of the ghost woman, she'd been little more than a shadow in a doorway, something I'd look out a window and know was there, always there, but distant still. Unspeaking, unreaching, merely there.

Not this night, however.

This night, Violet and I had come home to our new French *appartement* with a spring in our step, our bellies filled with good food, and a bottle of red wine in Violet's hand. Which we proceeded to drink from two of the newly beloved Mme Martin's glasses, sitting nude upon the soft sheets of our new bed, toasting our first night together in our new home.

The wine had heightened our optimism, and our desire, until the deep red Cabernet was put aside in favour of the sweetness of flesh, of the honey taste of our desire. We made love at first while laughing, and then again, more seriously, our eyes only on each other's gaze, as though we were each making promises to the other, to love and honour, to hold always.

And then the dream, ripping me from the night's soft hold, taking me further and further into the warren of stone streets, the buildings on either side leaning inwards at me.

She was there, my ghost, on my heels. No matter how often I ducked into a dark alley, how often I turned left, then right, then right then left, she was there behind me as though some grotesque shadow, or dashing out at me from an ink-dark doorway, until I was running, flinging terrified glances behind me always to see her right there, and I ran faster while her reaching fingertips grazed the air at the back of my neck.

Then finally, the scream that woke me, tearing from my lungs in my dream. In the moonlit room, it was still lodged in my throat, and Violet slept on, not woken by my terror.

I sat in the bed, sweat cooling on my bare skin, and tried to find the meaning in the dream. It had been haunting me – and yes, I intend the pun – since I was a child. Since, more or less, I realised now, staring out at the moon, my grandmother had told me the sad story of Vivi Madden, the artist who died in a mental asylum.

I got out of bed, and strode into the sitting room, going to the window and leaning panting against the glass. It was true – I had been having the dream since then. The two things were related; they had to be. I squeezed my eyes shut, thinking about it, trying to reason it out.

Was Violet the ghost in my dream? That would make sense, I thought. But I shook my head and rested it against the glass, ignoring my pale reflection. Violet was a dark will-o-wisp, but I was sure she wasn't the ghostly figure in my dreams. It was more an impression than anything else, I acknowledged, but the ghost was lighter, had lighter hair. More like mine than Violet's.

With a groan, I pushed away from the window. It was no use. I didn't know what it meant, this dream I kept having.

I'd told my grandmother about it once, and she'd been fascinated, laughing and telling me it was a past life making itself felt in this one. I'd laughed too, then, although not in the same way. I didn't believe in past lives. Things like that were the province of my grandmother and her cronies, discussed in reverent, hushed tones as they drank their cups of tea and upended them on their saucers, peering at the random patterns the leaves made. I didn't have time for all that nonsense.

'Fran!' There was an edge of fright to Violet's voice.

'It's all right, love,' I said, walking back into the room and smiling at her sitting there in the silvered light from the window, the blankets pooled in her lap. 'I just needed some water.'

She patted the bed beside her and I climbed in, drawing the sheets over the both of us. She curled into me like a warm kitten and I wrapped myself around her.

'I was afraid you were gone,' she mumbled, barely awake.

'I'm right here, my darling,' I said, holding her tight, listening to her breathing deepen again into sleep.

And it was true. I was right there.

But what if it didn't last?

How well I hid all this from Violet, I don't know. What I do know is that we settled in to our new life together during the day, Violet going off to work in the café each afternoon, and coming home face flushed with laughter, her eyes dancing as she poured wine and told me stories of the people she'd met that day, standing in the late sun, hands drawing pictures in the air, – and me, I was perfectly busy too, scouring the town for fittings for the shop, making list upon list of books I wanted to stock.

If anyone had seen those lists, I would have had a great deal of questions to answer. Always having had a good memory, it served me doubly well now, as I scrawled in a notebook all the names of authors writing in the beginning years of the twentieth century, and the names and dates of their books.

Virginia Woolfe – The Voyage out 1915, Mrs Dalloway 1925...
D H Lawrence – Sons and Lovers 1913, Women in Love 1920...

Violet wrote to her step-mother and her father's solicitor wrote to her. Then there was money, and the shop stopped being an empty room where the dust spun in lazy eddies, and became a real thing, and I walked amongst the shelves shaking my head in dizzy disbelief, touching the first editions of all my favourite writers, the books newly bound and smelling of fresh ink and paper under my fingers.

Violet spent her mornings painting, and every now and then I would find some pretext to dash up the stairs to our flat, and I would stand in the doorway of the little room she used as a studio, watching the small frown of concentration that crept into being between her dark brows, and I would feel a wash of contentment so strong it would threaten to buckle my knees.

And behind it would come a wave of panic to send me back down the stairs to the shop, where I would try thrusting it away in the pages of a newly-arrived book, or by talking to one of the browsing customers. They usually bought too, those customers, and within a month of opening, we were already gaining a reputation for stocking the all the most popular books – usually just before they became popular. My knowledge of the future came in handy.

It also terrified me. My lady ghost stalked me through the narrow streets of my dreams every night and I woke from them feeling ever more tenuous a grip on reality.

Because which was reality?

The more I thought on it, the less I could decide. I scratched at the lines on my palm until they became red and infected, and Violet took my hand in hers and dabbed salve on it every day until it healed, looking at me as she did so with troubled green eyes.

'You are still here,' she told me, and took to telling me every day as morning woke us with the scents and sounds of Nice. 'You are still here.'

She had stopped being afraid of me disappearing at the same time as the terror of it grew in me like a dark canker. I could feel it gnawing at the edges of my mind.

Sometimes on a quiet day, I would stand in the shop and close my eyes, reaching tentatively into the darkness behind my eyelids, probing in it for a creaking doorway behind which would be a hospital room, lights dimmed, grey machines still beeping, and me – lying motionless in the bed, my heartbeat a spiking and dipping green line on the display next to the head of the bed, and in my pale and drawn face my closed eyes would be moving in an ongoing and vivid dream.

Then I would shake myself back into a blinking survey of the shop, the dark shelving, the goose down armchairs, usually filled with a selection of absorbed readers, and on one of the walls, a selection of glowing paintings by Violet. I would stare at them and when that didn't work, I would go upstairs and find Violet, touching her lightly on the shoulder so that she turned to me and took my face in her hands, smearing paint on my cheeks, her lips warm against mine, tasting of berries and coffee, and as always, she smelt of night-flowering orchids. I would breathe her scent in, concentrate on her touch, and nod at her words.

'You are still here, my love,' she would tell me. Then she would stroke my hair, and press a kiss to my forehead, and I would nod and go back downstairs to wait until the night and the dream and the morning when perhaps I would wake up in a hospital bed instead of in Violet's arms.

CHAPTER THIRTY-FOUR

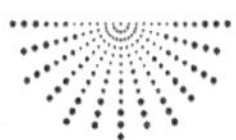

Violet was working behind Monsieur Dubois's counter, serving coffee and pastries as if it was second nature, and I had the afternoon off, the shop safely in the hands of a young man of uncertain health who would probably have been happy to work for books rather than francs. He spent most of his wages right there in the shop.

I stood outside the door of the bookshop and waved at Violet across the road. She blew me a kiss, and I waved again, before turning to follow the street up the hill towards my favourite purveyor of second hand books. Yes, I know it's strange to spend your free time in a bookshop when your working hours are also spent in one, but I'd decided to stock a small selection of used volumes, since many of my customers quite obviously had barely enough money to clothe and feed themselves let alone buy books.

But that is by the by – part of the minutiae of life that I was so in love with. Still am, as possibly you can tell.

The seasons had turned, summer leaving us long behind in favour of winter with its cold winds that blew through the streets like a cruel trick. I tried not to think about the men dying in the freezing mud of the Front, and I tried not to think about the image of myself lying in a hospital bed. I tried not to think of anything except Violet, our life together, our books, paintings, friends, love-making.

Chin tucked down in my collar, I hadn't been watching where I was walking – hadn't thought I'd needed to, I knew the way so well. Through the old town, its winding streets familiar now, to arrive to hear Monsieur Severn's cheery greeting and mug of hot coffee while we stood heads bent together talking books.

When I looked up, I didn't recognise the street I was on, unless I'd fallen asleep somewhere along my walk and arrived in my very own dream. I looked back the way I'd come, but the street showed me only blank buildings, leaning towards me, blocking out all but a sliver of cold white sky. I shivered, turned to continue, my shoes clattering on the cobblestones.

I was being silly. I was not in my dream – could I not see the sky? Was it not daylight? This was not my dream, and there would be no ghost behind me.

Not that I turned to look. I knew better than that. This was simply a part of town I'd not been in before, that I'd wandered into by mistake. I had, after all, been walking without paying attention, lost in amongst all the words in my head, as usual.

A snippet of a poem wound itself around my thoughts, and I whispered its words and shivered again.

> Because I could not stop for Death –
> He kindly stopped for me –

The Carriage held but just Ourselves –
And Immortality.

We slowly drove – He knew no haste
And I had put away
My labor and my leisure too,
For His Civility –

We passed the School, where Children
     strove
At Recess – in the Ring –
We passed the Fields of Gazing Grain –
We passed the Setting Sun –

Or rather – He passed Us –
The Dews drew quivering and Chill –
For only Gossamer, my Gown –
My Tippet – only Tulle –

We paused before a House that seemed
A Swelling of the Ground –
The Roof was scarcely visible –
The Cornice – in the Ground –

Since then – 'tis Centuries – and yet
Feels shorter than the Day
I first surmised the Horses' Heads
Were toward Eternity –

Emily Dickenson. Not one I would recite under the bedcovers for Violet. Not one with which to woo a beautiful woman, although we stocked a volume or two of her verse in the shop. Maybe that's why it popped unasked into my head, but it didn't feel like it. It felt like a portent. *Because I Could Not Stop For Death.*

I confess I screamed when the hand touched my elbow. Like a ten-year-old girl, which was another irrelevant thought – a quote from an old Doctor Who episode. He travelled in time too, and space, but definitely time.

'I did not mean to frighten you,' the person attached to the hand attached to my arm said, although it wasn't reassuring in the slightest. I looked at the woman, trying to regain my breath and feeling unravelled, scattered.

More so than usual. Which by then, was saying a lot.

'Well you did,' I said. 'You startled me.'

She bared her teeth in a grin and let go of my arm. I rubbed automatically at my elbow, where her fingers had felt sharp enough to puncture the skin.

'Who are you?' I asked.

She shook her head, pulling a dark shawl closer around herself. I tried to decide how old she was – fifty? A hundred?

'That's not the right question,' she said, and laughed.

'I don't understand.'

'That much, my dear, is obvious. I can tell just from looking at you.'

I stared at her a long, silent moment. We stood in a doorway, and there was a sign hammered to the door behind her, faded gold letters on a deep blue background.

Madame Celestine – fortune telling, divination.

I looked back at her in growing disquiet. Took a deep breath.

'What is the right question, then?' I asked.

That made her smile again, and a moment later, her hand was back on my arm, the fingers like hooks, and she drew me in through the doorway, pulling me along.

I have to tell you, I went with her. I couldn't help it.

'Sit,' she said, pointing to a chair placed at a round table, just the sort of table you'd expect from a lady in her realm of employment, draped with a heavy maroon velvet cloth, a cloudy crystal ball taking pride of place in the centre.

I sat.

Madame Celestine sat. Held out her hand.

I placed my own in it, palm up, the right one, the one with the twin lifelines. She leaned over them, brushing my fingers out of the way.

'What do they mean?' I asked past the lump in my throat.

'Two life lines,' she said. 'Is it not obvious?'

I confessed it wasn't. Or rather, it was, but not exactly what it meant. In practical terms, so to speak.

'Not completely,' was what I told her.

She stayed bent over my hand, her head slowly shaking from side to side. 'I have heard of this,' she said, almost to herself. 'But this is the first time I have seen it with my own eyes.'

I almost pulled my hand away. 'But what *is* it? What does it *mean*?' Not precisely what I wanted to ask, but as close as I could get without a lot of awkwardly unbelievable explanations.

She still raised her old black eyes in surprise. 'How is it that you do not know its meaning?' she asked, then blinked and lowered her gaze to my hand again. 'Two lives,' she murmured.

I sat in her small space, more cave than sitting room, close, dark, the crystal chandelier above us swaying ever so slightly with dim lights twinkling in the most odd manner.

'Tell me what to do,' I said, the words tumbling from my mouth before I could stop them.

Her eyes regarded me, my palm lying loosely in hers. 'How many lives do you have?' she asked.

I swallowed. 'Two.'

'And how many do you want?'

'Just the one.'

She smiled, her face creasing. 'Do you know which one?'

Did I? Yes. I nodded.

Madame Celestine folded my hand up and straightened. 'Then you must choose it.'

I blinked at her in the dim room. 'I have,' I said. 'I mean…I don't know what you mean.'

An elaborate shrug lifted her shoulders. 'You are haunted by your other life. Therefore you must banish it.'

She was speaking riddles. Or so I thought for a moment. Sitting back, I looked at her.

'I dream of being haunted,' I said. 'Every night. A woman follows me. A ghost.' My hands, back in my lap, plucked at the thick fabric of my skirt. 'I don't know what she wants.'

The fortune teller laughed. 'How is it possible that you do not know?'

'I don't even know who she is! Let alone what she wants.' I shivered, even in the over-warm room that smelled of coal and old fabric.

She shook her head at me. 'I do not believe you are this stupid. You – who have travelled so far!'

That made me shake my own head, hard and angry. 'I didn't choose this,' I said. 'I woke up here, and that's all I know. Everything else is a mystery.'

'All of life is a mystery.'

I wanted to slam my fists onto the table. She knew things I needed to know and here she was being cryptic. It was the same thing that had bothered me even as a child about my grandmother's cronies – they dressed everything in mystery.

'Everything is part of the great mystery,' she said, black eyes watching me like a bird's.

I stood. 'This is all bullshit,' I said, lapsing into my native twenty-first century language. I leaned over the table. 'Look, here's what I know. I had a life there. Then there was an accident. I woke up here.' I bit my lip. 'Now what I need to know is if I'm still alive there. If this is nothing but a dream I'm going to wake up from.'

'Of course you still are alive there – do you not haunt yourself?'

I stopped breathing, hands fisted on the table top, the crystal ball misty and glowing in the low light from the fire.

'What?'

She cocked her head to the side, her thick hair bundled loosely on her shoulders, black streaked through with grey. But she didn't say anything.

'I cannot live in two places at once,' I said at last, my voice low, strangled.

We looked at each other for a long moment. Then Madame Celestine, the fortune teller who seemed to know impossible things about myself, licked her lips and made a wide smile.

'Then you must choose,' she said. 'Choose which you want.'

'I have chosen!' I howled, straightening, clawing at my hair with hands with too many lifelines.

'Then why does your other life still follow you around?'

I stared at her. 'Are you referring to my dream?'

She raised an eyebrow and said nothing.

'Good god,' I said, closing my eyes. 'Can't you just tell me what to do?'

There was a rustling of skirts and when I opened my eyes, the old woman was standing, walking toward the door. 'Choose,' she said. 'Choose which one you want.'

'I have,' I said, tired, swept along behind her even though I wanted more answers. 'I have,' I repeated.

The front door was open onto the street and she gestured for me to leave, a smile on her face. 'Then do what must be done.'

Shaking my head, I stepped outside. It was raining, a slow, unhurried drumming of water against the cobblestones.

'You're not going to tell me how, are you?' I said, turning back towards her, but she was gone, the door closed. The sign was still there though, gold letters on a blue background. I reached out and touched them for a moment, then turned back to the street, stepping out into the rain, hunching over into my coat, ducking my head down and wondering exactly what it was I wasn't seeing.

CHAPTER THIRTY-FIVE

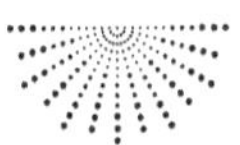

She was so beautiful it hurt. Shifting gently onto my side, I tried not to wake her. There was little moonlight from the window to touch her cheek, but I could still trace the beloved outline of Violet's face upon the pillow, even if I could not see the long, dark lashes, the warm rose of her lips. I wanted to touch her. I didn't want to wake her.

She moved slightly, slipping a hand up to curl under her chin and I wanted so very much to lean down and press a kiss to the paler shadow of her cheek. Instead, I picked up a strand of the dark hair she kept threatening to cut off – like I'd done to my own, grabbing a pair of Mme Martin's dressmaking shears I'd found in the drawer of one of the large tables downstairs, and hacking off the entire length of it so that it curled rather dubiously below my ears. But I liked Violet's long hair, I liked the silken feel of it on my bare skin, and I liked to hold it as I was now, a strand pressed between thumb and finger.

Her lips moved in the dimness of the room, and I wondered what she dreamed of. Did she dream of the painting that sat half-finished on her easel? I thought it might turn out to be my favourite yet, Violet painting a self-portrait, her green eyes magical even on canvas.

Or did she dream of serving warm croissants and hot coffee in the afternoons? A job she'd kept even though the bookshop was up and running, earning enough to keep the both of us. It was true though that she sat more often with the artists and writers who came into Monsieur Dubois' establishment than did she serve them. And often would she lead them later, coffee still in hand, across the street to our shop, and there they would ensconce themselves in the deep, shabby armchairs, smoking and talking and every now and then jumping up to snatch a book off a shelf, reading out loud a passage, a poem. It had become the place to be, to gather, just as Haven for Books had been back at home.

I rolled back over and stared up at the ceiling. Home. I'd just called Haven for Books, Bath, 2016, home. Was it habit? Or was it some veiled desire?

Habit, I whispered to the shadows of the room. Just habit. Here was home.

But there was home too, a traitorous voice hissed at me. Bronny, our friends. Stephen who worked for me, who pounced on each box of new books with an excitement that made me hope that he never wanted to move on to bigger and better things than my shop. My customers, who came for the books, the coffee, the muffins, the book groups, the social meetings.

Violet huffed out a soft breath next to me. Here was home. Here was another bookshop, new friends, Violet's artists, writers, some of whom I knew more about the course of their careers than they themselves did, a fact which still thrilled me whenever I saw them push the door open and step into the shop. I'll be stocking his book in two years, I'd think to myself. Hers in six months.

More than any of that though, was Violet herself.

I loved her.

She was home.

If I had to choose, then of course I chose her. She shifted again beside me, and a small, soft hand patted the mattress next to me, found me, and still sleeping, she moved closer, pressing her warmth against me, her hand tucking itself under my breast.

I would not live without Violet. Her of the gleaming green eyes, the mock-guilty looks when I discovered she'd taken up smoking again, Violet of the easy passion, arms flung around my neck, clothes shed with enthusiastic abandon, her flesh hot, needy, giving. Violet, who had my heart.

The thought of losing her was what had been making me afraid. I'd already made my choice. There was, in fact, no choice at all.

What had the fortune teller said? *Why does your other life follow you around?*

Impossible that she had been referring to my dream. I had been having that dream since I was a child. I had only been here in 1916 for a matter of months.

I rubbed at my hand. Those twin lifelines – they had been there, curving across the flesh of my palm since I was born. I squeezed my eyes shut and listened to the soft rhythm of Violet's breath.

A mystery. It was all so much of a mystery. My mind strained to make sense of it, but in the end, the fortune teller's words were all I could hear.

You must choose. You must banish the one you do not want.

What did that mean? Did that mean one of me had to die?

I sat up, the thought so sudden, shocking, that I did not think what I was doing.

'What is the matter?' Violet asked, her voice clogged with sleep.

My heart thumped too loudly. Picking up her hand, I kissed the knuckles. 'Nothing my love. I am thirsty, is all. Go back to sleep.'

She made a sound of snuffling agreement, and curled up against me again, her hand hooking around my thigh this time. Gently, I moved it, slid regretfully from the warmth of her body, and felt around in the dimness for my dressing gown.

I turned when I got to the doorway of our bedroom, of the room we slept together in each night, our bodies pressed against each other, arms and legs entwined. I could see the spread of her dark hair against the pillow and for a moment I wanted to go back and bury my face in it, breathe in the scent of the soap she used to clean it, then press my lips to the sweet hollow of her neck, feel the dancing flutter of her pulse,

'I love you,' I whispered. 'So very, very much.'

There was no reply except for a soft snuffling, but then, I did not want one. I wanted her to sleep on in the soft bed, my place beside her cooling while I did what I had to.

Walking into the sitting room, I realised I'd decided for certain what it was I had to do. As soon as the thought had hit me, I'd recognised it.

One of me had to die. Oh, I know how it sounds - melodramatic, but on that dark night, with the wind blowing a cold rain against the window, and underneath that, the distant wash of the sea, it didn't seem far-fetched at all. In fact, it seemed invincibly true.

Twenty-first century Fran Madden, lying in her hospital bed, attached to all manner of uncomfortable tubing, those machines counting off each measured breath and heartbeat, had to die.

So that I could live. Twentieth century Fran Madden, in love with the vibrant painter Vivi Madden; she was the one who had to live. I needed to be here, Violet needed me. Together we had saved her from the mental hospital, from the slow death that waited her there, but I knew it would always remain a spectre for her. Being together saved her from it again and again every day – and it saved me too, from the loneliness I'd never wanted to admit to, back in my upstairs flat eating Thai food standing in front of the fridge in the kitchen, from the feeling I'd always had but never understood of not quite being in the right place at the right time.

Well, now I was in the right place at the right time, and I needed to ensure that I stayed here. I could not live anymore with the thought that I might wake up again back in the wrong life.

I would not. It was eating me alive. It was causing Violet pain. It cost her every time she had to tell me that I was still with her. Because I knew too, that she feared my leaving more than anything else.

Twenty-first century Fran Madden had to die.

I chose, and I chose Violet. I chose life with her.

A gust of wind rattled the glass in the window, and I

looked around, thinking of how to do it. How to knock myself out so that I could do what had to be done.

The risks were high, I knew that – to knock myself out, there were no guarantee that I would wake again. And what did I intend to do once I'd achieved unconsciousness?

I had no idea. I only could think that this was how it all started, and it was how it could all be ended. Madame Celestine had said it could be done, and I discovered that I believed her.

But how to do it? How to achieve a blow to the head that would not kill me? People knocked their heads all the time – all I would need was a few seconds of unconsciousness, surely. But people did that by accident. It was a completely different proposition to do it purposefully.

The room offered no clues as to how I might achieve my desperate objective. There was the blue velvet sofa, black in the small light from the window. The table where we sat to eat our supper. The small occasional table piled with books, and one of Violet's scarves draped over them.

I clenched my fists and took a deep breath. I was being stupid, melodramatic, caught up with urgency, and I was missing the truth.

There was no need to knock myself out. To try to do so would only end up with me with some head injury, Violet waking up in an hour or two, finding the bed empty next to her and coming trailing out of the bedroom to find me, unconscious on the floor. Or dead.

I turned away from the table with the books and the scarf too, and the thought that I could wrap the scarf around my neck, pull it tight somehow, cutting off my supply of oxygen, until I passed out...

My mouth dried, and I trembled, standing there in the dim room, chastising myself. Wasn't the answer obvious? Hadn't I been seeing the ghost all my life – in my dreams?

Creeping back into the bedroom on silent cat feet, I went around the bed, to the little table at Violet's side. When I picked up the box of sleeping powders, it was with only the merest rustle. Violet sighed in her sleep, and her hand sought me again, only to find my pillow and rest there. It made me smile, to see her searching for me in her sleep, a dark curl over her closed eyes, and it made me more determined to do what had to be done.

I backed out of the room and went to our little kitchen, clutching the box in a white-knuckled hand. The water splashed into the glass, and on my hand. It was cold. I stirred in the powder, and downed it, standing there looking at the sofa.

I'd lie down on the sofa, I decided. Violet would wake in a while, and come looking for me, but I didn't need long, I was sure of it. If I went back to the bed and lay back down next to her warmth and seeking hand, I might wake her sooner, and I needed to do this. Needed to get this done.

A cushion under my head, and a light blanket over me, and I closed my eyes, ready. Violet's sleeping powder, which she used only occasionally, seeped through my system and pulled me under.

I let myself go.

CHAPTER THIRTY-SIX

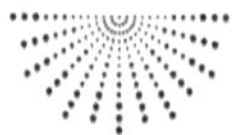

I was on the street.

Not the street outside the flat I shared with Violet in Nice. Not the one outside Haven for Books back in Bath either. This was the street from my dream – I knew it immediately.

The same street, the same buildings crowding in on me. And a moment later, I saw her, staring at me from a shadowed doorway, not much more than a shadow herself, but a familiar one. She stepped out and a hidden streetlamp flickered on, bathing her in a sickly yellow light.

She was no stranger. She was not Violet, or anyone else but myself, and looking at her, I realised I should have known that all along. Here was the 1916 version of myself, who had been me all along in some manner that I would never understand, a placeholder of sorts, and now symbol of my twin lives, beckoning me to cement my destiny, to choose between them, chasing me down because to live two lives at once is against the natural order of all we know.

She raised a hand, that ghostly me, and this time I did not run, but moved toward her on legs that felt unsubstantial. I was untethered from flesh and time, adrift in this strange dream world. Madame Celestine laughed at me in my head and I felt all the pieces come together.

My ghost was moving, fading back into the doorway, and I hurried after her, not wanting to lose sight of her for once, reaching out to touch her this time, instead of the other way around.

Except I did not touch her, stopping instead to look in shock at the doors she had led me to. My hand dropped, then went to press against my mouth, stifling the cry before it was born.

Two doors.

To the left, the door opened onto the bedroom I shared with Violet, and I saw her curled into a tight, beautiful knot, one hand flat against the sheet where I had lain only minutes before.

I started instinctively toward her.

Then stopped, eyes drawn to the other door, to the room behind it, and there it was – what I had always suspected, from the very first day. Fran Madden, the 2016 version, lying in a hospital bed, a green blanket drawn neatly up over her chest, a chest that moved steadily in and out with air artificially pumped in through a tube in her mouth. I could hear the quiet whoosh of it. In, then out. In, then out.

There were the machines, just as I'd imagined them, green lines spiking across the monitors, a soft hum, a quiet beep. My skin was the colour of swiss cheese, eyes closed, hands limp outside the blanket.

Bronny sat in a chair beside the bed, and my heart cried out to see her there, and I wanted to dash forward to touch her, to crush her in my arms, then hold her and stare at her. She looked tired, drawn, and I blinked, looked at Violet asleep in the other room, then back at Bronny, wondering how much time had gone by there, and how often she sat there like that.

There was a ring on her finger and I smiled. She and Louise had married. I was glad.

A gossamer touch on my shoulder and I glanced around to see the ghost woman staring at me. Her eyes were definitely my eyes, and I read the message there easily. It was time to live just the one life, and I had unfinished business to take care of. 1916 me couldn't take over my twenty first century life; she wasn't real enough, only designed to hold my place until I could come. I had conjured her, sitting on that ottoman in front of Vivi Madden's painting, and because time is not a linear thing, my conjuring filled all the spaces necessary to make it real.

I smiled at her, unafraid now, not understanding how I'd ever been frightened of her at all and nodded my head. There was no choice, not if I did not want to leave Violet on her own.

I slipped into the room, padding on ghostly feet of my own across the shiny floor and over to the bed. This would only take a moment, now that I knew what I needed to do.

Bending slightly, I brushed my lips against Bronny's burnished hair and touched her lightly on the shoulder. She looked up suddenly, the magazine she'd been reading sliding from numb, startled fingers.

She'd felt me. I watched her eyes turn to the figure in the bed, still unmoving except for the artificial breathing.

'Fran?' she whispered. 'Are you there?'

'Bronny,' I said. 'I love you dearly.'

'Fran?'

Slipping past her, I surveyed the medical equipment, trying to grasp the best way to do this. A glance back at the doorway and there was my dream ghost, staring at me, her eyes liquid and serious. She blinked, waiting, and I turned back to the machine I'd always imagined being there, counting the even thump thump of my heart. Then there was one that forced air in and out of me. That was the mostly likely one, I decided, and quickly, without any hesitation, I wrapped my ghostly hand around the tubes and yanked them free.

They did not come free. They did not dangle uselessly all of a sudden. But something happened to the other machine, the one that counted heartbeats. It counted for a little while longer, then screamed a warning into the room, the green line falling flat across the monitor. I waved a hand at it and it went silent, leaving me only to look at Bronny's panicked face.

'Hush, my dearest friend,' I whispered in her ear. 'Be happy.'

I left then, gliding past her on my ghostly feet, ignoring the body in the bed, air still in reality being forced uselessly in and out of its lungs even while blood stopped flowing through its veins and the flesh cooled between the sheets.

My other ghostly self met me outside the door, a smile on her face, and when I turned for one last curious glance, the door to the hospital room was gone, a bricked wall in its place.

Which left Violet. She was still there, and I breathed a sigh of relief despite being sure she would be. I moved to step through to her, to go to the bed and lean over her where she slept, to place a kiss upon that brow and wind a strand of that dark hair around a finger. To recite a poem into her sleeping ears. Yeats would do perfectly.

> I whispered, 'I am too young,'
> And then, 'I am old enough';
> Wherefore I threw a penny
> To find out if I might love.
> 'Go and love, go and love, young man,
> If the lady be young and fair.'
> Ah, penny, brown penny, brown penny,
> I am looped in the loops of her hair.
> O love is the crooked thing,
> There is nobody wise enough
> To find out all that is in it,
> For he would be thinking of love
> Till the stars had run away
> And the shadows eaten the moon.
> Ah, penny, brown penny, brown penny,
> One cannot begin it too soon.

Ahand on my arm stopped me in my tracks. I had forgotten my ghost. Was there something else I was supposed to do? I wanted nothing more of it, just for it to be done. I was good old practical Fran. I liked to-do lists and sorting books upon a shelf. I had a romantic side, that ran to poetry and Violet, but I wanted no more of this mystery. I wanted a normal life. With Violet.

She smiled at me, holding me there with her feather-touch upon my arm and I looked at her with an ill-tempered question in my eyes. I wanted to get back to Violet. I'd made my choice. It was finally over.

Then she shifted, my ghost, and apparently there was one more thing that had to be done, and it was, in a movement faster than I could see.

I felt it though, felt her step into me, fit herself inside me as though I were a glove she'd been waiting to draw on, as she was, since she'd been part of me all along. Part of my own soul conjured separately to show me the way.

I swallowed, blinked, and then when I opened my eyes, I was gazing into another's.

'Fran! What are you doing out here?' They were Violet's eyes, wide and dark in the half-light. She reached out a hand and touched the thin blanket draped over me where I lay on the sofa, her brows knitting together in confusion. 'What are you doing, Fran?'

I shook my head and sat, pushing my feet onto the floor and taking her hands. 'Help me up,' I said. 'The cold has made me stiff.'

She did, and without a further word, leading me back to

bed, climbing into the nest of blankets with me and wrapping herself around me to warm my chilled skin.

'What has happened?' she asked after a long moment. 'Something has happened.'

'I died, Violet,' I said, then winced at the melodrama of it. 'I mean…'

But she was sitting up, reaching past me to light the candle on the bedside table. Her face sprang into focus in the sudden warm light and I gazed upon it.

'I love you,' I told her.

She blinked at me. 'I love you too. What do you mean, you died?'

'I dreamed,' I said, opting not to tell her about the whole suffocation thing. 'I dreamed that I met my ghost and that she was actually me, the 1916 Fran, who was always actually me…'

'This is the ghost who has been haunting you in your dreams since you were a child? She was 1916 Fran?' Violet interrupted sharply.

I nodded, reaching out to touch her cheek, her hair, aware that I was smiling at her like an idiot. She ignored me.

'Carry on.'

'She took me to a place, where there were two rooms.' I looked around at our bed. 'One room was this one, with you asleep under the covers. The other was a hospital room.'

'A hospital room?'

'In 2016. Although, depending on how long I'd been lying in that hospital bed, I suppose it could have been 2017.' Just like 1917 was approaching here, Christmas drawing nearer in a surprisingly neat circle.

'And?' There was impatience in Violet's eyes. A touch of something else. Fear, perhaps. I stroked her cheek again.

'So I stepped into the hospital room and stopped the machines in there that were keeping me alive.' I didn't mention Bronny. There was no need.

Violet's mouth opened, but she was speechless.

'I don't think I was ever supposed to live two lives,' I said. 'How can you? Torn between two places, like that?'

'So you chose?' Violet's question was a whisper. 'You chose me?'

'Of course,' I said, and this time when I touched her, I drew her down into my arms and kissed that white cheek of hers. 'There was never any choice, really. I fell in love with you the first time I saw you.'

She giggled. 'You did not. You fell in lust.'

My turn to laugh. 'Perhaps, but it was strong, whichever it was.'

'I fell in love with you with the first poem you recited for me.'

I played with her hair. *Looped in the loops of her hair.* 'Do you remember which it was?'

'Of course,' she said, offended. 'She walks in beauty like the night.'

'Of cloudless climes and starry skies; and all that's best of dark and bright meet in her aspect and her eyes.' I kissed her. 'But I don't believe that was when you fell in love with me.'

Violet's eyes were bright at the teasing, dancing in the candlelight when she looked up at me. 'Perhaps not. Perhaps instead, it was after we'd made love for the first time, and I realised that when you touched me, you somehow managed to touch all of me.'

I stared at her in silence.

She smiled, dipped delicate fingertips to my breastbone. 'So now you'll always be here?' she asked, returning to the original conversation.

I nodded, throat thick with sudden tears. 'Yes,' I said. 'Always.'

'Because there is no other you, now?'

I nodded.

She looked at me for a long moment, then ducked her head to my shoulder and wrapped herself closer around me.

'Thank you,' she whispered.

'I wouldn't be anywhere else,' I said.

CHAPTER THIRTY-SEVEN

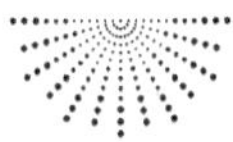

There's really only one more thing to tell you all, I expect, to round out this story of mine. Do you believe any of it? If it helps, I do not expect that you will. I am an old lady now, and the twentieth century has matured right along with me.

The first world war ended, and everyone celebrated, then the second reared its head and we all suffered, Violet and I still living in Nice, which was occupied this time, first by the Italians, then by the Germans. Those are years I prefer not to think upon. I knew they were coming, but history has its own momentum, and I am but one small anomaly in the great stream of it.

Of course, those were the big things, the years the whole world marks upon their calendars. We note them, we record versions of them in our history books, and teach them to our children, but they are not the real things that make up a life. Those are moments, dozens, hundreds of them, fleeting and magical. They are for me, the way Violet would come searching me out every day, a wicked, delighted smile on her beautiful face, showing off the smudge of paint that was invariably on her cheek.

They are the way her skin looked in the moonlight, pale alabaster, her dark, exotic hair hanging down her back, then later, when she finally did cut it, curling in sassy little question marks around her ears. It was the way she would touch her lips to mine, to my skin, the way we would make love as though we were dancing to music only we could hear.

It was the way she spoke with her hands, waving them about, her whole body animated as she debated and argued with her friends. I would watch her, forgetting to follow the actual conversation, so caught up in enjoying her obvious delight for life. And she would catch me looking, wide green eyes seeking me out and smiling at me, sharing the love, and the secret that we both held – that without each other, we would not have survived.

We survived. We thrived.

Violet painted, I bought books, and our shop became quite the hub for writers and artists – just the sort of community Violet had dreamed of way back at the beginning. We lived together as wife and wife, and none of our friends thought anything of it.

We went to Paris too, and met Gertrude Stein and Alice B. Toklas – I didn't manage to unstick my tongue much during that conversation, but Violet revelled in it, their interest in Picasso mutual. We met so many people I had only read about in my previous life that it seemed a complete fantasy, and it became a running joke between Violet and I that she would sidle up to me and deliver a sharp pinch to my elbow.

I wouldn't have exchanged any of it for the world.

Then came the day that begins the last part of my story.

Early spring, 1964, and we are no longer in our flat above the bookshop and we are no longer young things full of love and vigour. The love has not lessened, but we are no longer young, and though perhaps still vigorous in mind, our bodies stiffen and slow more each day.

'Violet?' I asked, coming across her on my way out of the kitchen, a red and white checked tea towel slung over my shoulder.

It is funny the details you remember.

She turned to me from her pose gazing at one of her paintings on the wall. I recognised the way she stood, one long finger pressed against her lips as though she had to force herself not to think out loud.

'Do you think it is time we did something about this?' she asked and flicked the finger at the painting.

I came and stood beside her, breakfast on the table in our snug little kitchen forgotten. I'd made eggs benedict, and they would be congealing on the plates, but looking up at the painting, I forgot all about them.

'Well?' Violet prompted, and I turned my gaze to her. She was still thin; I never had managed to get much in the way of padding on her bones. Her metabolism was as fast as her racing mind. She was also still beautiful, even in her seventies. Perhaps it is just love that makes one think their wife is lovely even when time has pressed itself into grooves and creases on their skin, but if so, it is still truthful.

Violet tugged my gaze back to the painting.

'She will be twenty-three this year.'

I nodded. My grandmother. Born 1941, the war just warming up, her father already left to fight, the baby and her mother left to hope for the best in Bristol. We'd thought of her a great deal over the last twenty years as she grew up, trying to figure out how it was all going to work.

'I think it's time,' Violet announced and staring at the painting I nodded again.

'Yes,' I said on a sigh. 'You're right of course. We're not getting any younger, and she's getting older…'

'And right now, at last, we know where she is.'

I laughed. 'Run off to Glastonbury with a hippie called Ronnie Madden.'

'From whom we get our name,' Violet said, leaning into me in the way she always did, to make it easier for me to put my arm around her. She had taken to using the name Madden when we moved to Nice. Not only when signing her paintings, but in everyday life.

I looked up at the painting on the wall, where it had hung since we'd moved here after the second world war, and thought about that long-ago day when she had given it to me as a gift, telling me to fetch a pen so that she could sign it for me. It was the painting that had started everything.

Violet tilted her head so that it rested against mine and I kissed her hair, which had turned a stunning white sometime in her sixties, and which I thought as magical as it had been when it was the opposite.

'I'll book the tickets after breakfast,' I said, then grimaced. 'Which will be a cold and congealed mess now.'

Violet turned and plucked the tea towel off me. 'I'll make us something else,' she said. 'While you make the calls.' She pursed her lips. 'Are we going to take the ferry?'

My eyes widened in horror. Then narrowed at her twitching lips.

'For nostalgia's sake,' Violet said, making a good effort to keep a straight face. 'It'll be our first time back in England.'

I raised an eyebrow.

'I think we'll take an aeroplane instead,' I said. 'Which is better for my stomach. I remember how sick that crossing made me, even if you don't.' I pretended to grumble but found myself grinning and smacking a kiss on Violet's cheek instead.

She looked tickled pink and smiled widely at me. 'I'm excited,' she said, moving into the kitchen with me.

'You're always excited when we plan a trip.'

'Because we always have a wonderful time.' She flicked the tea towel at me. 'Now make those reservations while I cook for you.'

I did as I was told, laughing, knowing that cooking in Violet terms was toast and coffee. Like most couples, we'd settled over the years into a rhythm that suited us. I did most of the cooking (which was little because we enjoyed eating out so much) and Violet did most of the housekeeping (which was little, because part of that job involved hiring a woman to clean for us twice a week).

'How soon?' I called to her, holding the telephone receiver in my hand.

'Soon as possible,' Violet replied, looking up from the counter. 'I feel like we should do it sooner than later.' A small frown puckered her brow and I wanted to question it. But it cleared, and she spoke again. 'Now that we've thought of it, you see.'

Fifteen minutes later, and we had seats booked on a BUA flight from Paris to London. It meant a train trip to Paris, another good reason to do it soon, because my hips had taken to screaming at me a few hours into such a trip and I didn't anticipate that improving with age.

When I hung up the phone, Violet came and sat at the table with me, putting a fresh cup of coffee in front of me. We looked at each other, all jokes put aside for now.

'Do we know what we're going to tell her?' she asked.

I looked at Violet sitting across from me and thought about the painting, its tangled garden and startling blooms. The name on the back, the story my grandmother had told me of the painting.

'The same one she told me?' I suggested.

Violet's forehead crinkled. 'I'm not sure you ever told me exactly what that was.'

Entirely possible. In fact, I knew I hadn't. I'd let her know the gist of it, but back then – during the story you've been reading – we were busy doing what needed to be done, and then we were busy living, and now here we were, two old ladies, having to think about it all again.

'You're chewing on your lip,' Violet said, giving me a laser green look. 'You do that when you want to obfuscate matters.'

A sigh, but not a disgruntled one. 'You know me too well,' I said.

'I do,' she agreed. 'So tell me it, my love. The entire story, this time.'

And so I told her. The whole, tragic story of Vivi Madden, her short life, her dark and lonely death at her own hands in a mental institution.

CHAPTER THIRTY-EIGHT

'You have to tell her the same story she told you.' Violet's mouth was set in the obstinate line that meant she would brook no further argument. And I wasn't entirely sure she was wrong, either.

'I know,' I sighed.

Her eyes, the turbulent colour of the water we'd not too long ago flown over, narrowed at me. 'Then why have you been disagreeing with me the whole trip?'

I took her hand as we walked through the station, a porter trundling our suitcases behind us.

'Because I don't want to tell that story,' I said.

She shook her head. 'That makes no sense at all – and I should know, since it is about me, since it is me we are talking about.' Violet stopped walking abruptly and pressed her palm to my chest, a gesture we'd repeated throughout our long history.

'There is no retrospectively protecting either of us,' she said. 'You have to tell your grandmother the exact story she told you, or perhaps it will not work. Are you really willing to take that risk?'

I pressed my lips together. Violet squinted at me.

'Okay,' I said. Held my hands up. 'All right.'

She stared at me a moment longer, searching my face for well-known signs of rebellion, then nodded in satisfaction. 'Good,' she said. 'It's important. You know that. The we have lived together is at stake, all of it.'

'I know,' I said, and movement behind her caught my attention. 'Come on,' I whispered. 'The porter is looking at us like we're crazy.'

Violet laughed like a school girl. 'It was the grandmother quip,' she said. 'No one our age could possibly still have a grandmother alive!'

I totted up the numbers. 'Well, technically, it is possible.' I rechecked the numbers. 'Just.'

A nice roll of her eyes. 'Well, just don't mention that in this case the grandmother is forty something years younger than the grandchild. I don't see you ever convincingly explaining that one.'

That plastered a happy grin on my face, and we stepped outside into a blustery spring day in Glastonbury. The bemused porter leapt forward to open the door of the nearest taxi, and we tumbled in as best as our travel-weary bodies would allow.

I held Violet's hand tightly in mine and waited for it to all unfold.

There was little reason to hesitate the next day, and both Violet and I were too restless to do more than take a hurried breakfast in the morning before she passed me the wrapped painting, now framed of course, and watched me with serious eyes as I stepped out of the hotel and blinked back at her.

'Go on,' she said. 'It will be all right.'

I nodded and swallowed down the lump in my throat. Turned my steps towards the tiny bookshop where I knew my twenty-three-year-old grandmother worked while she waited for the birth of my mother.

It was the same shop that she would later own, after she had birthed her baby and kicked out her erstwhile husband, and I had to stop to catch my breath when I stepped through the door. For a moment it seemed as though time wavered around me, a fragile thing, more not-there than there.

'Can I help you?' A sudden voice at my elbow that made the whole disorientation thing even more pronounced. It had been – I added it up – forty-seven years since I'd heard that voice.

A hand cupped itself under my arm. 'You're looking very shaky,' my grandmother said. 'Here, come and sit down. I'll make you a cup of tea. You've turned white as a ghost!'

I made myself look at her, and was met with a clear, blue-eyed gaze that made me wobble further. The hand under my arm tightened.

'Let me take this too,' she said, reaching for the wrapped painting. I let it go. She smiled at me.

'You're the first customer of the day,' she said, leading me to the back of the room and the counter, then standing for a moment looking nonplussed. 'You know,' she said, 'we really could do with some comfy seating, don't you think?'

I nodded, tried out my voice, which came out as rusty as I'd feared it would. 'Customers would appreciate it. It would make them feel this was a nice place to spend some time.'

'And spend some money!' my grandmother crowed. 'I really must suggest that to Frank. He's the owner.' She brought out a stool from behind the counter, and I sank gratefully onto it, meeting her eyes with my shaky gaze.

'Thank you,' I said. 'Suzanne, isn't it?'

Her eyes widened, then her face knotted in a frown. 'Yes, it is,' she said. 'But how did you know that? Have we met?'

I ignored the question for the moment. Nodded at her rounded belly. 'When are you due?'

Her hands went automatically to the baby inside her, fluttering over it in the way I've noticed all pregnant women do.

'Only five weeks to go,' she said. 'Thank goodness. This one's a real feisty bub.'

That made me smile. She'd stay feisty, my mother. Born wild, stayed that way, her mother – this woman in front of me – would tell me.

Suzanne was frowning at me again. 'I'm sorry,' she said. 'But there's something oddly familiar about you. Do we know each other? Please tell me if we do.'

I glanced about the shop. It was after all, different from the one I grew up in, now that I had time for second impressions.

'What do you stock?' I asked.

'What? In the shop?'

I nodded, and she looked around, confused. 'Just the usual, I suppose. Mostly the latest paperback novels although we have a good selection of history books, and our DIY section is always popular.'

I nodded. So the shop would be reborn as a purveyor of New Age knowledge when Suzanne took it over as her own. Interesting. I turned my attention back to my grandmother.

'I don't suppose we'd be able to have that cup of tea, would we?' I asked. 'I've come a long way to see you.'

'You have?' she asked. 'So we do know each other, then?'

I gave her my gentlest smile. 'I know you,' I said, and took a breath. 'And I've a gift for you, and quite a story.'

'We're related, aren't we?' She grinned, clasping her hands over her swollen belly. 'I knew we were! There's something about you that seems so familiar.'

'Yes,' I said. 'We are indeed related.'

She made the fastest cup of tea on earth, while I sat on the stool and looked around, wondering where the hell I was going to start this unlikely tale. Coming back, she slid a steaming cup in front of me, with a plate of biscuits, and pulled up another stool, climbing awkwardly onto it. I thought she'd overbalance for a moment, and topple right off again, but she gave me a triumphant grin and righted herself.

'Centre of balance isn't quite what it used to be,' she said.

I sipped at the hot tea. It was good. Very English, a thing I was no longer used to. 'Are you hoping for a girl or a boy?' I asked.

She patted her tummy again, giving it a fond look. 'I just want it to be healthy,' she said. Her eyes drifted back to my face, then down to the floor where she'd propped the painting. 'What's in there?' she asked.

'A painting,' I said. 'It's for you.'

'Me?' Surprise was written large over her face.

I nodded. 'And I'm afraid it comes with a rather unbelievable story.'

She gave me a sideways look. 'What's your name?' she asked. 'You haven't even told me your name, or how we're related.'

'And the story starts,' I said, and I caught the flash of curiosity in her eyes.

'Then you'd best tell me.' Her eyes narrowed. 'Wait, is this going to be a conversation I'll want to give my full attention to?'

'Yes,' I said. 'And it might take a while, I'm afraid.'

She put down her cup and clambered from the stool. 'I'm intrigued,' she said, disappearing down the aisles toward the front door. 'I'm going to lock this,' she called. 'Frank won't mind if we open late. Tuesday's our slowest day anyway.'

'Frank must trust you very well,' I said as she returned.

'Oh yes. I love this job. He tells me he'll sell the shop to me at a good price when he's ready to retire – and you know what? I think I'll take him up on the offer, if I can. It suits me here.'

'It does,' I agreed. 'Suzanne, would you be so kind as to unwrap the painting, so I can show it to you?

She picked it up with alacrity, fingers digging at the tape Violet had used to close the box it was in. I watched her in silence, still debating internally how to tell the story that went with the painting, Violet's stern instructions ringing in my ear.

Suzanne stared at it with wide eyes. 'It's beautiful,' she gasped, then after a long moment of contemplation, turned it over to see if it was signed.

'Vivi Madden,' she read, then lifted her eyes to mine. 'Madden,' she said. 'That is my name.'

'And mine,' I told her. 'My name is Fran Madden, and this painting was done by my cousin and the woman I have loved for forty-eight years.'

Suzanne stared at me, her mouth slightly open.

'Her name is actually Violet,' I continued. 'But she signs her work Vivi.' I couldn't help my smile. 'Because she thought that sounded more artistic. More fun. My Violet has a great capacity for fun, and adventure.'

My grandmother blinked at me.

'We've had the most extraordinary adventure together, Violet and I.' Suzanne looked from me to the painting, at the signature on the back of it, then me again. 'And you're part of it too.' I told her, taking a deep breath.

'Me?' she said. 'How am I part of it?' She frowned. 'When you say loved…'

'I mean we are lovers.'

'Oh.'

I smiled. 'Quite.'

She rallied. 'I had a friend at school, who had terrible crushes on other girls.'

'It happens. More than you know, probably.'

She nodded. Swallowed. 'Okay.' Smiled. 'What's the rest of the story? Where do I fit in?' Her eyes widened. 'How do I possibly fit in?'

Ah. The big questions. I took another sip of tea. Looked at Violet's painting. Floundered. My very young grandmother looked expectantly at me.

I cleared my throat. 'I want to tell you how Violet and I met,' I began. 'Would that be all right?'

'Ah, sure. I guess so.'

'Thank you. Because although you don't know it yet, you had a part in it.'

Suzanne laughed. 'How is that possible? You just finished telling me you and Violet met a long time ago.'

'Forty-eight years ago,' I agreed.

Then I went on to tell Suzanne Madden – who would, in three weeks, not five, give birth to a daughter who would in 1990 deposit another baby girl, this one three or so years old, into her arms before leaving on adventures of dubious destinations – the story of my meeting with Violet. Our ill-fated trip to the seaside, the interrupted kiss, our flight by train to the city, my father, Violet's father – his threats – the trip to France…

Suzanne's eyes were wide. 'He died? Violet's father died?'

A nod, then another sip of tea. It had cooled during the telling, but my throat had dried. 'Yes. He fell from the train.'

She pressed a hand to her mouth. 'But that is horrible. Poor Violet!'

We sat in silence for a moment until Suzanne lifted her head and looked at me again. 'Did you make it to Nice?'

'Yes, we did. And we've lived there ever since.'

'I've never been to France,' she said, and there was a slight wistfulness in her voice. I smiled at her.

'You've plenty of time yet,' I said.

She patted her stomach. 'Time perhaps,' she laughed. 'But maybe not opportunity.'

'True.' We both laughed and then Suzanne grew serious.

'I've enjoyed your story,' she said. 'It's like something out of a novel…'

'But you're not sure what it has to do with you?'

She shook her head.

This was where it would get sticky. And it was also where I was going to complete my swerve away from Violet's script. The one she and I had agreed upon. I couldn't fully articulate why I didn't simply want to leave the painting in Suzanne's possession, with the tale of it belonging to a distant relative of ours who had met an unfortunate and early end.

That was what I'd been supposed to tell my young grandmother, and it was the reason Violet was back in the hotel room, instead of sitting beside me helping to tell our fantastic story.

I'd been supposed to tell Suzanne I'd sought her out because I didn't have any other relatives, and I was a reasonably well-off old broad from France, and then I was supposed to leave the painting with her as part of an eccentric promise to leave all my money to her upon the occasion of my passing.

That last bit was true – Violet and I had already had the solicitor draw up our wills, leaving everything to Suzanne. Who else did we have to leave our few bits and pieces to, anyway?

Suzanne shifted uncomfortably on her stool, and I realised I was staring rather alarmingly at her.

Drawing breath, I prepared myself.

CHAPTER THIRTY-NINE

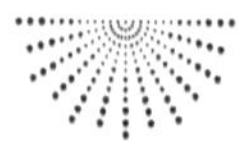

'Your name is Suzanne Ruth Madden, and you were married on the twenty second of August just last year.' I smiled. 'It was a small affair, in the outdoor area of a friend's café right here in Glastonbury – and afterwards you climbed to the Tor and got drunk on homemade strawberry wine.' As a kid, I'd always giggled when we got to the bit about the strawberry wine.

Suzanne's eyes widened, but I held up a hand and carried on. 'It was the perfect day, you thought, a cloudless sky, but one peculiar thing happened when you were up on that sacred hill, and it's puzzled you off and on ever since.'

'Who have you been talking to?' she asked. 'None of my family were at my wedding.'

'I know. Although your mother will write to you after she hears about the birth of the baby.'

Her eyes widened.

'Anyway,' I continued. 'I've often thought of the rainbow you saw that day as some sort of sign of things to come, but it's impossible to know.' I gave a Gallic shrug and a lopsided smile that was all my own, then leaned closer to the pregnant woman.

'Your baby will be born a week early, on the fourteenth of April, and you're going to call her Asphodel Ann Madden.' I leaned back and realised I was shaking. 'Your husband Ronnie wants to call her Daisy, which you personally think is a bit too cute and a bit too common.'

Her mouth was hanging open, and her hands were cupping the baby protectively.

'How...?'

'How do I know?'

Her eyes were round, startled.

'Because there was a bit of the story about Violet and me that I missed out when I was telling it. You're probably not going to believe it, you see, but I guess I'm going to tell you anyway.'

She shook her head. 'But how do you know about the name? I haven't told many people, and my friends would have said if they'd met you.'

I ignored her question and shifted my stiff old bones on the stool. Those things really are not designed for anything but young and plump little bottoms.

'My name is Frances Suzanne Madden, and Asphodel gave me your middle name because you were mad at her for getting pregnant.' I mused on it for a moment. 'I wonder if even then she suspected you'd end up doing more to raise me than she would, and she was giving us something in common.'

'What?' The word was little more than a gasp.

'I was born in 1987,' I said. 'In 2016, I fell from a ladder and hit my head. It knocked me right out, and when I came to, I was lying on a lawn in 1916.' I blinked at her, hoping she would remember to do the same instead of staring at me like a startled deer. 'I thought it was a dream, of course, but I never woke up from it.'

Suzanne was shaking her head. 'No,' she said. 'It's impossible.'

'I know. It is impossible. I know it is.'

She stared at me.

'And yet it happened. You, Suzanne, are my grandmother.' I nodded toward her round belly. 'Asphodel is my mother, but it will turn out that you are the one who raises me.' A glance around at the bookshop. 'Here,' I said. 'We will live in the flat above the bookshop – I've lived in a lot of flats above bookshops, come to think of it – and on the wall above the fireplace in the living room will be this painting.'

'You're telling me lies,' she whispered. 'I don't know why – tell me why you're lying to me. Who are you really?'

'I come to live with you when I'm three years old, my mother taking off to South Africa or somewhere. We don't know where for a long time.' I stop for a wetting sip of tea. The cup is almost empty. 'It's just you and me for my entire childhood. You're going to ask Ronnie to leave when Asphodel is four months old. You're thinking about it already, I bet.'

I'd hit a nerve; I saw it in the sudden paling of her freckled cheeks.

Suddenly I was tired. It was hard, telling my life's story, especially with little hope of it being believed. I looked at Suzanne, feeling old and sad, and missing Violet. I wanted to go back to her, let her pat me with those wondrous hands of hers, lie together on top of the strange bed and watch the sun crossing the window while we murmured to each other, little mumblings of the sort that you know, after long years of love, will comfort and bring consolation.

I slid from the stool, wincing as my circulation suddenly had access to limbs below the knees again.

'I was fascinated by this painting as a child, and you told me the story of its tragic artist, a woman who died too young.'

'Why are you telling me this?' she asked.

'Because I would be grateful if you would take this painting and put it on your wall. Just in case things turn out the way I'm saying they will.' I moved to pat her arm, then thought twice of it. She had a panicked, skittish look in her eyes. 'If you end up with a small girl who likes to sit on your Turkish ottoman and daydream about the painting, could you please tell her of a love story? Of a woman named Fran just like her, who fell in love with a beautiful, impetuous artist named Violet, and of how they defied their families to run away to France together?' I looked kindly at her. 'That's all I want.'

Suzanne's expression was numb, and I laid a hand on her arm after all. 'It's a small thing to do, either way, isn't it?' I straightened. 'And we are family, at least to me.' I looked around at the bookshop, smiling, seeing it as it would be – as it was when I was a child. 'Frank is going to sell you the bookshop, and you're going to have several comfy chairs for customers to sit in while they look through books.'

She shook her head. 'See, there's where you're wrong.' Her throat bobbed as she swallowed. 'He wants to retire next year. He wants to sell the shop next year. I don't have any money to buy it. There's no realistic way it's going to be mine. It's just a pipe-dream.' She slid awkwardly off her stool as well. 'So what you're saying will happen can't possibly.'

It was my turn to stare.

'What?' she asked, suddenly concerned. 'What is it? What have I said.'

The words, when they came, were cold in my mouth, vaguely metallic in taste. 'The money will come from us, my dear,' I said. 'Before we left to come here, Violet and I had wills drawn up to leave everything to you.' The cold of the shock receded, and I warmed again, smiled. 'It will be plenty to buy this shop, with the flat above it, and enough to completely restock, if you like.' Maybe she would too, I thought. Maybe she'd turn it into a New Age bookstore.

Suzanne clapped her hands to her mouth, the implications of what I'd said sinking in. Her head shook from side to side, telegraphing her horror.

'No,' she said.

Another shrug. 'It is of no matter,' I told her. 'I know too much and have lived with knowing too much for forty-eight years.'

'But I think I just told you that you're going to die next year!' She blinked. 'If all this you've told me is true.'

'Yes,' I said. 'And Violet. But we knew it would be soon.' I couldn't remember Suzanne ever telling me when she'd taken over the shop, and I realised why now. It could have been any time before I turned three. 'We've had the most marvellous life, Violet and I,' I told her. 'And now, if you'll excuse me, I must get back to her.'

Suzanne's hands were still covering her mouth and she moved them to press against her cheeks instead. 'But…'

'I know. I've come here and told you the most far-fetched

story. I don't really expect you to believe it.' One last look at the painting, the rose blooms as vibrant as ever. 'But please, just hang the painting on the wall for me. It won't do any harm and might make all the difference in the world for two women destined for each other.'

I was lapsing into maudlin ramblings. It was time to go.

CHAPTER FORTY

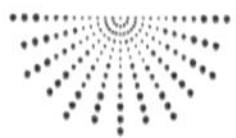

Violet and I were exhausted. I'd walked back to the hotel at half the pace, and she'd drawn me straight into her arms.

'Was it very terrible?' she asked. 'Was it very awkward?'

'Yes,' I said. 'It was both those things, and wonderful as well, and I told her everything.'

Violet had looked at me then, her eyes as green as the grass upon the Tor and then she'd nodded. 'I'd thought you would,' she said, the smile I loved so much finding her face.

'You did?'

'Of course.'

'But...'

She pressed her fingers to my lips. 'Hush my dearest,' she said. 'Of course I did. You are a book whose pages I have spent my life reading.'

I smiled, looking toward the bedroom, the sun slanting across the bed in a golden streak. Violet saw my look and led me there to lie in it, tucked up against each other, her eyes pools I was more than glad to lose myself in.

'It is a beautiful story, ours,' I whispered.

'Yes, indeed.' She traced the lines of my face. 'We inked in a great many words of love and adventure.'

'And illustrated it with paintings of all colours,' I answered, touching the spot on her cheek where she'd used to wipe the back of her hand, always – always – smearing a dabbed streak of paint there. I kissed the spot. 'So many beautiful paintings,' I said.

'So many beautiful poems.' She touched my hair, my shoulder, my neck, wrinkled now, but still able to feel the warmth of her hand just as it had when we were young. I took her hand and kissed the fingers, then put it back.

'So many wonderful years.'

'A love story that crossed the bounds of time.' An impish smile dimpled her cheeks. 'Literally.'

I laughed and wrapped my arms around her, and we drifted together in sunshine and the drowsy air of the afternoon, of a difficult day well done.

The knock, when it came, was tentative, and I lifted my head, unsure I'd heard anything at all. Perhaps a bird pecking at a tree in the garden.

'Someone's at the door,' Violet said, the words mushy with sleep.

'I'll see who it is.'

Violet sat up. 'It will be Suzanne.' She patted her hair and blinked at me. 'Who else would it be?'

She was right, of course. There was no one else it could be.

'I'm sorry to bother you,' Suzanne said as soon as I pulled the door open. I shook my head.

'You're not bothering us at all.'

She bit her lip and peered into the little sitting room. 'Violet is here too?'

'She is. Come in, Suzanne, and you can meet her.'

My grandmother nodded, looking ridiculously young, and she stepped inside, gazing around as though she were about to see a series of miracles. I suppose it seemed as though she was.

Violet came out of the bedroom and held out her hands. 'Suzanne,' she said. 'I'm so glad I get to meet you!' I realised, hearing Violet speak straight after Suzanne, that we both had French accents now. It made Violet sound wonderfully exotic and my heart swelled with love and pride.

Suzanne was carrying a small pile of books, and she looked awkwardly about for somewhere to put them. I took them from her and she let Violet hold her hands, getting a kiss on both cheeks.

But my attention was taken by the titles of the books in my hands.

'What are you grinning at, my love?' Violet asked. 'You look like a cat who just feasted on a nice, feathery treat.'

I looked up at her, then met my grandmother's eyes. Suzanne flushed, and came to take the volumes from me.

'I…ah…did some research after you left,' she said, looking at me, bright red spots roosting high on her cheeks.

'In the paranormal section,' I said, unable to stifle my laughter.

Violet clapped her hands in delight. 'But this is wonderful,' she said.

Suzanne swallowed. 'Your, ah, story was unbelievable, but ah, there have been other, sort of similar stories.' She blushed further. 'Kind of, anyway.'

She took back one of the books and flipped it open, pressed a fingertip to the thick paper of the page. 'Here,' she said. 'It's a story about a girl who got sick, went to sleep for three days, and when she woke up, she was a completely different person...' She looked up, eyes going to Violet, then me. The book snapped closed.

'I guess, it's not completely impossible, is what I'm trying to say.'

I nodded at her, giving her a grandmotherly smile, since I was the one old enough for that position.

'I'm going to make coffee,' Violet said, bustling away. 'We brought the beans with us. I know it is hard to find good roasts here. Do you want some, Suzanne?'

'Ah, coffee?' She was nonplussed.

But Violet was shaking her head anyway. 'No, of course not. It is bad for the baby. I will make tea for you.' She smiled, delighted. 'It is your granddaughter who made of me a coffee drinker. I always had tea before I met her, but not for many years now.'

Suzanne stood blinking in the middle of the room, the books clasped tightly against her breast. Her eyes turned to mine.

'Are you really my granddaughter?' she whispered, voice hoarse.

I nodded.

She looked down at her book, at the carpet. 'I really have been thinking of leaving Ronnie,' she said. 'But I've been afraid of, you know, bringing up the baby on my own.'

'You don't need to be. You do a fine job.'

Her eyes lifted to look in mine again, and I was struck by

their familiarity. Even across all these years, I recognised them.

'But she leaves you with me. Isn't that what you said? I must do something wrong with her if she abandons her own child.'

I shook my head. 'You have no blame for that. Asphodel is feisty now, and that's how she goes through life. Always chasing something. Some people are like that, is what I think. And as for me, I'm glad I got to live with you. I would never want that to be any different.'

She looked down, then nodded. 'Okay,' she whispered.

Violet brought over a tray with the drinks. I swapped a kiss for mine and sat down with a tired but contented sigh.

'So,' Violet said. 'You will hang the painting on the wall?'

Abruptly, Suzanne sank down on the closest chair. She looked at us, nodded. 'Yes,' she said, her voice a little strangled. 'This is all a great deal to take in, but of course I will hang the painting on the wall.'

'And if a little girl called Frances shows a fascination for it, will you tell her the story of Fran and Violet?' I asked, glancing at Violet, who looked at me, then nodded.

'I wanted Fran to tell you only the story you told her when she was a child,' Violet said. 'It didn't make sense to me to change anything – playing with fire, perhaps.'

Suzanne nodded slowly, and I could see the intelligence there that I'd grown up with, the sharp mind, especially now that I knew the reason for the obsession with subjects such as time-travel, ghosts, reincarnation.

'Fran has told me both versions,' she said. Her eyes bulged slightly. 'I was a little worried for a bit that it meant that this will be a never-ending sort of loop…'

'What do you mean?' Violet's voice was sharp.

'Well,' Suzanne said, looking abashed. 'I mean, that you will be born in...?'

'1987,' I supplied, and she nodded.

'In 1987, then go back in time to 1916, live a full life for many years...' Her eyes fled sideways and we all ignored the thought of next year being the end of said full life. She cleared her throat. 'And, ah, then being born again and going through the whole thing in an endless sort of loop.'

'Kind of like Groundhog Day,' I mused, thinking of the movie. When I looked up, both women were confused. 'Never mind.' I huffed in a deep breath. 'But you don't think so?'

'No. I think maybe you've already changed everything.' Suzanne said, and looked at us both. 'Don't you?'

My brows knitted. 'Well, yes,' I said. 'We have. This time around.' I blinked.

'But what about next time?' Violet asked.

Suzanne shook her head. 'I don't know that next time matters. You already went and changed everything.'

'But we need it to stay changed!' That was Violet. It could just as easily have been me.

We were all silent for a moment, drinks forgotten, and outside the day had drawn a long, weary breath towards dusk. The bed through the doorway was in shadow.

'I think it will,' Suzanne said at last. She patted the books in her lap again. 'Admittedly, I know nothing. Only the little bit I read this afternoon, and that wasn't much help.'

'Then how are you able to say?' Violet asked, and I squeezed her fingers again.

Suzanne smiled, the same, unruffled smile I knew so well

from my childhood. The one that told me not to worry, that all I could do was the best I could with what I had.

'Look at you two,' she said. 'It must have been something very strong that brought you together. It broke all known laws of time to do so.' The smile widened. 'I think that means something, don't you?'

Saying it like that made it seem so simple. I saw Violet think on it and come to the same conclusion.

'I think it's done,' Suzanne continued. 'I think it will always be done, whether I hang that painting or not. Whether this baby here…' She smoothed a hand over her belly. 'Has a baby of her own one day called Frances. Whether or not that happens, what you two did is done.'

'And can't be undone.' Violet turned to me. 'It feels true, darling. Don't you think it feels true?'

I looked at her beloved face, the same features I'd been gazing on with love for so many wonderful years. I nodded.

'Yes,' I said, with dawning delight. 'It does.'

'Nothing can change what you and I have achieved,' Violet said, and this time, it was her hand that squeezed mine.

'Of course, I'll keep the painting,' Suzanne said. 'And if I need to, I'll tell little Fran the story of two lovers who ran away to be together, and who loved each other more than anything.'

There were tears in my eyes.

'It is all we can ask for,' Violet murmured. Then looked at me. 'And if for some reason, we are wrong…'

'We had this life,' I finished.

'This wonderful, marvellous life.'

CHAPTER FORTY-ONE

So there it is. A story that no one will believe, and yet I could not help but write it down. All my life I have read books, quoted poetry, and admired those with stories to tell. Violet gave me this notebook for Christmas and told me to write it all down. So I have. You may think it fiction, if you like. It would probably be easier, if you did.

But as for me, I like to think the poets were writing the truth. That love is stronger and finer than anything else. That it fills the heavens, and our hearts.

We are looking at the end of our lives this coming year, or soon enough, anyway, Violet and I. But it does not bother us. We have had our adventure, and if there is one thing we've learnt – it's that time knows no bounds, when it comes to love.

Here she is now, my beautiful wife. I've not been able to marry her legally, but she will always be my wife.

'Are you done?' she asks, sitting beside me, her thighs still slender, still warm where they press against me.

'I am,' I say, putting these last few words on the page. She still smells of night flowers, my darling Violet. Of exotic blooms from far-away lands and enchanted nights.

She laughs, leaning over to read these last few words, but the kiss she puts on my cheek is as soft as ever, and her breath upon my skin still stirs me in all the same ways it always did.

Love knows no bounds, you see. If not my word, then take the good bard Shakespeare's, for I've my lady love here, to lie with one more time.

> Let me not to the marriage of true minds
> Admit impediments. Love is not love
> Which alters when it alteration finds,
> Or bends with the remover to remove.
> O no! it is an ever-fixed mark
> That looks on tempests and is never
>   shaken;
> It is the star to every wand'ring bark,
> Whose worth's unknown, although his
>   height be taken.
> Love's not Time's fool, though rosy lips
>   and cheeks
> Within his bending sickle's compass
>   come;
> Love alters not with his brief hours and
>   weeks,
> But bears it out even to the edge of
>   doom.
> If this be error and upon me prov'd,
> I never writ, nor no man ever lov'd.

ABOUT THE AUTHOR

Lily Hammond is the historical romance penname of Kate Genet, a New Zealand writer passionate about immersive and authentic stories of strong women who love other women. She lives in Dunedin, New Zealand with her American wife Valerie. Kate also writes contemporary romances under the name Ana McKenzie. If you enjoyed this book, please look for other titles by Ana McKenzie, Lily Hammond and Kate Genet (some of them are listed on the next page), and subscribe to the Sapphica Books mailing list for poetry, short stories, Lily Hammond postcards, and to hear about new releases, sales, and monthly giveaways of books and swag.